## "You're afraid," said Marius very softly.

She sat up straight and faced him squarely, her plain face animated into near beauty by her rage.

"How dare you?" Her pleasant voice was a little shrill but well under control. "Until you came I had my life planned and everything was... Can't you see you've stirred me up? I was happy before."

"Happy? With your broom and no chance of a glass slipper?" He got up and pulled her out of her chair and held her hand in his.

"Tabitha, shall we not be friends? After all, I expect to see a great deal of you in the future."

Tabitha stared ahead of her at his white drill coat. She was thinking that when he married Lilith it would be so much more comfortable if they all got on well together.

She said in a bewildered voice, "Could we be friends?"

Tabitha felt his hands tighten on her own. "Yes, Tabby." He let go of one hand and lifted her chin and gave her a long look, then kissed her on the cheek—a nice brotherly kiss, thought Tabitha.

Romance readers around the world will be sad to note the passing of **Betty Neels** in June 2001. Her career spanned thirty years, and she continued to write into her ninetieth year. To her millions of fans, Betty epitomized the romance writer, and yet she began writing almost by accident. She had retired from nursing, yet her inquiring mind still sought stimulation. Her new career was born when she heard a lady in her local library bemoaning the lack of good romance novels. Betty's first book, *Sister Peters in Amsterdam,* was published in 1969, and she eventually completed 134 books. Her novels offer a reassuring warmth that was very much a part of her own personality. She was a wonderful writer, and she will be greatly missed. Her spirit will live on in all her stories, including those yet to be published.

# THE BEST *of*
# BETTY NEELS

## TABITHA IN MOONLIGHT

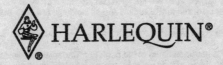

## HARLEQUIN®

TORONTO • NEW YORK • LONDON
AMSTERDAM • PARIS • SYDNEY • HAMBURG
STOCKHOLM • ATHENS • TOKYO • MILAN • MADRID
PRAGUE • WARSAW • BUDAPEST • AUCKLAND

ISBN 0-373-51222-8

TABITHA IN MOONLIGHT

First North American Publication 2001

Visit us at www.eHarlequin.com

**Printed in U.S.A.**

# CHAPTER ONE

MISS TABITHA CRAWLEY opened the door of Men's Orthopaedic ward with the outward calmness of manner for which she was famed throughout St Martin's Hospital, although inwardly she seethed with the frustration of having to leave her half-eaten supper, combined with the knowledge that within half an hour of going off duty after a tiresome day, it would be her almost certain lot to have to remain on duty to admit the emergency she had just been warned of. She had already calculated that the patient would arrive at about the same time as the night staff, which meant that she would have to admit him, for the night nurses would be instantly caught up in the machinery of night routine and the night sisters would be taking the day reports.

She frowned heavily, an act which did nothing to improve her looks, for her face was unremarkable enough with its undistinguished nose, wide mouth and hazel eyes, whose lashes, of the same pale brown of her hair, were thick enough but lacked both curl and length. Her hair was one of her few good points, for it was long and thick and straight, but as she wore it tidily drawn back into a plaited coil, its beauty was lost to all but the more discerning. Not that many of those she met bothered to look further than her face, to dismiss her as a nice, rather dull girl; if they had looked again they would have seen that she had a good figure and quite beautiful legs. The fact that they didn't look for a second time didn't bother Tabitha in the least—indeed, it gave her considerable amusement, for she was blessed with a sense of humour and was able to laugh at herself, which, she reminded herself upon occasion, was a very good thing. She had plenty of friends anyway, and although she was considered something of a martinet on the ward, the nurses liked her, for she was considerate and kind and didn't shirk a hard day's work.

Nurse Betts and Mrs Jeffs, the nursing auxiliary, tidying beds at the far end of the ward, watched her neat figure as she walked towards them, and Betts said softly:

'You know, Mrs Jeffs, she's got a marvelous shape and a lovely voice. If only she'd do something to her hair...' She broke off as Tabitha reached them.

'An emergency,' she said without preamble. 'Will you get one of the top beds ready, please? We'd better have him near the office—it's a compound fracture of tib and fib. He's eighty years old and he's been lying for hours before he was discovered. They're getting some blood into him now, but they won't do anything until tomorrow morning; he's too shocked. I'll lay up a trolley just the same.' She smiled a little and looked almost pretty.

The trolley done, she went back into the ward to start her last round, an undertaking which she always thought of as the Nightingale touch, but the men seemed to like it and it gave her the chance to wish each of them an individual good night as well as make sure that all was well as she paused for a few seconds by their beds. She started at the top of the ward, opposite to where Nurse Betts and Mrs Jeffs were still busy, coming to a halt beside a bed whose occupant was displaying a lively interest in what was going on. He was a young man of her own age, recovering from the effects of a too hearty rugger scrum, and he grinned at her cheerfully.

'Hullo, Sister—hard luck, just as you're due off. Hope it's someone with a bit of life in 'em.'

'Eighty,' said Tabitha crisply, 'and I fancy he's the one you should be sorry for. How's the leg?'

He swung its plastered length awkwardly. 'Fine. Pity old Sawbones is out of commission, he might have taken this lump of concrete off—I bet the new bloke'll keep it on for weeks. What's he like, Sister?'

'I haven't an idea,' said Tabitha, 'but be sure you'll do as he says. Now settle down, Jimmy, there's a good boy.' Her voice was motherly and he said instantly, just as though she were twice his age: 'Yes, Sister, OK. Goodnight.'

Tabitha went on down the neat row of beds, pausing by each

one to tuck in a blanket or shake a pillow and now and then feel a foot to make sure that its circulation was all it should be.

The ward was almost aggressively Victorian with its lofty ceiling and tall, narrow windows, and the faint breeze of the summer's evening seemed to emphasise this. Tabitha had a sudden longing to be home, instantly dismissed as she fetched up by Mr Prosser's bed. Mr Prosser had two broken legs because the brakes on his fish and chip van failed on a steep West Country hill when he was on his way to the more remote villages with his appetising load. Tabitha's nose twitched at the memory of the reek of fish and chips which had pervaded the ward for hours after his arrival. Even now, several weeks after his admission, the more humorous-minded of his companions in misfortune were apt to crack fishy jokes at his expense. Not that he minded; he was a cockney by birth and had migrated to the West Country several years earlier, satisfying a lifelong urge to live in the country while at the same time retaining his native humour. He said now:

''Ullo, ducks. What's all the bustle about? Some poor perisher cracked 'is legs like yours truly?'

Tabitha nodded. 'That's right—but only one. How are the toes?'

'All there, Sister—I wriggled 'em like you said. How's 'Is Nibs?'

'As comfortable as possible. I'll tell Mr Raynard you enquired, shall I?'

'Yes—'e's been 'oist with 'is own...' he hesitated.

'Petard,' finished Tabitha for him. 'Hard luck, wasn't it?'

She spoke with genuine sympathy. It was indeed hard luck for the senior orthopaedic surgeon to have fallen down in his own garden and broken his patella into two pieces. He had been brought in late that afternoon and had largely been the cause of Tabitha's tiresome day, for whereas his patients were willing to lie still and have done to them whatever was necessary for their good, Mr Raynard had felt compelled to order everyone about and even went so far as to say that if he wanted his damn knee properly attended to he'd better get up and do it himself, which piece of nonsense was properly ignored by those ministering to him. He had had the grace to beg everyone's pardon later on and had even gone so far as to thank God that he was in his own ward and in Tabitha's capable hands. Having thus made amends he then demanded the portable telephone to be fetched, and ignoring the fact that the staff were longing to get him settled in his bed, had a long conversation, his share of which enabled his hearers to guess without much difficulty that he was arranging for someone to do his work. He laid the receiver down at length and fixed Tabitha with, for him, a mild eye.

'That's settled. A colleague of mine has just given up his appointment prior to going on a series of lecture tours, he's coming down tomorrow to see to this—' he waved an impatient hand at his splinted knee. 'He'll take over for me until I can get about.' He grinned at her. 'He's an easy-going chap—he'll be a nice change from me, Tabby.'

She had said, 'Oh yes' in a neutral voice, thinking privately that probably the new man would be even worse than the other old friend of Mr Raynard's, who had come for a week when he was down with 'flu. He had been easy-going too—his rounds had been leisurely and totally lacking in instructions to either herself or the houseman, but hours later, usually as she was preparing to go off duty, he would return to the ward, full of splendid ideas which he wanted to put into operation immediately.

She walked on slowly down the ward, passing the time of day with each patient while she wondered why Mr Raynard chose to lie in discomfort and a fair amount of pain until this colleague of his should arrive in the morning, and then remembered that George Steele, his registrar, was out for the evening and wouldn't be back until very late, and there really wasn't anyone else.

She was on her way up the other side of the ward now and there were only Mr Pimm and Mr Oscar left before the two empty beds at the top of the ward. She stood between the two men, each of whom had a miniature chess board balanced on their chests, and Mr Pimm rumbled:

'He's got me, Sister—it's taken him the whole evening, but he's finally done it.'

'How?' asked Tabitha, remembering with a grief she still felt keenly the games of chess she and her father had played before he had married again. It was one of the memories she tried her best to forget, and she thrust it aside now and listened intelligently to Mr Oscar's triumphant explanation before wishing them a cheerful good night and going finally into the cubicle outside her office.

Mr Raynard was waiting for her, looking bad-tempered— something which she ignored, for she had long ago learned not to mind his bristling manner and sharp tongue. Now he asked; 'Is there something coming in?'

She told him briefly and added: 'If you're quite comfortable, sir, I won't stay—there are several things…I hope you'll sleep well. You've been written up for what you asked for and I hope you'll take it—you need a good sleep. Nothing after midnight, either, in case you go to theatre early—that depends upon your colleague, I imagine. I shall be here at eight o'clock anyway, and your pre-meds are written up.'

Mr Raynard snorted. 'All nicely arranged. You'll go with me to the theatre, of course.'

Tabitha raised her eyebrows. 'If you insist, sir—though I must remind you that it's theatre day tomorrow and there's a list from here to there; you made it out yourself last week.'

Mr Raynard looked sour. 'Well, you've got a staff nurse who's quite able to carry out your pernickety ideas.' He added reluctantly, 'You run the ward so efficiently that it could tick over very well by itself.'

Tabitha looked surprised. 'Fancy you saying that,' she remarked cheerfully. 'I'll be getting too big for my boots!' Her too-wide mouth curved into a smile. 'Just for that, I'll take you to theatre, sir.'

Her quick ear had caught the sound of trolley wheels coming down the corridor. 'There's our patient, I must go.'

The old man on the trolley looked like Father Christmas; he had a leonine head crowned with snow-white hair and his handsome old face was wreathed in whiskers. He groaned a little as he was lifted on to the bed, but didn't open his eyes. It was a few minutes later, after he had been tucked into the warmed and cradled bed and Tabitha had checked his pulse and turned back to take a second look at him, that she encountered his startlingly blue gaze. She said at once: 'Hullo, you're safe and sound in hospital. How do you feel?'

His voice came threadily. 'Not bad—not bad at all, thank you, Sister.'

She smiled. 'Good. Then will you close your eyes and go to sleep again? Presently, when you've had a rest and a little nap, one of us will answer any questions you may want to ask. Unless there's anything worrying you now?'

He closed his eyes, and Tabitha looked to the drip and checked his night drugs and was on the point of turning away when he said in a voice which was a little stronger: 'There are one or two questions. What is the time?'

She told him and he frowned so that she asked quickly: 'Is there someone who should know you are here? We got your address from your papers in Casualty, but there was no one home when the police called.'

'My cat—Podger—he'll wonder what's happened. My land-lady won't bother. He can't get out—he'll starve.'

'Indeed he won't,' said Tabitha instantly. 'I'm going home in a very few minutes. I live quite close to you, I'll feed your cat and see what arrangements I can make, so don't worry.'

He smiled a little. 'There isn't anyone...' he began. He closed his eyes and Tabitha waited for him to say something more, but he didn't; Pethedine and shock and weariness had carried him off between them to a merciful limbo.

It was almost ten o'clock by the time she left the hospital in her small Fiat. A few minutes' drive took her through the main streets of the city and into the older, shabbier quarter where she found her patient's house without difficulty. It was one of a row of two-storied Victorian houses which at one time would have been described as desirable family residences, although now they were let out in flats or rooms.

The woman who answered Tabitha's knock, had a flat Midlands accent which sounded harsh to Tabitha's West Country ears. She said stridently:

'What d'yer want?' and Tabitha felt a sudden pity for the old man she had just left, and for his cat. She explained why she had called and the woman stood aside to let her in with casual cheerfulness. 'Upstairs, dear—back room, and I 'opes no one expects me to look after 'is room or that cat of 'is. I've enough ter do.'

She opened a door and shuffled through it, shutting it firmly on Tabitha, who, left on her own, went briskly up the stairs and into the back room. She switched on the light, closed the door behind her and looked around. The room was small and very clean, and although most of its furniture was strictly of the sort found in furnished rooms, she was surprised to see what she took to be some good pictures on its walls, and several pieces of Wedgwood and Rockingham china on the mantelpiece. There was a desk in one corner of the room too—a beautiful piece of furniture which she thought to be Sheraton; it bore upon it a small ormolu clock and a pair of silver candlesticks which would probably have paid the rent for a year. It wasn't her business, anyway. She set about looking for Podger.

He was squeezed under the bed, a large black cat with a worried expression on his moonlike face. She gave him bread and milk which he gobbled noisily and then looked at her for more. It was impossible to leave him alone, at the mercy of anyone who chose to remember him. She gathered him up easily enough and went downstairs and knocked on the landlady's door. Podger cringed a little as it was opened and Tabitha said more firmly than she had meant to: 'I'll look after the cat. Perhaps you would be good enough to lock the door while…'

The woman eyed her with indulgent scorn. 'Till 'is rent's due I'll lock it. After that it's out with 'is things. I can't afford to leave me rooms empty.'

Tabitha put a gentle hand on Podger's bull neck. 'Yes, of course. I'll come back tomorrow evening—perhaps something could be arranged.'

She made her escape, and as she settled the trustful Podger

beside her in the car her mind was already busy with the problem of what was to be done. The old man must be hard up, even though some of his possessions, if sold, would keep him in comfort for some time. She started the car, and still pondering the problem, went back through the city to the quiet street where she had her flat.

As she parked the car outside the little house, she could see Meg standing in the open door, and as she crossed the road, Podger under one arm, she heard her soft Dorset voice. 'Miss Tabby, where have you been? It's all hours—and what's that you've got with you?'

Tabitha shut the street door firmly behind them and opened the door into the flat, then crossed the minute hall and went into the kitchen, where she put Podger on a chair. She said contritely: 'Meg dear, I'm so sorry. I'll tell you what happened, but I must feed this poor creature.' She rummaged around and found some cold ham and gave it to the cat, explaining as she did so. When she had finished, Meg clucked her tongue just as she had always done when Tabitha had been a very little girl and she had been her nanny.

'Well, what's done can't be undone,' she remarked comfortably, 'poor old man. Did you get your supper?'

'No,' confessed Tabitha, 'not all of it,' and was prevailed upon to sit down immediately at the table and given soup while Meg made sandwiches. With her mouth full, she said: 'You spoil me, Meg. You shouldn't, you know. You could get a marvelous job with an earl or a lord or someone instead of being cooped up here with me on a wage Father would have been ashamed to offer you.'

Her erstwhile nurse gave her a severe look. 'And what would I be doing with earls and lords and suchlike? Didn't I promise your dear mother that I'd look after you, and you didn't think that I would stay behind when you left home, now did you, miss?'

Tabitha offered Podger a morsel of cheese and jumped up to hug Meg. 'I'd be lost without you,' she declared soberly, and then: 'I don't want to go to Chidlake on Friday.'

'You must, Miss Tabitha. It's your stepsister's birthday

party, and though I know there's no love lost between you, nor yet that stepmother of yours, you've got to go. When you left Chidlake after your father married again you did promise him you'd go back, Christmas and birthdays and suchlike.'

'Oh, Meg, I know, but Father was alive then. Stepmother and Lilith don't really want me there.'

'Maybe not, but it's your home, Miss Tabby dear, whatever they say—you belong there and they never will. You can't leave the old house to strangers.'

Tabitha went over to the sink with her plate. She loved her home very much; Meg was right, she couldn't leave it completely. She said heavily: 'Of course I'll go, Meg. Now we'd better go to bed. I'll take Podger with me, shall I, in case he's lonely. And don't get up early, Meg. I'm on at eight and I'll have plenty of time to get something to eat before I go.' But Meg was already laying the table for breakfast; Tabitha knew that whatever she said, the older woman would be down before her in the morning, fiercely insisting that she ate the meal she had cooked. She yawned, suddenly tired, 'Today's been beastly,' she observed.

Meg gave her a shrewd look. 'Tomorrow's always a better day,' she stated firmly. 'Go and have your bath and I'll bring you up some hot milk—there's nothing like it for a good night's sleep.'

But hot milk or not, Tabitha found sleep elusive, perhaps because she had been talking about her home, and doing that had awakened old memories. She had had a happy childhood, accepting her happiness with the blissful, unconscious content of the very young. She had had loving parents, a beautiful home and no cares to spoil her days. She had been happy at school too, and because Chidlake had been in the family for a very long time, she had known everyone in the village as well as a great many people in nearby Lyme Regis. She had been fifteen when her mother died and almost twenty when her father married again, and by then she was a student nurse, living in hospital in the cathedral city some thirty miles away, so that she came home only for days off each week. At least, it had been each week to begin with, but she had come to dread them, for her stepmother made no pretence of her dislike of her and lost no opportunity of poking sly fun at Tabitha's lack of looks and young men, so that Tabitha, whose placid nature could turn to a fiery rage if sufficiently badgered, had made the journey home less and less frequently, and finally had thankfully qualified and with her increased salary and the small annuity her mother had left her, had set up house for herself in the tiny flat near the hospital. Her father had allowed her to choose enough furniture from Chidlake to take with her, and had raised no demur when Meg had announced that she had appointed herself housekeeper of the small menage.

Tabitha had continued to go to Chidlake from time to time, but after her father's death she went less and less—and only then because she had promised her father that she would and because she loved the old house so dearly. Sometimes she wondered what would happen to it, for her stepmother disliked it and Lilith hated it; probably it would be sold. When Tabitha allowed herself to think of this she longed to have the money to buy it, for it was, after all, hers by rights and she had been given to understand that her father had asked her stepmother to leave it to his elder daughter when she died. But Tabitha was only too well aware that that would be the last thing she would do, for she had bitterly opposed Tabitha's inheritance of a few small pieces of furniture and family silver and had ignored his request that she should make provision for Tabitha, although she had been powerless to prevent the payment of Tabitha's annuity and Meg's few hundred pounds.

Tabitha sat up in bed, switched on her bedside light and thumped her pillows into greater comfort. It was past twelve o'clock and she had to be up soon after six, but she had never felt so wide awake. She gazed around the room, soothed by its charm. Although small, the few pieces of furniture it contained showed up to advantage and the pink shade of the lamp gave the white walls a pleasant glow. She began to think about the weekend. Lilith's party was to be a big affair, and although she disliked Tabitha almost as much as her mother did, she had invited her with an outward show of friendliness because, after all, Tabitha knew a great many people around Chidlake; they would find it strange if she wasn't present. At least she had a new dress for the occasion—a green and blue shot silk with a tiny bodice, its low-cut neck frilled with lace and the same lace at the elbow-length sleeves. She had tried it on several times during the last week and had come to the conclusion that while she was unlikely to create a stir, she would at least be worth a glance.

Tired of lying awake, she rearranged her pillows once more, and Podger, who had settled at the end of her bed, opened a sleepy eye, yawned, stretched and then got up and padded across the quilt to settle against her. He was warm—too warm for the time of year, but comforting too. She put an arm round his portly little body and went to sleep.

She went to take a look at her newest patient as soon as she had taken the report the next morning, and found him more himself. He stared at her with his bright old eyes and said quite strongly: 'I've seen you before—I'm afraid I wasn't feeling quite myself.' He held out a rather shaky hand and she shook its frail boniness gravely. 'John Bow,' he said.

'Tabitha Crawley,' said Tabby, and gave him a nice smile. 'I'm glad to hear that you've had quite a good night—the surgeon will be along directly to decide what needs to be done.'

He nodded, not much interested. 'Podger?' he enquired.

She explained, glossing over the landlady's observations and telling him that they would have a little talk later on, before she crossed the ward to Mr Raynard's cubicle. He greeted her so crossly that she asked:

'What's the matter, sir? You sound put out.'

'My knee's the matter. I've hardly closed my eyes all night.'

Tabitha looked sympathetic, aware from the report that he had wakened for a couple of short periods only, but there was no point in arguing.

'I expect it seemed like all night,' she observed kindly.

'Bah! I told that fool of a night nurse to get me some more dope and she had the temerity to refuse because it wasn't written up.'

Tabitha took up a militant stance at the foot of his bed, ready to do battle on behalf of the night staff, who was a good girl anyway and knew what she was about.

'Nurse Smart did quite right, and well you know it, sir. A fine pickle we'd all be in if we handed out pills to any patient who asked for them. And you are a patient, Mr Raynard.'

He glared at her. 'When I'm on my feet I'll wring your neck…' he began, and stopped to laugh at someone behind her. She turned without haste; it would be George Steele, zealously coming to enquire about his chief—probably the new man had let him know what time the list would start and poor old George had had to get up early. It wasn't poor old George but a stranger; a tall, well-built man with a craggy, handsome face, pale sandy hair brushed back from a high forehead and calm grey eyes. He was wearing slacks and a cotton sweater and she had the instant impression that he was casual to the point of laziness. He said 'Hi there' to Mr Raynard before his eyes moved to meet hers, and then: 'Have I come all the way from Cumberland just in time to prevent you committing murder, Bill?'

Mr Raynard stopped laughing to say: 'I threaten the poor girl all the time, don't I, Tabby? This is Marius van Beek—Marius, meet Miss Tabitha Crawley, who rules this ward with a rod of iron in a velvet glove.'

Tabitha looked at him, her head on one side. 'You've got it wrong,' she observed. 'It's an iron hand in a velvet glove.'

Mr Raynard frowned at her. 'Woman, don't argue. Your hand isn't iron—it's soft and very comforting, if you must know.'

Tabitha said with equanimity: 'Well, I never—how kind,' and turned belatedly to Mr van Beek. 'How do you do, sir?' She half smiled as she spoke, thinking how delightful it would be if she were so pretty that he would really look at her and not just dismiss her with a quick glance as just another rather dull young woman wrapped up in her work, so she was all the more surprised when he didn't look away but stared at her with a cool leisure which brought a faint pink to her cheeks. He said at length in an unhurried deep voice that held the faintest trace of an accent:

'How do you do, Miss Crawley. You must forgive me for coming without giving you proper notice, but I was told it was so very urgent.'

He glanced at Mr Raynard, his sandy eyebrows raised, and Mr Raynard said hastily:

'It is—you're a good chap to come, Marius. Tabby, go away and whip up your nurses or whatever you do at this hour of the day and come back in half an hour. See that George is with you.'

Tabitha took these orders with a composure born of several years' association with Mr Raynard. She went to the door, saying merely: 'As you wish, sir. If you should want a nurse you have only to ring.'

She went away, resisting a desire to take a good look at Mr van Beek as she went. Half an hour later she was back again, her neat appearance giving no clue as to the amount of work she had managed to get through in that time. She stood quietly by George Steele, nothing in her plain little face betraying the delightful feeling of excitement she was experiencing at the sight of Mr van Beek, leaning against a wall with his hands in his pockets; he looked incapable of tying his own shoelaces, let alone putting broken bones together again. He half smiled at her, but it was Mr Raynard who spoke.

'Tabby, let me have my pre-med now, will you? The list will start at ten o'clock, so take Mar—Mr van Beek to see the other cases now, straight away.' He winced in pain. 'Remember you're coming to theatre with me, Sister Crawley.'

When he called her Sister Crawley like that she knew better than to answer back, even mildly. She said: 'Of course, sir,' and after passing on the news to Rogers, led the way into the ward with George Steele beside her and Mr van Beek strolling along behind as though he had all day.

She went straight to the cases which were already listed because she knew how Mr Bow would need to be talked over and looked at before it was decided if and when he was to have his bones set. She didn't think they would keep him waiting long though, because now that he had come out of shock it would be safe to operate. Surprisingly, Mr van Beek, despite his lazy appearance, seemed to have a very active mind, for he grasped the salient points of each case as they were put forward, so that they were standing by Mr Bow's bed much sooner than she had dared to hope. The old man opened his eyes as they approached the bed and a look of such astonishment came over his face that Tabitha glanced at the two men with her to find the reason, to find the same expression reflected upon Mr van Beek's handsome features. He said an explosive word in a language which certainly wasn't English and exclaimed: 'Knotty, by all that's wonderful! It must be years....' He put out a great hand and engulfed Mr Bow's gently in it and went on:

'The last time I heard from you was—let me see, five years ago—you were in Newcastle, because I wrote to you there and never had an answer.'

Mr Bow smiled. 'And now I'm here, and I hope you will be able to stick me together again.'

Mr van Beek gave him a long, thoughtful look. 'Yes, we'll have a long talk later, but now tell me what happened to you.'

He listened with patience to Mr Bow's meticulous and long-winded account of his accident, which included a great deal of superfluous information about Podger and a corollary concerning Tabitha's thoughtfulness of his pet's welfare, during the telling of which Mr van Beek said nothing at all, but stared very hard at Tabitha when Mr Bow got to the part about her rescue of Podger. Only when the old man at last fell silent, he remarked kindly:

'Well, don't worry, we'll get things sorted out for you— Podger is in good hands and I'm sure Sister will be able to arrange something about your rooms.' And Tabitha's heart warmed to him for making it sound as if Mr Bow rented something well-furnished in the best part of the city. The surgeon went on: 'The important thing is to get this leg of yours seen to as soon as possible, Knotty.'

He turned to George Steele and they examined the X-rays together, then Tabitha turned back the bedclothes and they looked at the bony old leg under its cage. Finally Mr van Beek said: 'We'll do Mr Bow after Mr Raynard, Sister.' He was writing as he spoke and when he had handed the chart to George Steele he looked directly at her. 'An open reduction and plaster, I think,' he glanced briefly at the Registrar and received a nodded agreement, 'and I should count it as a favour if you would take Mr Bow to theatre, Sister—he's a very old friend of mine.'

Tabitha rearranged the bedclothes. 'Yes, of course,' she answered matter-of-factly, aware at the same time that she would have to change her off duty with Staff Rogers to do so, but perhaps that was a good thing anyway, because then she could go to Mr Bow's lodgings on her way home—there would be a better chance of seeing the landlady in the evening.

Mr van Beek disappeared soon after and Tabitha, caught up in the ward routine, had no time to think about him, but presently, on her way to theatre with a determinedly chatty Mr Raynard, he was brought to her notice by that gentleman remarking on the coincidence of Mr Bow being Marius's tutor at Cambridge. 'Lost touch with each other,' droned Mr Raynard, faintly drowsy. 'Marius tells me they used to do a lot of sailing together—that would be getting on for twenty years ago.' He cocked a hazy eye at Tabitha walking beside the trolly. 'Marius is thirty-eight,' he offered.

'Indeed?' Tabitha wedged herself into the lift with the rest of the theatre party and sought for something to say. 'Quite old,' she ventured.

'At the height of his not inconsiderable success and a distinguished career,' snapped Mr Raynard, having a little difficulty with the long words. 'How old are you, Tabby?'

She gave him a rather blank look and he added: 'You can safely tell me, for I'm doped; I shall never remember.'

'I don't really mind if you do. I'm twenty-five.'

'Just? Or almost twenty-six?'

Tabitha frowned. How like a man to make her feel older than she was! 'Twenty-five,' she repeated. 'Today.'

The porters, who had been listening, chorused 'Happy birthday, Sister', and she thanked them; Mr Raynard, with a tongue rapidly becoming too large for his mouth, said: 'Yes, yes, of course. I shouldn't be surprised if you haven't been given the

best birthday present of your life.' Which remark Tabitha took
little notice of because, as he himself had said, Mr Raynard
was doped. In the anaesthetic room a few minutes later, Mr
van Beek, looking massive in a rubber apron, came to have a
last word with his patient. Mr Raynard opened his eyes, said
clearly, 'Birthday' and closed them again, and the anaesthetist,
pushing a needle into his colleague's arm, remarked, 'What a
way to spend it!' Tabitha, gowned and masked, saw no reason
to enlighten him as to whose birthday it was. He winked at her
over his mask. 'Coming in to hold his hand, Tabby?' he wanted
to know. 'Hard luck on Mrs Raynard—she only went to her
mother's yesterday, didn't she?'

Tabitha nodded. 'Yes, and Mr Raynard didn't want her to
know, but I telephoned her just now while he and Mr van Beek
were talking on the ward. He'll kill me when he finds out, but
someone had to tell her. She's on her way back now—with
any luck she'll be here by the time he comes round from the
anaesthetic. He'll be very happy to see her.'

The anaesthetist nodded; Mr Raynard was a happily married
man and made no secret of the fact, although Tabitha had often
wondered privately if he growled and grumbled at his wife and
children in the same way as he growled and grumbled at her.

They went into the theatre then and the white-clad figures
rearranged themselves in a group around the operating table—
rather like cricket, thought Tabby, taking up her prescribed
place by the patient's head and handing necessary odds and
ends to the anaesthetist a second before he asked for them. She
was very aware of Mr van Beek on the opposite side of the
table, although she didn't look at him. Instead, she concentrated
on the operation and could only admire the way the surgeon
wired the patella's two pieces back into one again. Watching
him, she found it strange that only an hour previously she had
thought him lazy; he worked fast and neatly and without fuss
while he carried on a casual conversation which had nothing
at all to do with the work in hand. He was just as quick putting
on the plaster too and far neater than Mr Raynard would have
been, for he invariably became bad-tempered and tended to get
plaster on everything and everyone around him, which Mr van

Beek didn't. When finally he had finished he said: 'OK, Sister, you know what to do. I'll be down later,' and walked over to the sink without looking at her.

They were going to have coffee before the next case, and Theatre Sister, who was one of her closest friends, said: 'I'll give you a ring when we're ready, Tabby—I say, I like the stand-in. Lucky you, seeing him every day. Is he married?' She was helping Tabitha drape the blanket over the patient and smiled across at her, and Tabitha, looking at her, thought for a second time that morning that it would be nice to be pretty, even half as pretty as Sue, whose blue eyes were laughing at her now.

'I don't know,' she answered, 'but I should think so, wouldn't you? I mean, he could take his pick, couldn't he?'

Sue laughed. 'I'm going to find out,' she said as she went back into the operating theatre.

Tabitha was surprised to have a summons to bring Mr Bow to theatre within five minutes of her returning to the ward with Mr Raynard. She barely had time to see him safely into his bed and station a nurse at his side before she was accompanying Mr Bow in his turn. She had imagined that Sue, with her blue eyes and pretty face, would have been reason enough for Mr van Beek to spend at least ten minutes getting to know her better. Perhaps he was married after all.

She saw Sue for a few seconds when they reached theatre, and although they were unable to speak Sue frowned and made a face beneath her mask which Tabitha took to mean disappointment of some sort, but she dismissed the subject from her mind as the anaesthetist signaled her to hold Mr Bow's arm steady. The operation took longer than she had expected, but both bones were broken and badly splintered and there was a lot of cleaning up to do before the wound could be partially closed and plaster applied to the leg. This time Mr van Beek made a little window above the wound so that it could be observed and dressed, and in the course of time, have its stitches out.

It was half past eleven by the time she returned to the ward for the second time and sent the next case up with Nurse Betts in attendance. She had a hasty word with Staff Rogers about off-duty, sent her to keep an eye on Mr Bow, and went herself to see how Mr Raynard fared. His wife, a small dark woman, pretty and elegant, had just arrived. She turned a worried face to Tabitha as she entered the cubicle and whispered: 'Hullo, Tabitha—thanks for letting me know. Aren't men awful sometimes?'

Tabitha didn't answer, because she didn't know enough about men to give an opinion, and in any case she imagined that Mrs Raynard's idea of awful meant having a husband who loved her so much that he couldn't bear to upset her when he fell down and broke his kneecap. She said instead:

'Mr Raynard said you weren't to be told, so he'll probably be very annoyed when he comes round—not at you, of course. I'll be close by if he wants to blast me.'

She went away again to confer with Rogers over Mr Bow, and then at Mrs Jeff's insistence, to drink a quick cup of coffee while she wrote up the treatment book, telephoned the hospital laundry and spoke sternly about the lack of draw-sheets on the ward, ironed out the difficulties of the two junior nurses who both wanted the same day off, and then, with a resigned and quick look in the little mirror hanging on the wall of her office, went back into the ward. Mr Raynard had come round; she could hear his wife talking to him. She went into his cubicle and met his baleful, still cloudy eyes.

His tongue was still unmanageable, he mumbled: 'You're nothing but a despot, Tabby. I said...'

Tabitha interposed: 'Yes, I know. I disobeyed you—I'm sorry, but isn't it nice to wake up and find Mrs Raynard here?'

He closed his eyes. 'Yes, dammit, it is.' Mrs Raynard looked across the bed and smiled at her, and Tabitha took his pulse and smiled back.

Mr Bow was coming round too. Tabitha sent Rogers to get the ward cleared for dinner and to look at the patient just back from theatre, and went to see the next one safely on his way; there was only one more now, with any luck, they would all be back soon after one o'clock. She went back to Mr Bow and found his eyes wide open while he frowned at the big cradle in the bed, under which his plastered leg was drying out. 'Hullo,' said Tabitha cheerfully, 'everything's finished and you're back in bed—your leg's in plaster and I expect it feels a little strange.' She took his pulse and was charting it when Mr van Beek came in. He nodded at her, half-smiling. 'Everything all right?' he wanted to know.

She told him in precise terms of pulse and temperature and blood pressure and he nodded again. 'Good—I'll just go and see Bill.'

'His wife's with him.'

'Muriel? I thought I heard her voice. Splendid, I'll have a word with her. Don't come—you must have enough to do.'

She was serving dinners in the kitchen when he put his head round the door. 'The last case will be back in twenty minutes, Sister. Steele's doing it. I'll come in again later on today. Steele will be around if you want anything.'

She nodded as she spooned fish on to the light diet's plates. He asked: 'When are you off?'

Tabitha added potato puree to the fish and said vaguely: 'Oh, this evening—Staff Nurse Rogers will be here...' She was interrupted by a subdued crash from the ward. 'Go and see what that is, Nurse Williams,' she said calmly, 'and take a peep at Mr Bow on your way.' She raised her eyes to the man waiting patiently at the door. 'Staff will be on until nine o'clock—if you want anyone after that there's Night Nurse...and Night Sister, of course.' She was interrupted once more by Nurse Williams bearing a horrid mess of stew and broken plate on a tray.

'Mr Bow's fine, Sister. This is Mr Prosser's and he's very sorry. It slipped.'

Tabitha ladled stew, wondering why Mr van Beek still stood watching. 'Do you want something, sir?' she enquired politely, half her mind on dinners.

He gave her a pleasant smile. 'Yes, Sister, but it can wait.' He was gone, leaving her to fret over the prunes and custard as to what exactly it was that he wanted, and whether it was something she hadn't got on the ward. Perhaps Sue would know; he might have said something to her. She would ask her at dinner.

Sue, although willing enough, was unhelpful. 'I've no idea,' she said. 'He used the usual instruments; he's fussy, but nice about it, and all orthopaedic surgeons are anyway. I tried to find out something about him, but he was closer than an oyster. He's a dear, though—a bit quiet; a pity, because he's got a lovely gravelly voice, hasn't he? Are you on or off?'

'On—I changed with Rogers because Mr Raynard wanted me to go to theatre—my morning was ruined!'

'Never mind, Tabby, it's your weekend.'

'So it is,' Tabitha replied gloomily.

The afternoon went in a flash. It was teatime before she had the opportunity to have a word with Mr Bow, who had made a surprisingly quick recovery from his anaesthetic and had asked for tea. She gave it to him, sip by sip, while they decided what to do.

'I'll have Podger,' said Tabitha, 'he's no trouble. It's your room I'm worried about. Do you want to keep it on?'

She could have bitten her tongue out the moment she had said it, because he answered with faint despair: 'Where else can I go?'

Before she could make a satisfactory answer, Mr van Beek spoke from behind her.

'I hope you'll give me the pleasure of staying with me when you leave hospital, Knotty. We have several years to talk over, have we not? Besides, I need to pick your brains concerning several ideas which have been simmering…. Why not give up your room? I can easily arrange to have your furniture stored.'

Mr Bow looked bewildered. 'But, my dear boy, I don't even know where you live.'

'Near enough,' said the dear boy cryptically, 'and when the time comes we can collect Podger.'

Mr Bow smiled. 'It sounds delightful.'

'Good—we'll fix things for you, if you'll leave it all to us. Now I'm going to ask Sister to get someone to settle you so that she can give you something for that niggling pain.'

He lifted a languid hand in salute and crossed the ward to

Mr Raynard's cubicle, and presently Tabitha heard him laughing there. He had a pleasant laugh, almost a chuckle. She sighed without reason, smiled at Mr Bow and went to find a nurse so that she could accompany Mr van Beek on his ward round. Afterwards, he went back to Mr Raynard again and Tabitha left them talking because it was time for her to go off duty and Rogers had to have the report. It didn't take long, for Rogers had only been away for the afternoon hours; Tabitha gave her the keys, put on her cuffs, took off her apron, and with it tucked under one arm, wished everyone a good evening and started off down the corridor. She was a quarter of the way down its length when the ward door flapped open and shut behind her and Mr van Beek's voice brought her to a halt. She turned round to face him and asked 'Now what?' in a resigned voice so that he smiled and said:

'Nothing—at least nothing to do with the ward. I was wondering—' he sounded diffident, 'if you're going to see about Mr Bow's rent and so forth, if I might come with you. Perhaps the landlady…?' He paused delicately and Tabitha thought that he must have possessed himself of quite a lot of inside information about Mr Bow's circumstances. It would indeed be helpful if he were to parley with the landlady. She said thoughtfully:

'Yes, I think it might be easier if you were to see her. I was going now, on my way home—I could give you a lift.'

'Your car? Can you leave it here—we'll use mine. Are you on duty early tomorrow?'

'No, not until eleven. I suppose I could catch a bus.'

'Right, that's settled.' He looked at his watch. 'Twenty minutes' time, then—the staff car park.' He went back into the ward without waiting for her to answer.

Tabitha went to the changing room and changed into the pale blue jersey dress she had worn to work that morning, wishing at the same time that she had worn something more eye-catching. Not that she had any hope of Mr van Beek's grey eyes resting on her for more than a few moments. How wonderful it would have been, she thought, if he had asked her out, not just to show him where Mr Bow lived, but because she was lovely to look at and amusing. She uttered an impatient sigh, tugged the pins impatiently from her hair and re-did it even tighter than usual, taking a perverse satisfaction in adding to the mediocrity of her appearance.

# CHAPTER TWO

THE SENIOR medical staff had a car park of their own on the right of the hospital forecourt. It was almost empty at this time of day, for the normal day's rounds were done and the theatres had finished at four o'clock and it was still too early for any possible extra visits to ill patients. There were only three cars in it, two of which Tabitha instantly recognized; the souped-up Mini Mr Jenkins, the gynae consultant, affected, and the elderly, beautifully kept Austin saloon the radiologist had bought some fifteen years previously and had never found necessary to change. The third car was a Bentley T convertible of a pleasing and unobtrusive shade of grey, in whose driving seat Mr van Beek was lounging. As Tabitha approached he got out, ushered her in to sit beside him and enquired in a friendly voice where Mr Bow lived.

'About five minutes' drive,' said Tabitha, and felt regret that it wasn't five hours. 'The quickest way is to turn left into the High Street, down Thomas Street and turn right at the bottom of the hill.'

He let in the clutch. 'Are you in a hurry?' he enquired mildly.

Tabitha blinked her thick short eyelashes. 'No,' she said in a practical voice, 'but I should think you would be—you must have had a hard day and I don't expect you want to waste your evening.' She gave him a brief enquiring look and wondered why he looked amused.

'No, I don't intend to,' he agreed gravely. 'Is this where we turn right?'

They were almost there; Tabitha wished she were Sue, who would have known how to turn even such a short encounter as this to good advantage. She said a little abruptly: 'It's this row of houses—the fourth from the end,' and even as she spoke he was bringing the car to a gentle halt. They were standing on

27

the doorstep waiting for someone to answer their ring when Tabitha asked: 'What are we going to say?'

Mr van Beek looked down at her earnest face and said lazily: 'If you wouldn't mind just mentioning who I am...' The door opened and the woman she had seen the previous evening stood in front of them. There was a cigarette dangling from her lip and her hair was caught up in orderly rows of curlers under a pink net. Without removing the cigarette, she said: 'Hullo, you again,' and gave Tabitha an unwilling smile which widened when she looked at Mr van Beek.

'Good evening,' said Tabitha, 'I said I should be coming...this is Mr van Beek who wishes to make some arrangement about Mr Bow.'

The woman stood aside willingly enough for them to go in and Mr van Beek thanked her with charm; still with charm but with a faint undertone of command he said: 'If you will be good enough to come with us—'and when the woman looked surprised, 'We intend to pack up Mr Bow's possessions. He is an old friend of mine and wishes me to arrange for them to be stored; he won't be coming back here.'

Mr Bow's landlady bridled as she opened the door. 'Not coming back, ain't 'e? I'll need a week's rent in lieu—and there's 'is washing.'

Mr van Beek was standing in the middle of the little room, looking at everything, his face inscrutable. 'You shall have whatever is owing to you,' he stated, and there was faint distaste in his quiet voice. 'Be good enough to tell us which of these things belong to Mr Bow and we will pack them up while you are making out your bill, then you might return, please, and make sure that we have forgotten nothing.'

The woman said carelessly: 'OK, if that's 'ow you want it. The silver's 'is and them pictures and the desk; there's a case under the bed too.' She crossed the room to open the drawers in a chest under the window. ''Ere's 'is clothes.' She went back to the door. 'Don't take nothing of mine,' she cautioned as she went.

Tabitha already had Mr Bow's case open on the bed. She

crossed the room and in her turn, started to investigate the chest of drawers.

'Poor old gentleman,' she observed, half to herself, 'how he must have hated it here.'

Mr van Beek had seated himself upon the table, swinging one long leg and looking around him in a thoughtful manner. 'Are you in a hurry?' he asked for the second time that evening.

Tabitha had scooped up an armful of clothes. 'Not really,' she answered cautiously as she bore them back to the bed. Was he going away to leave her to do all the work? Apparently not.

'Then do leave that for a moment and sit down.'

'Why?'

'Because I think that you are a sensible young woman and we have to get Knotty's future settled, more or less.'

Tabitha put her burden on the bed and perched on the bed beside it, wondering why his opinion of her good sense gave her so little pleasure. She crossed her hands tidily in her lap and said tranquilly: 'I'm listening.'

He said unexpectedly: 'You're a very restful girl. Most women are forever patting their hair or putting on lipstick or peering at themselves in those silly little mirrors they carry around.'

She made no answer. She felt fairly sure that doing all of these things would make little difference to her appearance, but there seemed little point in telling him so, for it was surely something he could see for himself. She suspected that he was a kind man, wishful of putting her at her ease. He smiled at her and she smiled back, and when he got out his pipe and enquired: 'Do you mind?' she shook her head, feeling at ease with him.

'Mr Bow,' he began, 'was my science tutor at university. We struck up quite a friendship, for he had known my father when he was alive and had been to our home several times. He was a keen sailor when he was younger—still is, I dare-say—and so am I. We did a good deal of sailing together, the pair of us. When I went back to Holland he visited me from time to time, then about five years ago he didn't answer my letters any more and when I went to his home, no one knew where he was. Each time I came to England I made an effort to find him, but without success, and then, today—there he was.' He looked round the room. 'Obviously fallen on bad times, if these few things are all he has left. He's a proud old man, which probably accounts for his silence and disappearance, and he'll be difficult to help. When he's better I think I could persuade him to come home with me for a holiday, but what then?'

Tabitha hadn't interrupted at all, but now she said: 'I don't know where you live, but if it's a town of any size, could he not teach—English perhaps if he's to live in Holland—just enough to make him feel independent? I know he's eighty, but there's nothing wrong with his brain.'

'I think you may be right. A holiday first, possibly with one or two others—Bill and Muriel Raynard perhaps. It's worth going into.'

He got up. 'Thank you for your suggestion. I believe I'll act upon it when the time comes. In the meantime we had better see to this stuff.'

Tabitha got to her feet. 'You'll need something to put the silver and china into. How about the desk drawers—are they locked?'

He tugged gently. 'No—if we can get everything into them, I can get someone to collect the desk.' He roamed around, collecting old newspapers, and started to wrap the silver carefully. Tabitha finished filling the suitcase, closed it, and began on the china. 'I'll take the case with me,' she promised, 'Mr Bow will want some things later.' Her eyes lighted on a pile of books in a corner of the room. 'I'd better take those as well.'

'No,' said Mr van Beek positively, 'I will—and the clothes. I'll put them in the car and drop them off at the hospital as I go past later on. Do you live close by?'

She thought he had probably had enough of her prosaic company. 'Oh yes. A few minutes' walk.' She added, to make it easier for him: 'I enjoy walking,' and when he replied: 'So do I,' it wasn't what she had expected him to say. The appearance of the landlady prevented further conversation and Tabitha sat down on the bed again and listened to Mr van Beek putting the woman in her place with a blandness which most effectively concealed his intention of having his own way, so that she presently went away again, clutching the money he had given her and looking bewildered, for she had gained the impression that he was one of those casual gentlemen who didn't bother to look at bills, only paid them.

'The shark!' observed Tabitha as the door closed upon the lady of the house. 'I wonder how many times she charged Mr Bow for laundry which never went.' She got to her feet once more and went round the room, opening and shutting cupboards and drawers to make sure nothing had been overlooked while her companion watched her with a little smile. 'Nothing,' she remarked unnecessarily and went to the door, waiting for him. He picked up the case and the books and led the way downstairs and out to the car where she said awkwardly: 'Well, goodbye, Mr van Beek—I hope your evening...' She got no further.

'Get in,' he said mildly. 'I've no intention of leaving you to walk home.'

Tabitha opened her mouth, but before she could utter, he said again: 'Do get in.' She did as she was told then, and when he had settled her in the seat beside him, she said: 'It's up Thomas Street and left at the traffic lights, straight on past the station, and then the first turning on the left.'

They talked only commonplaces during the short drive and when he drew up outside her flat she prepared to get out immediately, longing to ask him in but deciding against it because he might probably accept out of politeness. He leaned across her and opened the door and said casually:

'It's a full round tomorrow, so I'm told—we shall see each other then. Thank you for your help.'

She got out before she answered him. 'Yes—I'm on for the rounds. I—I was glad to help, although you made it all very easy.' She smiled, feeling a little shy, and was relieved when Meg flung the house door open and called in her soft voice: 'There you are, Miss Tabby, late again!' Which remark made it easy for Tabitha to say: 'Well, I must go—good night, sir.' She stood back and he closed the car door, lifted a hand in

salute and eased the big car slowly forward and away. She
watched it until a bend in the road hid it from sight, then went
indoors to answer Meg's questions.

Mr van Beek arrived dead on time for his ward round, which
Tabitha found a refreshing change from Mr Raynard, who had
a disconcerting habit of turning up either much too early or so
late that the whole ward routine was thrown out of gear. She
met the party at the door, looking calm and unruffled and very
neat, so that no one looking at her would have believed her if
she had recounted just how much work she had already got
through, and certainly no one thought to ask; Mr van Beek
gave her a pleasant and impersonal good morning and Mr
Steele and Tommy Bates, the houseman, had both said 'Hullo,
Tabby,' which was what they always said. In the ward they
would be careful to address her as Sister for the benefit of the
patients, which was a waste of time anyway, for she was aware
that they all called her Tabby behind her back. As George
Steele had once remarked, Tabby was such a cosy name. Tabby
had shuddered at his words, glimpsing a perpetual picture of
herself getting cosier and cosier over the years until someone,
some day, would prefix the Tabby with the word old.

This morning, however, there was no fear of that—indeed,
she looked a great deal younger than her twenty-five years, for
although her hair was still screwed ruthlessly into its severe
bun, there was a pinkness in her cheeks which gave her eyes
an added sparkle, although her greeting was sedate enough. She
had already done her morning round, and primed with her men-
tal list of plasters due for changing, extensions that needed
adjusting, pains for investigation and several urgent requests
from patients to go home, she advanced on Jimmy's bed, where
she stationed herself opposite Mr van Beek, handed him the
patient's board wordlessly, and waited while he read it.

'The plaster's due off, I see, Sister.' He glanced at Tommy
Bates. 'If Mr Bates would be good enough to do this, I will
come back presently and have a look.' He smiled at the jubilant
look on Jimmy's face. 'That doesn't mean that you're going to
get up and walk home—but we will have it X-rayed just once

more, and if the result is what I expect it to be, then we'll get you on your legs again. I'll discuss it with Sister presently.'

He turned away, leaving Jimmy grinning at Tommy Bates, who played rugger himself and was already wielding the plaster cutters with a masterly hand. Mr van Beek had reached the next bed when he asked over his shoulder:

'Where do you play, Jimmy?'

'Half-back, sir.'

'Ah yes—done during a tackle...'

'Rugger player yourself, sir?' ventured Jimmy.

Mr van Beek gave a half smile. 'Er—yes, but some years ago, I'm afraid.' He turned away and became instantly engrossed in a sub-capital fracture of femur which Mr Raynard had dealt with a few weeks previously, by means of a metal prosthesis. Old Mr Dale was a difficult patient, now he saw a new face to which he might grumble. Which he did at some length, while Mr van Beek listened with an impassive face and Tabitha and George Steele stood impassively by, listening to Mr Dale blackening their characters with no sign of discomfort, for they shared the view that an irascible old gentleman of well over seventy who had grumbled all his life was now too old to change his ways, and as neither of them had done any of the things of which they were accused, they didn't allow him to worry them. Nor, it seemed, did Mr van Beek, for when the old gentleman had at last finished complaining, he said soothingly:

'Yes—we all appreciate how tiresome it is for you to stay in bed, Mr Dale, and how irksome it is for you not to be able to sit in a chair. I feel sure that it has been explained to you why this is. However, as it distresses you so much, I fancy we may be able to help.' He looked at Tabitha, his grey eyes twinkling. 'Gentle traction here, I think, Sister, don't you?' He removed his gaze to Mr Steele. 'I'll leave you to deal with that, if I may, Steele. A couple of weeks should suffice—that will bring us to a month after the operation, will it not? Time enough for the prosthesis to have become firm.'

He turned back to the patient and explained, in a reasonable voice which brooked no contradiction, why the treatment was to be changed, and added: 'And I should prefer it, Mr Dale, if you refrain from complaining about my colleagues without reason. Mr Raynard operated most successfully upon your hip, and, if you will allow it, your treatment is equally successful.' He smiled, the gentle smile Tabitha liked to see. 'You should join the team, not fight against it, you know.'

They were at the next bed when they heard Mr Dale chuckle, and Tabitha, who had been envisaging the horrors of getting traction on the recalcitrant old man, smiled and caught Mr van Beek's eye. Mr van Beek winked.

Mr Prosser welcomed them with all the pleasure of a host inviting old friends in for a drink, and a great deal of time was lost while he and Mr van Beek discussed the nutritional value of fish and chips and the psychological effect of eating them from newspaper. 'Adds a bit of interest,' declared Mr Prosser. 'Tell you what, you bring Sister 'ere down to my place when I get 'ome—I'll give yer the finest bit o' cod you've ever 'ad.'

Mr van Beek said mildly: 'Well, that won't be for a little while yet, you know, but I'll accept your invitation, as I'm sure Sister will.'

They both looked at Tabitha, who said hurriedly: 'Oh, yes— that would be delightful,' because that seemed to be the answer they expected of her, although privately she was unable to visualize Mr van Beek doing any such thing, and certainly not in her company, but by the time Mr Prosser got back home the man standing opposite her would be lecturing in some other land, or at best, back in his own country. She wondered whereabouts he lived in Holland, a country about which she knew almost nothing. She was struggling to remember a little of its geography when Mr van Beek's voice, patiently requesting her to hand him an X-ray form, penetrated her thoughts. She said: 'Oh, sorry, sir,' and went rather a pretty pink, causing Mr Prosser to remark: 'You look bobbish, Sister—come up on the pools, ducks?'

She laughed then, as did the two men with her as they moved down the ward.

Mr Bow, when they got to him, was looking considerably better. His plastered leg seemed to take up most of the bed and his face was pale, but his eyes were clear and as blue as ever. Tabitha had already seen him, of course, but she had left Mr van Beek to explain what had been done, which he did now, with a masterly absence of the more gruesome details and a good deal of humour. 'I'll be back to have a chat, Knotty,' he concluded, 'Saturday at some time.' He glanced at Tabitha as he spoke and she murmured: 'Of course, sir,' while regretting bitterly that she would be at Chidlake and would miss him.

Mr Raynard was better too; his knee dealt with and encased in plaster, he had allowed himself to relax sufficiently to sample the pile of thrillers his wife had thoughtfully provided. He put his book down as Tabitha pulled aside the cubicle curtain and said: 'Tabby, where have you been? I've not seen you the whole morning.'

'I don't expect you have, sir,' she replied with composure. 'You were fast asleep when I came to see you at eight o'clock, and when I came back from Matron's office you had had your breakfast and had gone to sleep again.' She added kindly: 'Plenty of sleep is good for you.'

He growled something at her and then said: 'Well, come here—I've something for you,' and when she obeyed, he produced an envelope from under the bedclothes and offered it to her. 'Your birthday present,' he said gruffly, 'a day late, but I got Muriel to do something about it. Open it.'

She did so and gave a chortle of mingled pleasure and laughter. It was a year's subscription to *Vogue*—it would be delightful to leaf through its extravagant pages, although her stepmother and Lilith would laugh at the notion of her taking any of its advice. But they didn't have to know and there was no reason why she shouldn't wear pretty clothes even if she were plain. She said warmly: 'You're a dear, sir—it's a gorgeous present. Thank you very much.'

'Glad you like it—did you have lots of presents?'

Tabitha said: 'Oh, yes, heaps,' and looked up to see Mr van Beek's discerning eyes upon her, just as though he knew that the only present she had had was a scarf from Meg. She flushed guiltily and made for the door saying: 'I've just remembered—something I had to tell Staff…' and made her escape to the office, where she allowed her cheeks to cool before going back again, her usual calm self.

Mr van Beek had begun a highly technical discussion with his friend into which he drew her at once, almost as though he hadn't noticed that she had been gone; she joined in, almost convinced that she had been oversensitive and that he hadn't given her that peculiarly penetrating look after all. By the time they were ready to go back to see Jimmy's now unplastered leg, she was persuaded that she had been rather silly.

The male members of the party, having viewed the leg, fell to a lively discussion on the game of Rugby football and she stood patiently listening until the smell of the patient's dinners reminded her that the round had taken longer than usual. She sent Mr Steele a speaking glance which Mr van Beek intercepted. 'Ah, dinners, Sister—am I right?' He led the way to the ward door, where, probably unaware that the roast beef and Yorkshire pudding were getting cold, he paused to thank her agreeably for her assistance and wish her a good day. She watched the three men walk away without haste up the corridor, Mr van Beek looming head and shoulders above his companions.

She saw him only very briefly the next day and in the evening she went to Chidlake.

It was a beautiful early evening, and because she was in no hurry, she took a cross-country route which led her along narrow, high-hedged lanes which wound in and out of villages well away from the main roads and still preserving an old-world charm quite hidden from the motorists on the highway. She stopped briefly at Ottery St Mary for petrol, and took a small back road which climbed steeply towards the coast, and after a while crossed the main coastal road into a country lane roofed with overhanging trees. The lane wound its way casually for a mile or so down to the village and although she couldn't see the sea yet, it was close by. Presently the trees parted, leaving the lane to go on by itself between fields and an occasional house or row of cottages. Tabitha stopped then, for now she could see Chidlake and, beyond its roof, the sea, with the Dorset coast spreading itself grandly away into the evening's dimness. The view was magnificent; she sat back and enjoyed it, longing to be going home to her mother and father, instead of to two people who had no love for her; no liking even. She was only too well aware that the only reason she had been invited now was because her stepmother felt that it was the right thing to do.

Tabitha started up the car and went on down the hill towards her home. She wasn't looking forward to the next two days, but at least she would see some old friends at the dance, and that would be pleasant. She turned off the lane and up the short drive to the house, a pleasant Georgian edifice, not large, but roomy enough to shelter a fair-sized family in its rambling interior. She stopped in front of the rose-covered porch and got out, taking her case with her, and went indoors.

The hall extended from front to back of the house and she could see the garden through its open door, still colourful in the evening light, as she went into the sitting room. It was large and low-ceilinged with French windows leading to the lawn beyond. Its furniture was the same as Tabitha remembered from her earliest childhood; beautiful, graceful pieces which had been in the family for many years, and although her stepmother hadn't liked them, she had had to admit that they suited the house, so they had been allowed, mercifully, to stay. Her stepmother was seated by a window, reading, and although she put down her book when Tabitha went in, she didn't get up but said sharply: 'You're late. We had dinner, but I daresay there's something in the kitchen if you want it.' She eyed Tabitha with cool amusement. 'That's a pretty dress you're wearing, but what a pity it's wasted on you. I must say, Tabitha, you don't grow any better looking. What a good thing you have the sort of job where looks don't matter.'

Tabitha said dryly: 'Yes, isn't it?' and prepared to leave the room again; she had heard it all before, and would doubtless hear it all again at some time or other. She asked: 'The usual room, I suppose?' and when Mrs Crawley nodded, went upstairs. At the head of the staircase she crossed the landing, and passing the room which used to be hers but which her stepmother had argued was unnecessary to keep as hers now that

she lived away from home, went on up a smaller flight of stairs
to the floor above, where she went into a small room at the
back of the house which she used on her infrequent visits. It
was pleasant enough, simply furnished and with a wide view
of Lyme Bay which almost compensated Tabitha for the loss
of her own room. She unpacked her own things quickly, hung
the new dress carefully in the wardrobe, and went back downstairs to the kitchen where the cook and her husband, the gardener and odd-job man, were eating their supper.

They were a nice enough couple whom her stepmother had
engaged after her father's death, when the old cook and even
older gardener had been dismissed by her as being too elderly
for their jobs. They had gone willingly enough, for Tabitha's
father had remembered them generously enough in his will,
and now they lived in the village where they had spent their
lives and Tabitha made a point of visiting them each time she
went to Chidlake and remembering their birthdays and Christmas, for they had loved her parents and home almost as much
as she did herself. Now she accepted a plate of cold ham and
salad and carried it into the dining room, where she ate her
solitary meal at the rosewood table which could seat twelve so
easily. It had been fully extended; no doubt there would be
people to dinner before the dance.

She took her plate back to the kitchen, wished her stepmother good night and went to her room, where she spent a
long time doing her nails, which were pink and prettily shaped
and one of her small vanities. This done to her satisfaction, she
sat down before the mirror, loosened her hair from its tight bun
and piled it high. It took a long time and she lost patience
several times before it was exactly as she wanted it, but when
it was at last finished, she was pleased enough with the result.
She would do it that way for the dance, she decided, as she
took it down again and brushed it slowly, thinking about Mr
van Beek. She was still thinking about him when she got into
bed; he was nice, she wanted to know more of him, though
there wasn't much chance of that. She supposed he would stay
until Mr Raynard could get back to work once more, and if Mr
Raynard chose to clump around in a plaster, that wouldn't be

long. Then, presumably, he would be off on his lecturing tour and she would never see him again. She sighed, wishing that she was as pretty as Lilith, for if she had been, he would probably have taken her out just for the pleasure of being seen with her. As it was she would have to be content with their brief businesslike trip to Mr Bow's room. She remembered that he had said that she was a restful girl and smiled, and smiling, went to sleep.

There was a lot to do the next day. Lilith, who didn't appear until halfway through the morning, was taken up with the hairdresser, countless telephone calls and endless discussions as to her appearance, which meant that Tabitha had to run several errands in the village, help with the flowers and then assist her stepmother to her room because her head ached. It was lunchtime by then, a hurried meal over which Tabitha and Lilith wasted no time; they had little to say to each other, and beyond remarking that Tabitha looked tired already and pointing out several grey hairs she was sure Tabitha hadn't noticed for herself, Lilith had nothing of importance to say. Tabitha knew about the grey hairs, and ignoring the remark about her tired looks, she got up from the table saying she had several things to do for herself, and made her escape.

It was a pity she couldn't like Lilith; she had tried hard at first, for Lilith was exactly the kind of young sister she would have liked to have; small and dainty and blonde and so pretty that everyone looked at her twice at least. It had taken Tabitha an unhappy year to discover that Lilith was shallow by nature, spiteful by instinct, and only spoke the truth when it suited her. Also she hated Tabitha. Tabitha thought about that as she took out the present she had brought with her for Lilith's birthday. It was an old silver locket and chain and she had chosen it with care because although she had no affection for Lilith, it would still be her birthday and nothing should spoil it.

She spent the afternoon with Jenny and Tom in their little cottage, drinking strong tea and talking about old times, and then walked along the top of the cliffs and over the fields to the house. It looked beautiful in the sunshine and would be even more lovely later on in the evening, for the roses were

well out and the balcony at the back of the house had been
decorated with masses of summer flowers. She went indoors to
the drawing room, cleared for dancing and just as lavishly decorated. She went through the double doors at the end of the
room and up the staircase and met Lilith on the landing. 'There
you are,' said her stepsister. 'How untidy you look! I hope
you'll do better than that this evening. I'm coming to see your
dress.'

Tabitha paused at the foot of the little stairs. 'I don't think
I want you to,' she said quietly. 'I promise you it's quite suitable and I shan't disgrace you.'

She went on up the stairs and Lilith followed her. 'Come
on, Tabitha,' she wheedled, 'it's my birthday—I'm supposed
to be happy all day, and I shan't be if I can't see your dress.'

Tabitha sighed. 'Very well, though I assure you it's nothing
to get excited about.'

She took it out of the cupboard and laid it on the bed, and
Lilith said instantly in a furious voice: 'You can't wear it—
you can't!'

'Why not?' Tabitha was too surprised to feel angry.

'The colour will clash with mine. It's blue—pale blue—that
dress of yours will make it look faded.' She stamped her foot.
'You shan't wear it! You've done it on purpose so that I shan't
look prettier than everyone else.'

'Don't be silly,' said Tabitha bracingly. 'Why should I do
that? And how was I to know what colour you intended to
wear—besides, we're not going to stand together all the evening.'

Lilith didn't reply but ran out of the room; Tabitha could
hear her voice, shrill with temper, raced downstairs, and braced
herself for her stepmother's inevitable intervention on her
daughter's behalf. Mrs Crawley swept in, the little smile Tabitha had learned to dread on her face. Her voice was pleasant
and brisk.

'What's all this fuss about your dress, Tabitha?' Her eyes
studied it, lying on the bed. 'My dear, even if it didn't clash
with Lilith's, you couldn't really wear it. I mean, it just isn't
you, is it? Were you persuaded by some super sales-woman

into buying it? There's that pretty grey and white striped dress you had last year—so suitable. I'm sure you wouldn't want to spoil Lilith's birthday party—it is her party; you know—besides, there's someone she met at the Johnsons' the other evening and she wants to look her best for him, and there's no one you particularly want to impress, is there?'

Tabitha had gone a little white, for she had a fine temper, but she had learned to control it during the last few difficult years. She said now very evenly: 'No, no one. It makes no difference at all what I wear.' And then because she was so angry, she added: 'Would you rather I didn't come?'

Her stepmother looked genuinely shocked. 'Not come? Of course you must come—what would everyone say?'

Tabitha smiled; her stepmother saw it and frowned angrily as she turned to leave. 'Dinner's at eight,' she said shortly. 'You know everyone who's coming. We'll give Lilith her presents while we're having drinks. Everyone else will come about nine or thereabouts.'

After she had gone Tabitha sat down on the bed and cried. She cried for her new dress and for the birthday parties she hadn't had for the last five years, and for the bedroom which had always been hers and wasn't any longer, and because she was lonely. And underneath all these, only half realizing it, she cried for Mr van Beek.

Presently she blew her nose, wiped her eyes and set about repairing the damage—something that she did so well that by half past seven she was dressed in the grey and white stripes, her face nicely made up and her hair piled in intricate little puffs on top of her head, showing off a surprisingly pretty neck. She had pinned a pink velvet bow in front of her coiffure, and after a final appraising look in her mirror she went downstairs, her head held defiantly high, to meet her stepmother and Lilith once more before greeting their dinner guests. Half of their number were friends of Lilith's own age, but the remainder were older people, who had known her parents and herself from a baby, and as she was seated between the vicar, who had christened her, and the doctor who had attended her birth, she enjoyed her dinner. The doctor was long past retiring age, although he still worked on with a young assistant to do the more arduous work. Neither of them had seen her for some time and had a great many questions to ask her which she answered as lightheartedly as possible. Nevertheless, towards the end of the meal the doctor leaned a little nearer and said quietly:

'Tabby, we've worried about you a little. When your father died did he leave provision for you? This may seem like an impertinence, but we have your wellbeing at heart, my dear.'

Tabitha gave him a warm smile. 'Yes, I know, and thank you. Father didn't leave me anything; you see, he hadn't made a will since Mother died. He kept meaning to…I had some trinkets of Mother's and some of the silver. There was an understanding that…' She paused, not liking to say what was in her mind. 'I believe my stepmother misunderstood,' she finished lamely.

'Quite so,' said her companion, 'but I suppose the house will revert to you eventually?'

Tabitha shook her head. 'No—I've been told that it's to be Lilith's.'

The vicar, listening from the other side, looked astounded. 'But she has no connection—Chidlake has been in your family for years—your father must have meant you to have it so that it would pass to your children.'

'Well, I don't see much chance of marrying,' said Tabitha prosaically, 'but I think that's what he intended, because he used to say so when I was a little girl. Still, I have a good job, you know,' she smiled reassuringly at their worried old faces. 'Next time you're out our way, you must come and see the ward.'

The dinner party broke up shortly afterwards and everyone went to the drawing room to await the arrival of the other guests, who presently came in a never-ending stream, laughing and talking and handing a radiant Lilith her presents, and when the small band struck up, taking to the floor in the pleasantly full room. Tabitha danced in turn with the doctor, the vicar and several friends of her parents and once or twice with young men who were Lilith's friends and strangers to the village. Their conversation was limited to asking her who she was and

then expressing surprise at her answer. They danced badly,
something which she did very well, so that when she saw a
young man in a plum-coloured velvet suit and a pink frilled
shirt making his way towards her she slipped away using the
bulky frames of the doctor and his wife as a shield, and went
outside on the balcony. It was a glorious night, with the last
brightness of the sun still lingering over the distant headlands
of Torbay. She wandered away from the drawing room, so that
the music and noise was dimmed a little and leaned over the
balustrade to sniff at the roses below. It was then that she
became aware of Lilith's voice, very gay and excited. She must
have left the drawing room too, although she would of course
have a partner. Tabitha straightened up; if she walked on
quickly, Lilith wouldn't see her. But it was too late, for several
paces away, Lilith cried:

'Tabitha? All alone? Have you run out of partners already?'
She gave a tinkle of laughter. 'We should have got some older
men for you.'

Tabitha turned round. She began quietly: 'That would have
been a good...' Her voice faltered into silence, for the man
with Lilith was Mr van Beek.

Her first reaction was one of deep regret that she wasn't
wearing the new dress, the second that his elegance, in contrast
to his appearance when they had first met, was striking. She
thanked heaven silently for the kindly moonlight and said in a
voice from which she had carefully sponged all surprise: 'Good
evening, Mr van Beek.'

Lilith looked surprised, frowned and then said incredulously:
'You know each other?'

Mr van Beek smiled charmingly at her. 'Indeed we do.' He
turned the same smile on Tabitha, who didn't smile back.

'How very delightful to meet you here, Miss Crawley, and
how providential, for one or two matters of importance have
cropped up—perhaps if Lilith would forgive me, we might settle them now.'

'Settle what?' Lilith wanted to know.

'Oh, some very dull matters concerning patients,' he answered easily. 'Nothing you would want to bother your pretty

head about. Go back and dance with as many of your young men as you can in ten minutes, then you will have all the more time for me.'

Lilith smiled, looking up at him through her long curling lashes.

'All right, Marius, you shall have your ten minutes, though it all sounds very dull.' She didn't bother to look at Tabitha but danced off, the picture of prettiness, to disappear into the drawing room.

Tabitha had stood quietly while they had been talking, and now that Lilith had gone she still made no move. It was Mr van Beek who spoke first. He said, to astonish her: 'Tabitha in moonlight—how charming you look.'

'There's no need,' began Tabitha firmly, 'to flatter me just because you've discovered that I'm Lilith's stepsister.'

His brows lifted. 'That seems a most peculiar reason for flattery, which, by the way, isn't flattery. I did know that you were stepsisters. You do look charming—you've done your hair differently too.'

He smiled at her so kindly that she burst out: 'Moonlight's kind. Wait until you see me indoors, I'm as plain as ever I was.'

He came and leant on the balustrade beside her. 'I'm sure your mother and father never told you that you were plain.'

'Of course they didn't.'

'Then why do you think you are?'

She looked at him in astonishment. 'I grew up knowing it,' she frowned. 'At least, I guessed I would be.' She fumbled for words. 'I—I knew, that is, before I was told.'

'And who told you?'

Tabitha had a sudden vivid memory of standing before the mirror in the hall, doing something to her hair. It had been soon after her father had brought his second wife home, and already Tabitha had become aware that she wasn't liked. Her stepmother had stopped and looked at her reflection over her shoulder and said, gently mocking: 'Why do you fuss so, Tabitha, surely you know by now that there is nothing much you can do to improve matters? You're a plain girl, my dear.' Tabitha could still hear that light mocking voice.

'Well, go on,' prompted Mr van Beek gently, but she shook her head and then changed her mind to say uncertainly: 'Well, she only told me something I guessed was true, only I didn't want to admit it…!'

'You should never guess,' he stated firmly. 'Now you've got an *idée fixe* about it, haven't you? All you need is treatment.'

She eyed him suspiciously. 'Treatment? What sort of treatment?'

'At some convenient time I will answer that, Tabitha. Now shall we go indoors and finish this dance?'

Tabitha agreed, thinking that he was getting bored. The conversation had hardly been a sparkling one, and that had been her fault. The music had started some time earlier; he would only have to partner her once or twice round the drawing room. She was right, or almost so, for they had circled the floor exactly one and a half times when the band stopped playing and she muttered some excuse about speaking to an old friend, and went to sit by old Lady Tripp, who was indeed an old friend of her mother's when she had been alive. Tabitha plunged into an awkward conversation; her companion was deaf and everything had to be said at least twice, so that the thread was quickly lost.

In a minute or two she looked cautiously round the room and saw Mr van Beek dancing with Lilith. Even from the other end of the room, she could see that Lilith was sparkling, her lovely face alight with pleasure, which apparently Mr van Beek shared, for he was smiling down at her, and whatever it was he was saying made her laugh happily. Tabitha smiled herself, albeit with difficulty, while she listened with sympathy to Lady Tripp's detailed description of her arthritis, at the same time wondering how and where Lilith had met Mr van Beek. Her stepmother had said that Lilith had met someone at the Johnsons', and as far as she could see, he was the someone—and just the sort of man Lilith would marry. He was a good deal too old for her, of course, but did that really matter if he had a good position and money to give her all the luxuries she demanded of life? Lilith was undoubtedly the sort of girl a man would want for a wife, especially an older, successful man, and presumably Mr van Beek was successful. She wasn't sure, but it seemed unlikely that he could afford to run a Bentley like his unless he had a very good practice or money of his own—Mr Raynard had said that he was at the height of his career. She was roused sharply from her thoughts by Lady Tripp, who wanted to know, in the kindest possible way, if she had a young man yet. She was attempting to answer this question when she was asked to dance, and although it was one of the very young men trailing attendance on Lilith, Tabitha welcomed him with rather more enthusiasm than she felt and followed him on to the dance floor to twist and whirl and weave with a gracefulness which Mr van Beek, who was talking to the vicar, watched with a lazy enjoyment which sadly enough she failed to observe.

Despite the lateness of the hour when she had gone to bed, Tabitha was up early the next morning. She would go back to St Martin's after tea—before, if she could manage to get away, but now the sun was shining and a walk would be delightful before breakfast. She dressed and went down to the kitchen and made herself some tea and stood drinking it at the open kitchen door, thinking about the dance. It had been, according to her stepmother, a great success, even the fact that Tabitha had already met Mr van Beek hadn't spoiled Lilith's triumph, for she had been extravagant in her praise of him and full of plans in which he largely figured.

'He's got a Bentley,' she told Tabitha with glee. 'I shall ask him to take me to Bournemouth or Torquay for the day.'

Tabitha had said nothing, although she wondered if Mr van Beek was quite the man to enjoy either of these resorts during the summer months; she had an idea that his tastes might run to something quieter. In answer to Lilith's close questioning about her acquaintance with him, she had been briskly offhand. She had made no mention of Mr Bow, and Lilith, whose knowledge of hospital life was fragmental, imagined that as a surgeon he had merely to walk into the theatre, operate and go home again, and Tabitha saw no reason to enlighten her. She couldn't stop Lilith getting Mr van Beek if she wanted him, but she certainly wasn't going to help her; she was vague to the point of stupidity when Lilith demanded to know when he was likely to be free and which days of the week he could be expected to operate, and even more vague as to the length of time he would be likely to remain at the hospital.

She finished her tea, dismissed her thoughts because they weren't very happy ones, and prepared to enjoy her walk. She crossed the fields towards the sea as she had done the previous afternoon, and walked, in the coolness of the early morning, down to Lyme Regis and out along the Cobb. There were few people about, mostly exercising their dogs, and at the end of the Cobb, a handful of enthusiastic people getting ready to sail. Tabitha went and sat on the edge of the stone wall and watched them, carrying on a casual conversation the while. She was getting to her feet once more when Mr van Beek said from behind her: 'Good morning—I imagined you would still be in bed.'

Tabitha turned round slowly, not attempting to hide her pleasure at seeing him and at the same time resolutely recognizing his remark as a figure of speech and no more. She said cheerfully: 'Hullo—not on a morning like this.' Her eye fell on an elderly dog with a woolly coat standing beside him. 'That's Fred, isn't it—unless you own his double.'

He laughed. 'The Johnsons' dog, not mine. You know him, I see.'

'For years. He must be twelve now—he used to come swimming with me.'

He asked abruptly: 'You were happy, weren't you? Here in your lovely home, with all your friends. Has your family been here long?'

'About a hundred and fifty years—the house was built during the Regency period.'

'And what will happen to it now—is it to be yours, or will your stepmother…?'

Tabitha turned away so that he wouldn't be able to see her face. She spoke steadily. 'My father didn't leave—that is, he didn't make a will. My stepmother owns it, naturally. I expect when Lilith marries she will live there.'

He sounded surprised. 'Lilith live there? I simply can't imagine it. She likes London, I imagine—a flat in a modern block of skyscrapers and Harrods just around the corner.' He spoke lightly, almost jokingly, and she answered carefully.

'Lilith is pretty and very popular—she has dozens of friends. Of course she likes a carefree life, but she'll settle down in a year or so.'

He didn't answer. She stooped to pat Fred. 'Well, I must be getting back.' She edged away, but not fast enough, for he reached out and caught her bare arm.

'I'll run you back—I've got the car at the end of the Cobb. There's no hurry.'

She said 'No,' quickly, and then because he gave her such a strange look, went on: 'It's kind of you, but I like walking. I wouldn't like to disturb my sister and stepmother, they're still sleeping.'

Mr van Beek gave her a long considering look. 'I see that you have another *idée fixe,*' he observed mildly, although he didn't tell her what it was this time. 'In which case, since you don't care for me to drive you back, I will, if I may, walk with you.'

Tabitha caught her breath. 'No—yes, well it's two miles across the fields and along the cliff path.' She looked at him anxiously.

His face bore no expression other than that of polite interest. 'Yes? In that case I daresay Fred and I shall give up about halfway. We are neither of us as young as we were.' If he heard Tabitha's sigh of relief he gave no sign, and now that the danger of arriving at Chidlake with him and being seen by a furious Lilith was averted, Tabitha became quite cheerful.

They started to walk back along the Cobb with Fred lumbering beside them. They were halfway along its length when Mr van Beek said:

'You should wear your hair like that more often.'

Tabitha slowed her pace to look at him. 'Like this?' she

asked in an amazed voice. 'Just hanging—I've tied it back anyhow.'

'And very nice too, although I do appreciate that it might not do under a sister's cap.'

'Oh, I couldn't,' her voice was matter-of-fact, 'it took hours and I'd never have time in the morning.'

He stooped and picked up a pebble and threw it for Fred, so that they had to stand and wait while he shuffled after it. 'Yes, I daresay, but surely after a little practice you would be quicker?'

She accepted Fred's proffered pebble and gave him an affectionate pat before she replied: 'I suppose I could try. But what's the point?'

'Why, to prove to yourself that you aren't plain, of course.'

Tabitha felt temper well up inside her. 'Oh, don't be ridiculous,' she cried, 'and stop patronizing me just because you're sorry for me. You've got Lilith…'

They were off the Cobb now, climbing the steep road to the footpath. She started to run, not looking back, and didn't stop until she was almost at the end of the path, with Chidlake in sight across the fields.

She went back before tea, pleading an interview with Matron which couldn't be avoided. That Matron would wish to interview any of her staff on a Sunday was highly improbable, but it was the only excuse Tabitha had been able to think of and in any case neither of her listeners were sufficiently interested to want to know more. She said her goodbyes thankfully and drove the Fiat out of the gate and up the hill, away from the village and the sea. At the top she stopped and looked back. It was a very clear day, Chidlake stood out sharply against its panoramic background. She could see every window and every chimney, even the roses at the front door. She saw something else too—the Bentley gliding up the hill below the house, then turning in at its gate to stop before the door. She didn't wait to see Mr van Beek get out, but started the little car's engine with a savagery quite alien to her nature and drove, a great deal faster than was her habit, back to her own little flat.

# CHAPTER THREE

TABITHA had regained her usual calm by the time Mr van Beek arrived on the ward the next day. She wished him good morning in a stony voice and pretended not to see his swift glance at the fiercely screwed-up bun beneath her starched cap. She led him firmly round the ward, speaking when spoken to and not otherwise, and then only on matters connected with her patients' broken limbs. George Steele and Tommy looked at her first with astonishment and then frankly puzzled, and when George enquired, sotto voce, if she was sickening for something and had his head bitten off for his pains, they exchanged a bewildered look, for this wasn't their good-natured Tabby at all. Only Mr van Beek, going impassively about his business, appeared oblivious of anything amiss. At Mr Bow's bedside he paused for a minute after examining the leg exposed for his inspection.

'You're doing well, Knotty,' he offered. 'We'll have you in a boat before the summer's out, even if we do have to carry you.'

The old man smiled. 'You were always a man to get your own way, Marius, so I'll not contradict you.' He sighed. 'I must say it sounds tempting.'

'Leave it to me,' said Mr van Beek. 'I have everything planned, even Podger.'

They all moved away, Tabitha wondering what the plans for Podger might be. It seemed she wasn't to be told until Mr van Beek saw fit, which annoyed her to the point of frowning, and Mr Raynard snapped: 'What's bitten you, Tabby? Where's all the womanly charm? You look as though you're encased in metal armour plating. Wasn't the weekend a success?'

She was about to answer this when Mr van Beek answered for her.

'Miss Tabitha Crawley danced the lot of us into the floor,'

he remarked, 'and looked delightful doing it too. What is more, she was up with the sun the next morning. I know, because I was up too, exercising my host's dog. We met.'

He smiled at Tabitha, who stared woodenly back and uttered a brief and equally wooden 'Yes'. But if she had hoped to discourage him from recalling the happenings of the weekend, she failed lamentably, for he went on to describe it in detail in a lazy, good-natured manner, even remarking upon the extreme good looks of Lilith.

'A bit young,' remarked Mr Raynard obscurely. 'I met her mother once—terrifying woman, always smiling.' He coughed and added hastily: 'Sorry, Tabby—quite forgot. I'm sure she's very—er—competent,' he finished inadequately.

What at? wondered Tabitha, unless it's making me out to be a halfwit with a face that ought to be veiled and no taste in clothes. She frowned again and changed it quickly into a smile because the men were looking at her.

'Shall I get someone to bring your coffee in here?' she enquired, a little haughty because they had all been staring so. 'Unless there's anyone else Mr van Beek wants to see.'

They agreed, still puzzled, because it had become the custom for them all to crowd into Tabitha's office after a ward round and drink their coffee there, wreathed in pipe smoke and eating their way steadily through her week's supply of biscuits. So Nurse Betts, a little mystified, took a tray into Mr Raynard's cubicle, and presently Tabitha, drinking her own Nescafé while she wrestled with the off duty, listened to the hum of cheerful talk coming from his bedside. Someone was being very amusing, judging from the bellows of laughter. She gave up the off duty after a few minutes and went along to the linen cupboard to see if there were enough sheets. They were on the top shelf and she had climbed on to the shelf below the better to count them, when the door opened behind her. She froze, because the nursing staff were supposed to use the steps, not climb around the cupboard like monkeys, and whoever it was, Matron, or worse, Fanny Adams, the Assistant Matron, would point this out to her in the tone of voice used by someone who had discovered wrongdoing and felt justified in censuring it.

She took a firmer grip on the upright of the top shelf and looked down behind her. Mr van Beek was lounging in the doorway, his hands in his pockets, watching her with interest. She waited for him to make the obvious remark about the steps and when he didn't, felt compelled to say: 'This is so much easier than those little steps. I thought you were Matron.'

'Heaven forbid!' he murmured gravely. 'Come down, I want to talk to you.'

Tabitha stayed where she was. 'I'm busy, sir, counting sheets.' A sudden thought struck her. 'Unless it's urgent?'

'It's urgent,' he said instantly.

'Then I'll come down,' said Tabitha, to find herself instantly clasped round her waist and lifted to the ground. The linen room was small, a mere cupboard, and they were forced to stand very close. She put a hand to her cap and said a trifle anxiously: 'Not Mr Bow…he was fine.'

'And still is. Why did you run away?'

A question Tabitha didn't wish to answer. She said instead: 'It was urgent.'

'I consider it urgent, and I should like an answer.'

She saw that she would have to give him one or stay imprisoned with the sheets and pillowcases for an unlimited period. She drew a breath and began quietly: 'I don't want to be pitied. To be compared with Lilith and then pitied is more than I can stand—it makes me bad-tempered and envious and I try not to be, and then you come along and stir me up.'

'Good,' said Mr van Beek with lazy satisfaction.

Tabitha flashed him a cross look and found his eyes, very calm and clear, contemplating her. Her voice throbbed with the beginnings of temper. 'It's nothing of the sort. I've made a life for myself; I've a home and Meg and a job that I can keep for the rest of my life.'

'God forbid!' interposed Mr van Beek with deep sincerity, and when she gaped at him he added: 'No, no—I don't mean that you're not a splendid nurse—you are, but there are other things. You seem to think you're not entitled to any of them.'

She made a small sound, half snort, half sigh. 'You're not a girl.'

His lips twitched. 'No—meaning that I am unable to understand?'

'Yes,' said Tabitha baldly, 'that's exactly what I do mean. And now if there's nothing more you want to say, I think I should get on with my work.'

His eyes twinkled. 'Shall I lift you up, since I lifted you down?'

She shook her head and he turned away from the door and then paused to ask:

'Would it be possible to do the Wednesday round half an hour earlier? That beguiling young sister of yours has teased me into taking her to Torquay, and if I could get away by eleven…'

Tabitha fought a violent desire to burst into tears, box Mr van Beek's ears and find Lilith at once and do her some injury. She was still feeling surprise at her strong feelings as she said stonily: 'That will be perfectly all right, sir,' and stood waiting for him to go, and when he saw that she wasn't going to say anything more, he said: 'Well, goodbye.' He stretched out a large, well-shaped hand and touched her hair lightly.

'Still determined to be Cinderella?' he enquired as he went.

Tabitha prayed wickedly for a cyclone, a terrific thunderstorm, or just a steady downpour of rain, starting just before eleven o'clock on Wednesday, but the faint promise of rain on Tuesday evening had evaporated before a clear blue sky when she went on duty the following morning, and by the time the round began the sun was blazing down from a cloudless sky, justifying Mr van Beek's elegant summer suiting and beautiful silk shirt.

Tabitha, handing X-rays and reports and whisking bedclothes off plastered arms and legs, wondered where he would take Lilith. There was an hotel in Torquay famed for its food—she couldn't remember its name, but she felt sure that that was where Lilith would expect to go, and no doubt Mr van Beek would spend his money very freely indeed just for the pleasure of having such a pretty girl for his companion. She scowled fiercely at Mr Prosser, who was so taken by surprise that for once he was left speechless.

The round was businesslike, and although Mr van Beek did all that was expected of him by each of the patients, he wasted no time on unnecessary chatter. Even Mr Bow received only the briefest of remarks and when they reached Mr Raynard, that gentleman besought his friend not to hang around; he was doing nicely enough, and unless Tabby chose to kill him off in the meantime, he would still be there on the following day. As the party moved towards the door Tabitha spoke.

'You would rather not wait for coffee, I expect, Mr van Beek.' She went through the door into the office ahead of the others and turned to smile bleakly at him. 'I hope you have a very pleasant day,' she added insincerely, and smiled warmly at George Steele and Tommy, indicating with a little nod the coffee tray ready on her desk. Mr van Beek paused for the smallest moment of time, his eyebrows lifted. Then his eyes narrowed.

He said smoothly: 'Thank you. The pleasures of the day will doubtless make up for the lack of coffee now.'

He stalked away and Tabitha watched him go, feeling wretched and miserable because he had seemed to mind so much, and excusing her own bad temper as concern that a man as nice as he was should fall for someone like Lilith. She attempted to throw off the peculiar sense of loss she was sustaining by being extra bright and chatty to George and Tommy, leaving them even more puzzled. They went away presently, shaking their heads over her, for they liked her very much, having a brotherly fondness for her which allowed them to appreciate her good points without noticing her plain face.

The day dragged; Tabitha took an afternoon off duty so that Staff Nurse Rogers could have a half day—Mrs Burns, the part-time staff nurse, would stay until five o'clock. She went home to the flat and helped Meg turn out cupboards, then sat idly with Podger on her lap, trying not to think about Lilith and Mr van Beek. Sunbathing, she supposed, or having tea on the terrace of some hotel and then later, dinner and a drive back in the moonlight. She found her imagination unbearable and got up so quickly that Podger let out a protesting miaouw and only allowed his ruffled feelings to be soothed by a saucer of milk and the small portions of sandwich with which he was fed when Meg came in with the tea.

'A nice beast,' observed Meg, 'makes a bit of life about the place. You haven't told me about the dance, Miss Tabby.'

'Well,' said Tabitha, 'it wasn't all that exciting—not for me, anyway.' She explained about not wearing the new dress and Meg tut-tutted in a comforting voice.

'Never you mind, child,' she consoled. 'You'll get the chance to wear it, you see if you don't.'

'Yes, I know. The Christmas Ball at the hospital. Even though I've never worn it, it'll seem old, if you see what I mean.' She looked at her watch. 'I must fly, Meg dear, I'm a bit short-handed this evening, so don't worry if I'm late.'

But on the whole, it was a quiet evening. There had been an admission, it was true, which had gone straight to theatre to have a broken arm put in plaster, but the patient would go home again very soon and presented no great strain on the ward staff. There were a couple of men admitted for laminectomy for the following day too, but they were allowed to sit in the day room, watching the television with anyone else who could manage to get as far, and the remaining patients were quiet enough. Even Mr Raynard, deep in a thriller, gave less trouble than he usually did. He had been sat out for a short period during the day, and so had old Mr Bow; they had faced each other across the ward, their legs carefully propped up before them, while they boasted to each other how soon they would be on their feet again, and while Mr Bow didn't exactly smirk with satisfaction when Tabitha did her evening round, he certainly seemed to have taken on a new lease of life, a fact which Mr Raynard noted when she reached his bed.

'Nice old fellow,' he commented, 'clear as a bell on top too—splendid brain, I shouldn't wonder. We must have a chat some time.' Tabitha forbore from pointing out to him that they had been shouting to each other for most of the afternoon and took this as a strong hint that they should be arranged within normal talking distance of each other. 'You shall sit together tomorrow,' she promised. 'I don't see why you shouldn't have

a wheelchair, but we'd better wait until Mr van Beek comes—
he'll be in early to look at those two laminectomies.'

'If he's back in time,' commented Mr Raynard darkly, to
which remark Tabitha made no reply, for there was none to
make.

The evening was fading before the pale moon as she reached
home, and although she was tired she thought how nice it
would be to go out for an hour, out of the city and into the
country, or perhaps take the coast road to the sea, preferably
in a Bentley. She opened the flat door and called to Meg as
she always did, and Meg came to the kitchen door and said in
a faintly scolding voice: 'There you are at last—I've just
popped something on a tray in the sitting room for you. You
go in and have it straight away.'

'Why can't I have it in the kitchen with you?' demanded
Tabitha, and Meg gave her a strange look and said: 'All right,
Miss Tabby, you go and fetch it if you'd like that better.' She
turned away. 'I'm busy.'

The sitting room looked pretty; there was a small lamp
lighted on the little table by the fireplace and a tray set invit-
ingly beside it. Opposite, in the winged armchair she had
brought from Chidlake, sat Mr van Beek, looking very much
at his ease. Tabitha stood just inside the door, watching him
unfold his length, conscious of a peculiar sensation at the sight
of him and quite unable to think of anything to say. It was a
relief when he asked mildly: 'You don't mind, I hope? Lilith
asked me to call and give you these.'

He indicated a large box of chocolates which Tabitha stared
at unbelievingly, rather in the manner of one confronted by a
deadly serpent.

'Chocolates—from Lilith? Why?'

He laughed a little. 'I imagine she thought you might like
them,' he murmured. 'Aren't you going to sit down and eat
your sandwiches?'

She sat down and saw that there were two cups on the tray.

So he expected coffee. She poured it out and handed him a
cup and said at length:

'How—how nice. I—it's a bit unexpected.'

His eyes crinkled into laughter lines. 'Unexpected presents are always nice. Have you been busy?'

'Yes—no—not too bad. How—why—that is, you could have brought the chocolates with you tomorrow.'

A muscle twitched at the corners of his mouth. 'I had plenty of time to spare. Lilith met some of her young friends in Torquay, they asked us to join them for dinner. She thought it might be rather pleasant. After all, to come back early in the evening as I had warned her we should have to do was a tame ending to the day in face of dancing until all hours.'

Tabitha bit into a sandwich, and then, remembering her manners, offered him one.

'She stayed—I can't believe it!' She looked at his quiet face and corrected herself. 'Oh, I see. She thought you would stay despite the fact that you had said you had planned to return early. She must have been surprised.'

Mr van Beek said gently: 'Er—yes, I believe so. I imagine she is a young lady who usually gets her own charming way.' He gave her a sharp glance. 'What are you thinking?'

'How clever you are—none of Lilith's young men stand a chance against you—none of them would have dared to cross her, it will intrigue her. I expect you're very experienced.'

She looked up and found him laughing silently. His voice was bland.

'Probably. How's Podger?'

Tabitha had gone a little red in the face because he had snubbed her, gently it was true, but a snub all the same, and she was sensitive to snubs. She discussed Podger's well-being politely, and just as politely enquired if her companion would like more coffee, and when he declined asked: 'What is to happen to Podger? Mr Bow is devoted to him. Have you—that is, do you know anywhere where they can be together?'

Mr van Beek got slowly to his large, well-shod feet. 'Oh, yes, I've thought all that sort of thing out. I believe it will work very well. I'll go, you must be tired and I didn't intend to stay so long.'

Tabitha went to the door with him, seething silently because he had snubbed her for the second time. She thanked him once more for bringing the chocolates and added: 'Please thank Lilith for me when you see her. I—I don't go home very often, I'm sure you'll see her before I shall.'

He nodded in a casual manner as he got into the Bentley. His goodbye was equally casual.

Meg eyed the almost untouched sandwiches which Tabitha took into the kitchen.

'You've hardly eaten a thing, Miss Tabby. What a nice gentleman that was. I felt sure you would want him to stay until you got back from the hospital.' She gave Tabitha an innocent look and Tabitha cried:

'Meg, you didn't say that! You didn't persuade him to stay?'

Meg was indignant. 'Of course not, love—he just said did I mind if he waited for you, and he looked so pleasant and friendly, I just couldn't imagine anyone not wanting to talk to him. I didn't do wrong, did I, love? Don't you like him?'

Tabitha was at the sink and she didn't turn round. 'Yes, I like him very much, Meg,' she said, and changed the subject quickly before Meg could ask any more questions.

It was later, as she got ready for bed, that she allowed herself to think about Mr van Beek's visit and its reason. There was only one good answer—he wanted to get on good terms with her, so that he would have an ally to plead his cause if Lilith should prove capricious. Probably he didn't realize that she and Lilith avoided each other as much as possible, and what reason had he for thinking so when Lilith asked him to deliver chocolates to her stepsister? She could hardly tell him that Lilith had sent them as a token of a triumph which she didn't want Tabitha to miss. It was the kind of gibe in which she excelled, although he would have seen it as a thoughtful gesture from the girl he was attracted to, to a possible sister-in-law. She frowned at the thought; she didn't want to be Mr van Beek's sister-in-law, she wanted to be his wife: The knowledge of this exploded inside her head like a bomb and left her trembling. She said out loud with only Podger to hear: 'I must be mad! Whatever induced me to…oh, Podger, what shall I do?'

Podger was asleep; as though she might get an answer from the mirror she went to it and stared at her reflection, which stared back at her, solemn-faced and sad. He had called her Cinderella; she hadn't much liked it at the time, now it vexed her. She began to hunt through the dressing table drawers until she found what she sought—a beauty case the nurses had given her last Christmas and which her stepmother had advised her, quite kindly, not to make use of—as she had pointed out in her light, cold voice, Tabitha's face was better without anything other than a little powder and lipstick, by which Tabitha understood her to mean that it was best not to draw too much attention to a plain face. So she had buried it away beneath a pile of undies and almost forgotten it, but now she opened it, poking among its contents and selecting them with experimental fingers. When she was satisfied with her choice, she fetched the current copy of *Vogue,* opened it at its beauty page, and started doing things to her face.

She was up half an hour earlier the next morning and spent the whole of that time before her mirror, where she repeated last night's efforts to such good effect that when she went down to breakfast Meg gave her a long loving look and said at once: 'That's nice, Miss Tabitha. I like that bit of colour on your eyelids and that pretty lipstick. And your hair—that'll look fine with your cap.'

Tabitha, gobbling toast, said uncertainly: 'Really, Meg? It doesn't look silly?'

'My dear soul, you couldn't look silly if you tried. You just go like that, all prettied up. It suits you.'

Thus encouraged, Tabitha swallowed her tea, hugged Meg with the enthusiasm of a small girl and departed for St Martin's, to enter her ward shortly afterwards, feeling selfconscious until she encountered Nurse Betts' surprised and admiring stare. All the same, she felt a little shy as she started her morning round, but she held her head high on her slender neck and although the patients stared, none of them voiced their surprise at her changed appearance; only the incorrigible Mr Prosser spoke up, and that in a voice loud enough for the entire ward to hear.

'Well, ducks,' he cried cheerfully, 'I always said 'as 'ow you was a nice enough bird if yer let yourself go.' To which

remark Tabitha found no answer, so she asked him rather more
severely than usual how he did, to which he replied that he did
all the better for seeing her all perked up. It seemed prudent
to nod her well-arranged topknot and pass on to Mr Bow.

That old gentleman, beyond giving her a searching look,
made no remark about her appearance; he was far too anxious
to have a report on Podger, and she obliged him with this while
she examined his plastered leg, peering at its little window to
make sure all was well beneath it before feeling his toes. It
was only as, satisfied as to his condition, she was moving away
from the bed that he said:

'They say that beauty is but skin deep; but there are other
kinds of beauty than the obvious one, and they are vastly more
important.'

Tabitha, who wasn't sure if he was speaking to her or thinking out loud—a habit of the elderly, she had long ago discovered—said gently: 'Yes, I daresay you're right, Mr Bow,' and
went to say good morning to Mr Raynard who, as usual at that
early hour, was feeling bad-tempered. He grumbled 'morning'
at her without bothering to look up, but when she bent over
his leg and said in her composed voice: 'I should think you
might be allowed to do more weight-bearing exercises soon'
he glanced at her and then, after a first long stare, remarked:
'Well, well, Tabby, you've been at the paint-pot.'

'If you mean,' said Tabitha with dignity, 'that I've used
rather more make-up than usual, I have.' She gave him an
anxious glance. 'Does it look awful?' she wanted to know.

He studied her carefully. 'No—you look different, but it suits
you.'

'What suits who?' asked Mr van Beek from the doorway.
Tabitha hadn't expected him, at least, not until after the list
that morning. There were several patients—two of them the
laminectomies admitted the day before, now lying very quiet
and clean in their theatre gowns, awaiting the telephone call
which would send them on their way, each in his turn, to the
operating table. But before this could happen, Mr van Beek
needed to be there, scrubbed and waiting for them. As it was,
he was leaning against the end of Mr Raynard's bed, looking

so idle and elegant that it was hard to imagine that in half an hour he would be stooping over a supine body, working with meticulous care on that same body's spinal column. Tabitha peeped at him from under her eyelashes; she thought he looked as though he intended doing nothing more strenuous than taking a stroll round the nearest park. He looked up quickly and caught her peeping and held her glance with a bright one of his own which was so searching that she reddened painfully under it, wondering what he was going to say, but when he did speak it was about something quite different.

'I've arranged for Mr Bow's things to be collected this evening—I suppose you wouldn't be so kind as to come with me and see them off the premises?' he added vaguely. 'If anything were to get broken or lost,' and then still more vaguely, 'witnesses, you know.'

It sounded reasonable enough, and even if it hadn't been she was well aware that she would have jumped at the chance to be with him on even such a prosaic errand as this one. She said pleasantly:

'Yes, all right. I'm off at six, if that's OK.'

He nodded and turned away, lifting a vague hand in greeting and farewell to Mr Raynard. At the door he said in a businesslike way: 'I had a look at those two laminectomies last night, the first one—Butt, isn't it? seems straightforward; I'm not sure about Mr Dennis, though, I fancy he'll prove to be difficult. I thought you might like to know so that you can deploy your staff accordingly.' He gave her a brisk nod as he went out of the door.

He was right, the second case held everything else up, so that the list dragged to a close at tea time; by then Tabitha was wishing her day at an end, what with Matron's round, the physiotherapists and visitors and Mrs Jeffs not coming because the children had measles, she was beginning to wish that she hadn't promised to accompany Mr van Beek that evening. She spent her tea break re-doing her face and hair at the cost of a second cup, so that by the time she had given Rogers the report and was ready to leave, she was both hungry and thirsty, and in consequence, a little peevish as well.

She hadn't seen Mr van Beek all day; she didn't count his hasty visit to the ward to see his first two cases after dinner, before theatre started its afternoon session, for the only conversation they had had concerned the patients. She went along to the car park, convinced that he wouldn't be there, and found that he was. He settled her beside him and as if he sensed her mood, talked with sympathy about their busy day until he drew up outside Mr Bow's lodgings.

No one came when he knocked on the door; he knocked again and stood back to look at the curtained windows. 'There should be someone at home,' he observed, and in the small silence which followed Tabitha exclaimed: 'There is—at least, there's a funny noise.'

They listened. The noise was faint and irregular, and it was Mr van Beek who said: 'I believe it is someone calling for help, do you?'

Tabitha didn't answer; her nose twitched, she said urgently: 'I can smell something burning.'

She looked at the calm face of the man standing beside her, waiting for him to do something. When he said: 'Give me a hairpin, Tabitha,' she did so without question and watched silently while he picked the lock of the front door, opened it, handed her back her pin, and went inside with her closely at his heels. There was no one in the first room they entered—a sitting room, rather cold and stiff, with unused furniture and a great many artificial flowers in monstrous glass vases; nor was there anyone in the poky little room behind it, which unlike its neighbour was very much lived in, with a large bed against one wall, the remains of a meal on the table, an oppressively large television dominating the room from one corner, and a highly decorative wallpaper which was in direct variance with the carpet. They closed the door with relief and went to the kitchen, where they found the landlady lying on the floor. She appeared to be semi-conscious, but opened her eyes and said 'Help' before closing them again. She looked pale and her hair was sticky with blood.

Mr van Beek got down on one knee beside her and gently tried out her arms and legs before picking her up and carrying her into the little back room and laying her on the bed. He said matter-of-factly, 'My bag's in the car, I'll fetch it—see if you can find out where the fire is.'

Tabitha went back into the kitchen where the smell was stronger. It was a small room with so many built-in cupboards that there was barely room to turn round to get anything out of them. One of the cupboard doors stood open though, and inside, down among the sugar and tea and flour, was a smouldering cigarette. The fire was still in its embryo stage, but the sugar had caught, which was why the smell was so pungent. Tabitha hauled out the groceries, put the cigarette and the smouldering sugar in the sink and went to join Mr van Beek. He was examining the woman's head and said without looking up: 'There's a torch in my bag—shine it here, there's a good girl.'

There were two cuts, not very deep, but like all scalp wounds, bleeding freely. 'A couple of stitches,' murmured Mr van Beek. 'You'll find some scissors in my case. Cut away the hair, will you—I'll give her a local.'

Tabitha did as she was bid and then went into the kitchen to see what he was doing. 'A saucepan,' he murmured, 'to boil up the needleholder and so forth—I can't see one.'

Tabitha started on the cupboards; at the third she produced one and put it on to boil, took the instruments from him, popped them in, put the lid on with a satisfied little clash and said: 'I wonder if there's a bathroom where you can wash your hands?'

He was prowling round, looking for a clean towel. 'I'll manage at the sink—how hard it is to find even the most commonplace things in other people's houses.'

'Yes,' Tabitha agreed, 'and do take off that jacket, you may get blood on it.'

She went back to have a look at their patient and found her with her eyes open. 'Oh, lor',' said the landlady in a puzzled voice, 'whatever's 'appened?'

'You must have fallen down,' said Tabitha, 'and bumped your head. It's cut a little, the doctor will see to it for you.'

'I didn't send for no doctor.'

'No,' explained Tabitha, 'we came to see about Mr Bow's things, and Mr van Beek heard you calling and we came in.' She thought it best not to mention the picked lock at that moment. 'He's in the kitchen, boiling some things.'

'My 'ead! What things?'

Tabitha was saved from explanation by Mr van Beek's entry, carrying the saucepan and a small pudding basin, and she made haste to clear a small table of its potted plant and carry it to the bedside, where she spread it with the day's newspaper. Mr van Beek arranged his saucepan to his satisfaction, requested that the bowl should be filled with Savlon solution and swabs, and departed again, presumably to scrub his hands in the sugar-filled sink.

The landlady didn't care about having her head stitched; she said so with a good deal of vehemence, jerking her head about in such a fashion that Tabitha was hard put to it to keep it steady while Mr van Beek inserted first the local anaesthetic and then the stitches. When he had finished, he warned her that her headache would trouble her for several days, produced some tablets for her relief, and set about clearing up while Tabitha arranged a bandage around the sufferer's head.

'Is there anyone coming home?' she enquired. 'It might be a good idea if you went to bed.' She looked doubtfully at the television and wondered if going to bed in that room would make an atom of difference. 'Somewhere quiet?' she ventured.

'There's a put-u-up in the front room. My old man'll be 'ome in a minute, 'e'll see to it.' She was interrupted by the thunderous knock on the door. 'That'll be the moving men.'

Mr van Beek came soft-footed into the room and Tabitha got to her feet.

'Let them in, there's a good girl,' he begged. 'Take them up to Knotty's room, will you, while I find out how this good soul cut her head and who her doctor is—I think she'll be all right now. Whoever he is, I'll warn him and he can visit tomorrow.'

There wasn't much to do in Mr Bow's room. The men appeared to know exactly what was required of them; she signed some papers, went through the cupboards and drawers once more, and returned downstairs where Mr van Beek was waiting.

In the car he asked. 'Home?' and when she said, 'Yes, please,' went on, 'I'm sorry about that, but I was glad to have you with me; if I'd been on my own I daresay I should have still been looking for a saucepan. The odds and ends were safely collected?'

Tabitha said yes, they were and sat silent until he stopped outside the flat, to stay sitting quietly beside her, making no attempt to open the door. She was searching for something to say and had her hand on the door when he said, his voice plaintive: 'I've had no tea.'

Tabitha, who had been sitting in a dim world of her own dreaming, became at once practical. He might not care a row of beans for her, but that was no reason for refusing him a meal. She said, her pretty voice motherly, as though he were one of her patients: 'Come in and have some now, and I'm sure Meg will have a cake or some sandwiches.'

He agreed with an alacrity which she hadn't quite expected and they were in the flat's tiny hall before she had had time to decide if she had been foolish to ask him or not. But Meg had no qualms at all, for when she heard that their visitor had gone tea-less, she bustled them both into the sitting room with the promise of a suitable meal within a brace of shakes, which promise she carried out very rapidly with Tabitha's help. Presently the two of them sat down to boiled eggs, bread, jam and thick, rich cream and a very large seedcake, with Meg pouring the tea and listening to their reason for being late and making her wise, rather dry comments as they told her, and finally wanting to know if the nice old gentleman's things had been safely disposed of.

Mr van Beek removed the top of his third egg with surgical expertise.

'Oh yes, Meg, they're safe and sound until such time as he should need them again, which won't, I hope, be long. I shall take him back home with me until I start my lecture tour and after that we must see.'

The conversation became general after that, and when Meg

went back into the kitchen to wash up he showed no sign of
getting up to go, but asked instead if he might smoke and then
sat back in the only chair large enough to accommodate him
in comfort, and talked at some length about a new type of
artificial hip joint he was interested in. And Tabitha, listening
intelligently and making the right comments at the right times,
wondered what it was about her that encouraged him to con-
tinue upon such a dull topic—her ability to listen, perhaps,
which was something she had noticed that pretty girls didn't
need to do, and her dislike of hurting people's feelings by not
being interested. She should, she supposed, be grateful to be
given the chance to hold even such a dry conversation as this
one with him. She tried to imagine Lilith in her place and
wondered what she would have done to divert him to some
lighter topic, but of course he would never have started on it
in the first place if it had been Lilith. Mr van Beek said suddenly, making her jump guiltily:

'Why do I bore you with all this? But I told you did I not,
that you are a very restful woman, and what is more, you look
interested.'

'Oh, I am,' said Tabitha mendaciously, and jumped again
when he went on.

'I'm glad to see that you've stopped playing the Cinderella,
and very nice you look too. Does it take very long?'

She gave him a suspicious look to make sure he wasn't
mocking her, but his face was grave and enquiring; he really
wanted to know.

'Well, I get up half an hour earlier than usual, but I expect
I shall get quicker.' She drew a breath, then: 'Have you—have
you seen Lilith?'

He looked surprised. 'No—was I supposed to? I've not had
time, for one thing, have I? I daresay I shall run into her at the
weekend, for I shall be with the Johnsons at Lyme. Do you
want me to give her a message?'

He hadn't asked her if she was going to Lyme; she fought
disappointment at his lack of interest and said steadily: 'No,
thank you—I—I just asked.'

But his next question sent her spirits soaring. 'When do you intend to go to Chidlake?' he wanted to know.

'I—that is, I don't often go, not any more.'

His voice was gentle. 'Isn't it your home?'

She didn't look at him. 'It belongs to my stepmother now.' She had tried to make her voice light and when he said; 'Tabitha,' looked at him with a determined smile. He bent his head before she could draw back and kissed her cheek, and she thought she detected pity in his eyes before he dropped their lids, but she couldn't be sure. He said on a little laugh:

'Isn't it time the prince came along with the glass slipper, my dear girl?'

'I don't know any princes.' Her voice was sour and he ignored her remark, still smiling. 'What a lot of Tabithas there are,' he mused. 'Efficient Tabitha on the ward, outdoor Tabitha on the Cobb, kind Tabitha coming to Knotty's aid, Tabitha in moonlight and—er—cross Tabitha.'

She had to laugh. 'I'm not cross, only you say things…'

'Just as long as you listen,' he answered blandly, and got up to go.

She stood where he had left her until Meg came from the kitchen to rouse her from her thoughts with a prosaic: 'Now, now, Miss Tabitha, day-dreaming again, and you promised you'd run up and see Mrs Diment about that bathroom drain.'

'So I did,' said Tabitha without any enthusiasm at all; her landlady was a pleasant enough person but given to a nice chat at any time of the day. She didn't want to go; she would have preferred to stay just where she was, thinking about Marius van Beek. She said for the second time: 'So I did,' and went unwillingly out of the front door of the little flat and up the stairs to Mrs Diment's own flat.

She saw quite a lot of Mr van Beek during the next few days, but on none of these occasions did he give any sign that he remembered any part of their conversation; he was polite, pleasantly friendly even, but their talk was confined to patients and their bones, so that by the end of the week Tabitha began to wonder if her stepmother was right after all, and it was indeed a waste of time trying to improve her looks. She went

off duty on Saturday evening, glad that she had changed her
day off with Rogers who wanted to go to a wedding on the
Monday. All the week she had gone on duty eager to see Marius van Beek; perhaps a day away from hospital with no chance
of seeing him at all would bring her to her senses. Meg would
be going to her sister's, she would have the flat to herself. She
spent the short journey thinking of all the things she could do.
Sunday loomed, inexpressibly dull, before her.

Meg's sister lived in Ottery St Mary. Tabitha ran her there
in the Fiat after an early breakfast and then went back to the
flat. It was going to be a delightful day, warm even for summer,
with a vivid blue sky which made Tabitha disinclined for any
of the chores she had told herself she would do. Nevertheless,
she got her bucket and suds and cloths and started to clean the
car; a job she detested but which was long overdue. She had
been working without much enthusiasm for ten minutes or so
when the Bentley crept up noiselessly behind her and Mr van
Beek, looking cool and elegant and lazier than ever, stepped
out and strolled towards her. Tabitha dropped the sponge back
into the bucket with a tremendous splash and said with artificial
calm:

'Good morning. I thought you were at the Johnsons'.'

'Hullo. Yes, I am…' before he could go on she said quickly,
without thinking: 'Lilith's not home.'

He half smiled at some secret joke she felt she wasn't sharing. 'No, she isn't. I wondered if you would like a day out. I
feel like a breath of sea air. I hope you do too.'

So that was it, thought Tabitha; Lilith had refused to spend
the day with him and the next best thing was herself, because
she was after all Lilith's stepsister and one of the family—or
so he imagined. What more natural than for a man to cultivate
the good offices of his future sister-in-law? She spent a few
anxious moments warring with her pride, knowing that the battle was lost before she had offered herself even the mildest of
reasons as to why she should refuse. She said amiably:

'Yes, that would be nice, but I'm in the middle of doing
this.'

He held out a hand and took the sponge from her. 'Go and

fetch whatever you swim in,' he advised. 'I'll finish this for you. I suppose there isn't any coffee?'

She turned at the door. 'By the time you're done, it'll be ready,' she promised.

He was putting the final polish to the roof of the car when she returned. In twenty minutes or so she had not only made coffee but changed her dress, re-done her hair and touched up her face, as well as finding a beach bag and her swimsuit. She packed it rather impatiently, because only that week she had intended to buy herself a bikini, something rather dashing and colourful, and somehow hadn't got around to it. Now she would have to wear her last year's swimsuit—not, she assured herself, that it would make a scrap of difference what she wore.

'Coffee's ready!' she called, and as he came towards her with the bucket in one hand, 'Thank you, Mr van Beek.'

He stopped short in front of her. 'I know it wouldn't be quite the thing to call me Marius in the ward, but couldn't you bring yourself to do so at all other times? It makes me feel very old, for one thing, and for another, it gives me the disagreeable sensation that you don't approve of me.'

Tabitha said briskly: 'How ridiculous! Why shouldn't I approve of you? And I certainly don't consider you old.' She added kindly: 'I'm twenty-five myself, you know, and women get older much faster than men.'

'And that,' said Marius as he took his mug of coffee, 'is the sort of comforting remark which you can be relied upon to make at all times.'

Tabitha thought he was joking; it wasn't until they had sat down opposite each other at the kitchen table that she looked at his face and saw that he was serious and knew that he had meant every word—a fact which she found didn't please her at all; it merely proved that he thought of her as Tabby—kind Tabby, if you like—but Tabby, just as everyone else did.

'Very good coffee,' said Marius pleasantly, and she nodded, unaware that he had been watching her closely. 'We make excellent coffee in my country—you should try it some time.'

And so I would, thought Tabitha, still put out, if I had a socking great Bentley to take me there. 'I've not been to Holland,' she said out loud. 'I've not been abroad since my father died.'

'You like travelling?'

She nodded. 'Very much, though I haven't been far.'

He wanted to know where and she found herself telling him, reluctantly at first and then thawing to his charm and friendliness so that by the time they got up to go she found herself quite good-humoured again.

'Would you like to swim first?' he asked as they got into the car. 'I thought we might take the Totnes road and cut down to Stoke Fleming. We've plenty of time, and there's a good place for lunch at Churston Ferrers.'

'That sounds nice.' Tabitha's voice was cool, hiding the delight welling up inside her. She thanked heaven in fervent silence that she could swim.

The beach was almost deserted. Tabitha, behind a convenient rock, put on the despised suit, bundled her hair into a sensible white cap, and ran down to the water's edge, where she stopped because despite the heat of the day, the water felt unexpectedly cold; it was only Marius's voice calling to her from some way out that made her plunge in, to forget the chilliness of the water in the delight of swimming. She swam as she danced, with grace and energy; it took her no time at all to catch up with Marius, loitering in shallow water, she suspected, to see if she was up to his standard. Side by side, they swam strongly out to sea and then turning, swam back, more slowly now, to the beach, where they stretched out, the waves breaking over their feet. Tabitha took off her cap and her hair streamed down in an untidy mass, shedding pins. She lay quiet in the sunshine while Marius picked them up one by one and made a tidy heap of them beside her. She eyed them worriedly. 'I'll never get my hair up again—it takes ages, and I've only a tiny mirror with me.'

'Well, I'm not surprised. There's yards of it, isn't there? Can't you put it up when we get to Churston Court? Put it all back in again and I'll race you out to that dinghy.'

They swam for another half hour or so and finally left the water to lie down again, pleasantly tired, in the warmth of the sun. Presently Marius rolled over and propped his head on an elbow. 'Nice,' he observed laconically. 'Peaceful and warm and delightful scenery—what more could one want?'

Tabitha opened one eye and found him looking at her, his face a good deal too close for her peace of mind. She shut the eye again and said, for lack of anything else, 'Um', thinking that Lilith would have known exactly what to say. Her stepmother had once told her that she had no sparkle and Tabitha, for once, agreed with her. She was still searching feverishly for some scintillating topic of conversation when Marius said:

'You're peaceful too. I don't feel I have to be forever talking trivialities.'

Tabitha, without opening her eyes, said thank you, fuming silently. He made her sound like a feather pillow, or a middle-aged aunt, or anything else comfortable which could be ignored until wanted. She frowned and he continued: 'Of course, you have misconstrued my meaning, but for the moment that doesn't matter. I like your eyelashes.'

This time Tabitha opened her eyes and sat up. 'You what?' she queried in astonishment.

'Like your eyelashes,' he repeated patiently. 'Most women have black spiky ones, but yours are thick and brown and the length they are meant to be. They look like those camel-hair brushes artists use.'

She went pink, recognizing a compliment and hoping it wasn't just because she was Lilith's stepsister. 'Thank you,' she said gravely. 'I think I'll dress.' Marius got up and pulled her to her feet.

'You don't believe a word of it,' he sounded resigned, 'but of course these things take time.'

She was still puzzling out this remark when he caught her by the shoulders and kissed her without haste. The kiss was as gentle as his voice had been.

Churston Ferrers was near the river, between Dartmouth and Totnes. The restaurant was in a restored Queen Anne house, handsomely decorated and obviously expensive. Tabitha, in a powder room of sweet-smelling luxury, re-did her hair and her face too and went to join Marius in the bar, where over their

Dubonnet they discussed what they should eat with the deep interest of people who were really hungry. They settled for prawn and oyster cocktails, filet steak with a salad, and strawberries and cream. The meal was delicious and they lingered over it, talking easily. They had reached the strawberries before Tabitha asked:

'What part of Holland do you come from—that is, where is your home?'

Marius helped himself to cream. 'Veere—a very small town on Walcheren island, that's in Zeeland, in the south. My family have lived there for many years—one of my ancestors married a Scotswoman during the reign of James the First, and since that time there have been other marriages with both English and Scotswomen. My father's brother is married to an English-woman—I was staying with them when I had Bill Raynard's telephone call.'

Tabitha asked quickly before he could talk about something else: 'Have you a practice?'

'No—a few patients come to the house, but I have rooms in Rotterdam. I'm on the staff of one of the Rotterdam hospitals and I have some beds in Middelburg hospital as well.'

'Oh, a consultant.' Tabitha thought how unassuming his answer had been, and like him more than ever, which although it had nothing to do with loving him was, to her mind, almost as important. Hadn't Mr Raynard said that he was embarked on a successful career? She remembered something else. 'But you lecture—Mr Raynard said you were going...'

'That's right. I've been over here to team up with some orthopaedic chaps who are on to something new. I went up to Ambleside afterwards—it seemed a good idea to have a holiday before I start my lectures again.'

She wanted to ask where he was going, but didn't; instead she asked:

'You like that? More than surgery?'

He smiled slowly, his eyes crinkling nicely at their corners. 'It suits me very well at present, though I imagine that when I marry I shall give up a great deal of the lecturing and concentrate on consultant surgery. You see, I should like to see as much as possible of my wife and children.'

Tabitha blinked her paintbrush eyelashes. 'Yes, of course. Will you tell me some more about Veere?'

But presently, when they were in the car again, she found that they were talking about Chidlake and Mrs Crawley and Lilith. It seemed to her that he wanted to know a lot about Lilith, which, she reminded herself, was only to be expected— probably he'd brought her out for that very reason—so she was careful to colour her answers in Lilith's favour, because even though she knew that she loved him so much that she would never want to marry anyone else—supposing that anyone else should ask her—she couldn't stand in his way. She considered that Lilith wouldn't make him a good wife, but that was hardly her business, so that when he wanted to know why Lilith wasn't earning her own living, Tabitha made haste to point out that she was only just eighteen and hadn't quite made up her mind, whereupon Marius wanted to know if she herself had made up her mind at that age, to which she hastily replied that yes, she had, but that had been different, and was shocked into silence by his bland: 'Ah, yes—Cinderella.'

They crossed Dartmoor, pausing often to admire the scenery, and stopped at Chagford for tea. By now they had stopped talking about herself and her family and to her relief the conversation became the pleasant exchange of ideas and opinions. She was a voracious reader herself; it was nice to find someone who shared her pleasure in books and whose tastes were similar to her own. She discovered, too, that they enjoyed the same music and admired the same pictures too; it seemed inevitable that they should dislike the same things in life. They were still comparing notes on this interesting discovery when they arrived at Meg's sister's house, and as they went up the garden path together Tabitha was conscious of regret that they wouldn't be able to finish their talk.

They went inside to wait while Meg got ready to leave and stayed for a cup of tea while flowers were picked from the garden and the best of the young peas and beans were gathered for them to take home. It was seven o'clock by the time they

were on the road again, with Meg in the back seat, telling them
about her day in her soft Dorset voice and asking questions
about theirs. Outside the flat Tabitha turned to thank Marius
for her day, but he cut her short by saying in the pleasantest
possible manner: 'Oh, but I'm coming in if I may', and did so.
They all went into the kitchen where Podger was waiting anxiously for his supper, and Marius sat quietly while the beast
was petted and fed, and only then did Tabitha remember her
manners sufficiently to say: 'Oh, I do beg your pardon, only
he was hungry—I'll make some coffee and we can go into the
sitting room.'

Mr van Beek didn't move. 'It's a lovely evening,' he observed. 'I know of a nice place at Dulverton where we could
have dinner.'

He glanced as he spoke at Meg and smiled and she said
instantly: 'Now that's a good idea, Miss Tabby—you go along,
that'll give me a chance to do one or two things.'

'What things?' asked Tabitha with faint suspicion.

'Now, love, you leave that to me.' Meg sounded exactly as
she had used to do when Tabitha had queried something that
wasn't her business when she had been a little girl and Tabitha
responded unconsciously to her old nanny's firm voice. She
turned to Marius and asked: 'But aren't you tired?'

He said blandly: 'After such a delightfully relaxing day? Not
in the least. Shall I wait here and talk to Meg while you go
and powder your nose?'

She powdered her nose; she would have liked to change her
dress too, but felt it would hardly do because he was in slacks
and a sports shirt and they weren't likely to go anywhere grand,
although she was sure she had seen a jacket on the back seat.
She was ready in ten minutes, looking as neat and fresh as
when they had set out that morning. The only concession to
the occasion she allowed herself was a careful spraying of
Fleurs de Rochelle, which maybe accounted for his 'Very nice,'
when she went back into the kitchen.

They talked shop all the way to Dulverton, which was only
a little more than half an hour's drive away; they talked about
Mr Bow too, although Marius gave her no inkling as to what

he intended to do about his old friend when he was fully recovered. By the time they drew up outside the Carnavon Arms she was still none the wiser and had discovered that if her companion didn't want to answer a question he had a gentle but firm way of not doing so. But she forgot this in the pleasure of his company; he could be an amusing companion when he chose and seemed intent on making her evening an enjoyable one. They dined off lobster Thermidor and a crême brulée and washed these delicacies down with a dry white Burgundy, followed by brandy with their coffee, which must have accounted for Tabitha's feeling of well-being as they drove back to the flat, a feeling which evaporated slowly as he bade her a pleasant good night at the front door, refusing her offer of more coffee and making only the most conventional remarks about their day together.

By the time she was in bed, the evaporation was complete. Looking back over the day, she was unable to recall one single remark that she had made that had been witty, clever, funny or even faintly interesting. No wonder he hadn't wanted to come in; he must have been glad to be rid of her. She fell asleep, convinced that she might just as well scrape her hair back and not bother with her make-up. She woke in the night, suddenly and piercingly aware of how much she loved him and, if he married Lilith, just as aware that she would have to go away because seeing them together would be more than she could bear, just as meeting him would be impossible. He would call her Tabby—probably Old Tabby, in a horribly kind brotherly fashion. She went to sleep much later, her cheeks still damp where she hadn't bothered to wipe away her tears.

# CHAPTER FOUR

IT WAS DURING the next morning, while George Steele was doing a round, that Tabitha learned that Marius would be operating on four days that week, and when she enquired why, George mentioned that Mr van Beek was due to go on a short lecture tour in five days' time and intended to clear as much of the waiting list as he could before he went.

'Oh,' said Tabitha, 'he's not coming back! Will you be able to manage on your own, George?'

She didn't really care in the least if George could manage or not, but she had to say something—anything, to take her mind off the fact that Marius was going away and she wouldn't see him.

'Of course he's not going,' said George patiently. 'Only for a week—Sweden, I believe—it was arranged long before he heard from Mr Raynard. He'll come back and take over again until the Old Man's on his feet.'

The Old Man himself substantiated George's statement himself when Tabitha paid him her morning visit. He was sitting up in bed, surrounded by an untidy welter of case notes, screwed-up pieces of paper, several lists and a calendar. He thrust an impatient arm out as she approached the bed and shot most of the clutter on to the floor.

'Tut-tut,' said Tabitha severely, 'you're by far the untidiest patient we've ever had.' She picked everything up, sorted it neatly and laid the little pile back on the bed.

He glowered at her. 'Stuff,' he tapped the lists with an impatient finger. 'I want to get these sorted out for Marius—you've a busy week ahead of you, my girl, so make up your mind to that.'

Tabitha tucked a pillow in exactly where he needed it most. 'I don't mind,' she said sunnily, and gave him a broad smile because Marius was coming back and so the day had turned into something wonderful; a week would go quickly enough, and however hard Mr Raynard tried, he wasn't going to be fit to return to work for quite a while yet.

Mr Raynard gave her a suspicious look. 'What have you got to look so pleased about?' he demanded. 'Had a weekend in Paris?'

Before Tabitha could reply to this pleasantry, Marius spoke from the door.

'Not Paris, or for that matter, a weekend. Just a very delightful day swimming and doing nothing. We enjoyed ourselves.' He smiled and gave her a friendly nod and then ignored her, going over to the bed to pick up the lists scattered upon it. He cast his eye over the first of them and asked: 'Which days shall you want me to operate? I'd rather like to be free on Thursday.' He looked at Tabitha as he spoke. 'Sister?'

'That's fine,' she said quickly. She had a day off herself on Thursday. She stood silently, wondering how he was going to spend his day. Mr Raynard did more than wonder; he asked: 'Got plans, eh? What are you going to do?'

'That is something I shall leave my companion to decide,' said Mr van Beek smoothly, and gave Tabitha the ghost of a smile. She went away presently, a prey to chaotic thoughts. Could he possibly be going to ask her out again—he could have found out that she was free on Thursday easily enough; the off duty list was in the office. Even as she savoured this delectable idea, her common sense told her that it was extremely unlikely. She went into the office and stared at her face in the mirror on the wall.

'What a fool you are,' she chided her reflection. All the same, she decided to buy the bikini that very day; if she missed dinner she would have time enough.

She got back to work with a bare minute to spare to find Marius in the office, sitting at her desk. As she went in he got to his feet, remarking idly: 'What a lot of housekeeping you appear to do—doesn't it bore you?'

She took the sewing book, the repair book and the request for repair book from his hand. A little breathless, she stammered: 'No—not at all—at least...'

He didn't allow her to finish. 'You've been shopping?'

She went faintly pink, although she kept her voice matter-of-fact enough.

'Yes. On theatre days I always have an evening, you see, and the shops are shut by the time I get away.'

He nodded and then pointed out. 'But you have days off, don't you? Surely you could shop then?'

She wasn't going to tell him that she spent those, or the greater part of them, helping Meg to give the flat a weekly clean. Meg wasn't old, but neither was she all that young any more. Without the subject being mentioned between them, Tabitha had gradually taken over the heavier jobs, which weren't all that arduous in the little flat, but they took time, and when they were finished she usually took Meg out for a run in the car. Her days off weren't exciting, nor were they wholly her own.

Marius was at the door. 'Nice of you not to make a fuss about Thursday,' and when she lifted her nondescript brows in surprise, he went on: 'Oh, you could have done, you know. Not enough staff—altering the off duty, laundry not back—I can think of a dozen good reasons why you should object if you wish.'

Tabitha examined the laundry book in her hand with great care. 'But I don't object,' she stated calmly—far more calmly than her heart was beating. 'As it happens it's most convenient, as I have the day off myself.'

Marius put his hands in his pockets. He said suavely: 'Yes—I know. I looked at the list. What do you think of Knotty?'

The change of subject was so abrupt that she took a few seconds to adjust her thoughts. 'He's doing very nicely. There's still a little discharge around the stitches, but he has almost no pain, and begs for crutches.'

Marius took his hands out of his pockets and opened the door.

'Yes, he's mad keen to get on his feet again. I should like him X-rayed, this week and—er—Mr Raynard too. Leave a couple of forms out, will you, and ask George to do the necessary.'

He nodded rather vaguely and went out, shutting the door gently behind him, and Tabitha sat down at her desk, still with the books clutched in one hand and the bag containing the new bikini in the other. She had been greatly daring telling him about her day off, and he had known all the time. If he had wanted to take her out, he had certainly had the opportunity to say so. But he hadn't. She cast the books on the desk with a thump and flung the bag pettishly into the corner of the little room.

The next two days were busy; the lists were long and heavy, and, she thought wearily at the end of the first day, she might just as well not be there for all she saw of Marius. It was true he paid a visit to the ward after he had finished the list, but then he was his other self—the surgeon intent on his patients and nothing else; there was no trace of the placid, almost lazy man who talked idly about anything under the sun other than his work.

Wednesday was worse, because one of the student nurses had a sore throat and had to go off duty, and an emergency was admitted who died before anything other than emergency treatment could be done for him. Marius and George were operating when the case was admitted and although Marius had come down almost immediately, there was really nothing to be done. Tabitha, consoling the young wife as best she could over cups of tea in her office, was seized with frustration at the futility of their efforts, and when the girl's mother arrived and she was able to hand her over to someone else's care, she took the tea tray to the kitchen and washed up the cups and saucers, giving vent to her feelings by crashing and banging the crockery. She had just smashed the teapot into wet tea-leafy fragments all over the floor when Marius came in. She gave him a furious look, said 'Oh, damn,' and on the verge of tears, bent to clear up the mess. He bent to help her and after one look at her unhappy face, said gently:

'I know how you feel. I'm sorry there was nothing to do for that poor chap.' He shoveled the bits tidily into the bin under the sink and went on with deliberate briskness:

'That first case—he bled a lot in theatre—I think he'll be

OK, but keep an eye on him, will you? George has all the details.'

He walked to the door and held it open for her and then went to the ward door and opened that for her too. She thought that he was going in with her, but he stayed where he was. He spoke casually. 'I shall be seeing Mrs Crawley and Lilith to-morrow—have you any message for them?'

She remembered then that the next day was Thursday. She might have known that he would go and see Lilith, but all the same, disappointment left its bitter taste in her mouth. She had been a fool, indulging in wishful thinking; she wouldn't do that again. She found her voice and was glad to hear its normality.

'No, I can't think of any, thank you. I hope you have a pleasant day.'

She gave him a brief glance and a smile that barely curved her mouth and flew into the ward.

Friday and Saturday followed the exacting pattern laid down by Tuesday and Wednesday. When she spoke to Marius, and that seldom, it was to do with the patients and nothing else, and on the Saturday evening when he came to do a final round after theatre and spent quite some time with Mr Bow and Mr Raynard, she was careful to be busy as far away from him as possible. So she only had herself to blame when from behind Mr Prosser's curtains she heard Marius enquire from Betts where she was, and when Betts told him, his voice, telling the nurse not to disturb her but to convey his regards. She took so long over Mr Prosser afterwards that that astute gentleman actually fell as silent as she had become; only as at length she pulled the curtains back did he say: 'Well, Sister, we'll miss that Dutchman—a nice chap even though 'e's a foreigner. I 'ear 'e's coming back.'

Tabitha paused at the foot of the bed. 'That's right, Mr Prosser—he's only going for a week.'

She was conscious, as she spoke, that she had said that as much to comfort herself as to enlighten Mr Prosser. Later on, when she was home, sitting with Podger on her knee, she had to admit to herself that as things were, it could make no difference whatsoever to her whether Marius was away for a week or a year. At least, she corrected herself, it could make no difference to him.

The week was unending, and made worse by a visit from Lilith one evening, ostensibly to bring some fruit from Chidlake—something she had never done before, and it was obvious to Tabitha within a very few minutes that it was more than the fruit which had brought her stepsister. Lilith settled down in her chair, accepted the cup of coffee she was offered and embarked on a meaningless chatter which Tabitha considered a waste of time. But she sat quietly, listening to Lilith's talk forced as she did so to admit to herself that Lilith looked prettier than ever in a dress that must have cost a great deal of money. Tabitha sighed soundlessly; if only her father had left her provided for... She roused herself to hear Lilith say: 'It was gorgeous—Marius is such fun even though he's so much older, and we get on so well, just as though we'd known each other all our lives. He's sweet with Mummy too, but of course it's me he comes to see.' She gave Tabitha a sharp look and Tabitha steeled herself to look serenely back.

'Yes,' she agreed, 'he seems very nice. But isn't he a little old for you, Lilith?'

She shouldn't have said it. Lilith smiled, a smile very like her mother's and one which Tabitha dreaded. 'Sour grapes?' she queried on a little laugh. 'Poor Tabby, it must be ghastly to be as plain as you are.' She studied Tabitha with her head on one side. 'You've done something to your hair and I do believe you've got make-up on your eyes—how Mummy will laugh when I tell her! About Marius—I'm going to get him, you know. I'm not quite sure about marrying him, not until I know if he's got enough money, but he's marvelous at taking a girl out, and he looks at me—you know,' she laughed again and murmured cruelly, 'No, of course you wouldn't know. He's very interested in Chidlake too—he thinks I love it, but you just wait, if I do decide to marry him, we'll never go near the place again. He can work in Wimpole Street or wherever it is.' She broke off to ask: 'How much do doctors earn—I mean doctors like Marius?'

A wave of rage swept over Tabitha. Here was Lilith coolly

considering marriage with Marius and she didn't know the difference between a doctor and a surgeon! She said evenly:

'Mr van Beek is a surgeon—he specializes in orthopaedics. I have no idea what his income might be.' She couldn't resist adding: 'How should I? I'm not in the habit of being on such friendly terms with the consultant staff.' As she said it she recalled the Sunday she had spent with Marius; that at least was something Lilith didn't know about. She said slowly: 'Aren't you being mercenary, Lilith?'

Her stepsister laughed. 'What a fool you are, Tabby. Why shouldn't I have an eye to the main chance? You're quite soft with your silly out-of-date ideas. I shall marry someone with plenty of money, and if he's as good-looking as Marius, so much the better.' She got up and stretched. 'I'm off—you're not exactly lively company, are you, Tabby?'

'Why did you come?' Tabitha asked with curiosity.

Lilith giggled. 'Oh, my dear, I should have thought of it, but when Marius was at Chidlake the other evening, we walked round the garden and he remarked that of course we kept you supplied with stuff from the garden. I said yes—I should have been a fool to have said anything else, shouldn't I? Now I can tell him that I took you a whole basketful and he'll think that I'm a sweet, thoughtful little sister and fall in love with me just a little bit more.'

Tabitha had nothing to say to this, although she longed to speak her mind, but if she did, there was the danger of Lilith guessing that Marius was something more than just another consultant. She held her tongue until Lilith had got into her sports car and driven away, and then went into the kitchen, where to her own surprise she burst into tears and mumbled the whole sad story into the ample comfort of Meg's bosom. She felt better when she had told the whole; and sniffed and gulped for a little while before she spoke.

'Oh, Meg, if only I were just a tiny bit pretty, so that he'd look at me—he looks at me now sometimes, but only because he's giving me instructions about a patient or something, and even when we had that lovely day together he stared at me as though—as though he were sorry for me.'

'Rubbish,' said Meg. 'Was he the one who told you to change your hair-style?'

Tabitha lifted a puffy face. 'Yes—so you see...'

'I see nothing, Miss Tabitha, but he must have looked at you long enough to have seen that a different way of doing your hair would make you look prettier.'

Tabitha sniffed. 'Dear kind Meg—but don't you see that he only said that because I'm Lilith's stepsister and he wanted me to like him so that I'd be on his side? He may have thought that as I was older she would ask me for advice—about him, I mean—so that she'd fall in love with him.'

Meg said rubbish again, rather more forcibly. 'Miss Lilith's incapable of falling in love,' she declared roundly, 'and Mr van Beek, now he's not a man to need pushing when he picks himself a wife.' She handed Tabitha a large snowy handkerchief. 'Dry your eyes, love, we'll have a cup of tea and you'll feel better; that girl always upsets you, drat her.'

She went to put the kettle on and busied herself laying a tray. 'He's always been very nice to you, Miss Tabby.'

Tabitha sat down at the table. She said in a stony little voice: 'He's nice to everyone, Meg—old and young and plain and ugly, even that awful woman where Mr Bow lived—you see, he's kind. Sue says he never loses his temper while he's operating, and he's not impatient. The other day her new junior brushed against him and he had to re-scrub and regown, and he just told her not to worry—anyone else would have torn the poor girl apart. And the men like him.'

'And you like him too, don't you, love?'

Tabitha poured tea for the two of them. 'Yes, Meg.'

Meg sipped her tea. 'Love's never wasted, Miss Tabby—there doesn't seem to be any rhyme or reason to it now, but there surely will be.'

Tabitha put down her cup. She had gone a little pale. 'Meg, how did you know?' She put her cup down with a little clatter in its saucer. 'Meg—no one else—he—?'

'No, Miss Tabby love, but I've known you all your life, haven't I? I can't help but know. But if you don't want to talk about it I won't say another word.'

There was no sign of Marius on Monday morning; it wasn't theatre day, but there was the out-patients' clinic at two o'clock; it looked as though George Steele would have to take it as well as examining the new patients who were filling the empty beds. Tabitha had had her coffee and was explaining for the hundredth time to Mr Bow why he couldn't walk for a few more weeks when she heard the swing of the ward door and then Marius's unhurried step, so that she had time enough to compose her face into its habitual calm before he reached her side. He said at once:

'Are you very annoyed with me? I should have been here a great deal earlier.'

She achieved a smile, bade him a polite good morning and went on: 'I hope your lecture tour was a success.'

'I believe so—though I don't feel I'm the one to ask. Is there anything new in?' He wasn't looking at her, but smiling at Knotty. Tabitha had turned away to ask Rogers to telephone George Steele, now she looked at Marius and said pleasantly: 'Yes, sir. Mr Steele will be here in a minute. I expect you would like to talk to Mr Raynard.'

Mr van Beek's mouth twisted at its corners, but all he said was:

'To be sure I should. I'll let you know when I'm ready to do a round, Sister.'

She nodded rather austerely and went away to get Jimmy on to his legs; he had a walking iron now, and a new, lighter plaster, and was going home that afternoon. Naturally enough, he was in tearing high spirits, so that Tabitha became a great deal more cheerfully herself; she was chuckling over his grossly exaggerated picture of how he intended to stump down the aisle at his approaching wedding when he interrupted himself to say: 'Of course you'll come, won't you, Sister—and you, sir?'

Tabitha hadn't heard Marius—he was standing behind her and said readily enough: 'Of course—I shall be delighted.' He smiled at Tabitha, who pretended not to see. 'That makes two invitations we have jointly accepted, does it not, Sister?'

Tabitha looked up from her task of fitting a thick sock over Jimmy's large foot. 'Two?' she queried blankly, 'jointly?'

Marius said gravely, his eyes twinkling: 'Yes—this invitation we have just accepted for—when was it, Jimmy?—two weeks today—and Mr Prosser's kind invitation to sample his fish and chips.'

She felt a little glow of pleasure spreading itself under her apron bib. 'Oh, yes—I didn't think you were serious.'

'I was. When you are ready, Sister, I should like to do a round.'

The round proved to be a lighthearted affair. George, glad to have a load of work taken off his shoulders, was inclined to be talkative, Tommy was always cheerful anyway and Marius seemed glad to be back. Knotty and Mr Raynard, sitting propped up side by side, had been left until last and when the party reached them it seemed obvious that they were prepared to settle down to a lengthy chat with these two gentlemen. The vexed question as to how much longer both should stay had to be threshed out, and as for some reason best known to themselves, and presumably Marius, they wished to leave at the same time, it took a good deal of discussion for them all to arrive at a date some three weeks ahead. This done, the talk degenerated into a lively exchange of opinion on the joys of sailing, the vagaries of the weather as applied to that sport, and the uses of a pair of bumkins on a small sailing boat. Tabitha, who hadn't the least idea what these might be and in any case wanted to get on with the patients' dinners, took a cautious step backwards in the hope that she could drift away unnoticed.

But not quite, for Marius said: 'Yes, do go, Sister—we're wasting your time, I'm afraid.'

Dinners were over and Tabitha, leaving Staff in charge, went to her own meal. The men had gone at last, still talking, nodding polite, rather vague thank-yous as they went. She had the impression that they hadn't really seen her; whatever it was they had been talking about must have been of the most absorbing interest. Tabitha thought this over while she ate her cold beef and salad in an absent-minded manner.

'Sickening for something?' Sue wanted to know. 'You look peaky.'

It was Mary, the women's medical ward sister, who asked: 'Has that handsome Mr van Beek been running you off your feet? Not,' she added, 'that I would mind him running me off mine. I only see him in the distance—he looks fab.'

'He is,' put in Sue. 'Every theatre sister's dream come true, and nice with it—not exactly a lady's man, though—none of that "Come hither, girl," stuff. What do you say, Tabby?'

Tabitha agreed with her friend, thinking privately that it would be nice if she could have disagreed. She smiled at Sue as she spoke; she had a great many friends in hospital not one of whom had ever referred, even obliquely, to her plain face. Even now, Sue had managed to imply that she had as good a chance of having a pass made at her as the prettiest girl there. Tabitha suddenly felt almost pretty; it was surprising what a few kind words could do to a girl's morale. She went back to the ward feeling positively thrilled.

The ward was fairly quiet; Tabitha caught up on her books and then spent an hour showing the newest student just how traction worked and why, and then because she was off at five she decided to have a cup of tea in the office and not go down to the dining room; she could be planning the next two weeks' off duty while she drank it. She made her way up the ward and paused by Mr Raynard and Mr Bow, sitting with their heads bent over a map.

'Planning to run away?' she wanted to know.

Mr Raynard gave her a considered glance. 'You might call it that,' he agreed, 'eh, Knotty?'

Mr Bow coughed. 'Yes, I suppose one might put it like that. Tell me, Sister, how is my dear Podger doing? It is so kind of you to have him, I fear he may outstay his welcome.'

'Not he,' said Tabitha cheerfully. 'He's quite happy—or as happy as he can be without you. Meg loves him.'

'Meg? Ah, yes, your companion and housekeeper. I am indebted to you both.'

'He's no trouble, Mr Bow. We're glad to have him until you're able to have him again.'

Mr Bow and Mr Raynard exchanged glances. Tabitha thought they looked like small boys bottling up a secret. 'That, I hope, will not be too far distant, Sister,' said Mr Bow. His rich sonorous voice sounded gleeful.

Tabitha prepared to move on. 'I know,' she replied, 'three weeks at the earliest.' She walked away and then came back to stand by Mr Bow once more. 'I don't know what your plans are, Mr Bow, but if you want any help I'll be glad to do what I can, and if it's beyond me, I'll get the social worker to come and see you.'

Mr Bow smiled gently. 'You are a kind and thoughtful young woman,' he pronounced, 'but I believe my future is already in good hands.'

Tabitha nodded and went on her way quickly, otherwise it might look as though she was curious—which she was. Marius had fixed things for his old friend, she supposed. Doubtless she would know nothing more until she was asked to return Podger. Perhaps Mr Bow was going to stay permanently with Marius, but this wasn't a very fruitful line of thought because she hadn't the least idea where he was living. He seemed to spend his weekends with the Johnsons, but he surely didn't go to and fro each day, and he didn't live in the hospital or she would have heard about it through the grapevine. She pulled the off duty book towards her and looked unseeingly at its neatly ruled pages, ready for her to fill in. She was aware that she was wasting too much time thinking about Marius; it simply would not do. No effort on her part to attract him would stand a chance against Lilith's pale beauty; besides, she didn't know how to set about it.

She sighed loudly and was glad to be interrupted by Mrs Jeffs coming in with the tea tray. There were two cups on it and Tabitha asked idly:

'Hullo, who's having tea with me?'

'Mr van Beek, Sister. He popped his head round the kitchen door and asked if there was a cup to spare. Men need their tea,' she added comfortably. 'I did a little bit of buttered toast for you both.' She beamed at Tabitha and turned round as there was a knock on the half-open door and Marius walked in.

'That's right, sir, you come in and keep Sister company—
there's nothing like a nice cuppa and a chat.' She gave them
each a motherly smile and squeezed her plump person past
Marius. 'Too fat, aren't I?' she remarked cheerfully, 'but my
hubby says he can't miss a pound of me.'

She chuckled richly as she shut the door.

Tabitha had had plenty of time to acquire calm. She said
now in the tones of a polite hostess: 'Do sit down, Mrs Jeffs
makes a lovely pot of tea and there's toast too.'

Marius settled himself in the only other chair in the little
room.

'Mrs Jeffs treats me with all the cosy warmth of an affectionate aunt,' he observed.

'You don't mind, I hope? You see, she's not had any training, only what we've been able to give her, so she's not very
well up on hospital etiquette. She has a husband and sons and
several grandchildren and I expect she forgets you're a senior
member of the staff. She doesn't mean...'

He crossed one leg over the other, taking up most of the
available space in doing so. 'Why should I mind? Mrs Jeffs is
a treasure and it's delightful when someone forgets who I am—
there are those who don't.'

He looked at her with a little mocking smile and she went
bright red. The mockery went, leaving only kindness. 'I didn't
mean to upset you, Tabby. You must find it difficult remembering to call me sir in hospital and then treating me just like
anyone else outside it.'

Tabitha handed him the toast. 'Well, yes, I suppose so. Are
you glad to be back?'

'Yes. Lecturing is all very well when you can do it in one
place all the time. I keep forgetting where I am.'

She laughed. 'Do you talk in English?'

'Sometimes—sometimes German or Dutch, according to
where I am. Why do you look so pale?' He bent an intense
gaze upon her. 'Aren't you well?'

Tabitha choked on her tea. 'Yes, thank you. I—I didn't know
I looked any different from usual. You've a long list for tomorrow.'

He studied her carefully before he replied. 'All right, don't tell me if you don't want to,' he remarked mildly. 'Yes, it is a big list, the first case will take quite a time, but that's the only one presenting any difficulties. George and I should polish off the rest quickly enough. You'll be on all day?'

She nodded. 'Until the evening.'

They drank their tea in silence after that while Tabitha sought vainly for some topic of conversation. It was a pity that she could think of nothing at all to say; she wasn't in the least surprised when he got to his feet and said: 'Well, thanks for the tea and the peace,' and was gone before she could so much as say goodbye.

The week passed and the weather, warm and bright, showed up the ward's old-fashioned drawbacks so that everybody, staff and patients alike, was inclined to be a little irritable. Marius came and went, good-natured as always, seemingly unaware of the tiresomely old-fashioned surroundings. But then he was free to go at the end of the day's work in the operating theatre; it was the nurses who had to stay, working in the out-of-date sluices, walking with tired feet up and down the bare wooden floors. There would be, in some distant future, a splendid new hospital, equipped with every modern aid to nursing which could be devised. Tabitha, writing up the Kardex in her stuffy office, wondered how many years it would be before it was built and if she would still be at St Martin's then.

She laid down her pen at length and went to do her last round. Jimmy had gone, of course; she would be going to his wedding soon. The man in his bed was middle-aged and a little aggressive and she missed Jimmy's cheerful face; it would be nice to see him married, though. She had bought a new hat for the occasion, a large floppy one with a wavy brim which she considered suited her very well because it hid her face. It was a pretty shade of pink and would help to liven up the rather plain oyster colour silk dress she intended to wear. She had arranged a day off for the wedding so that she would have plenty of time to drive to Bradninch where Jimmy lived, and for a little while at least she had wondered if Marius would suggest that they should go together, but he had said nothing;

possibly he had forgotten all about it, for village weddings, she deduced shrewdly, were by no means the only social occasions in the lives of such men as Marius.

She went slowly down one side of the ward and just as slowly up the other, giving her attention to each patient in turn until she came to Mr Bow, who was sitting up in bed making knots with a short length of rope.

'What are you doing?' asked Tabitha. 'Did the physio people give you that to do?'

'I'm practicing seamen's knots, Sister, and Marius brought me the rope. A good idea, don't you think?'

'Well, yes, I suppose so if you like such things,' said Tabitha. 'At least it keeps your fingers supple.'

Mr Bow executed something complicated with admirable dexterity. 'Indeed, yes.' He gave her a brief glance from his blue eyes. 'I am very comfortable, thank you, Sister.'

Tabitha felt herself dismissed, so she said good night and moved on to Mr Raynard's cubicle. He was deep in a book, but he put a finger carefully in its pages to mark where he had got to and said: 'Hullo, Tabby Nightingale, still dragging your weary feet from bed to bed?'

'Well, really,' she responded indignantly, 'you make it sound as though I've got varicose veins or bunions! You and Mr Bow are very quiet this evening—aren't you speaking?'

'Good lord, girl, what queer notions you do get into your head. Of course we're speaking, but at the moment we are occupied. How is he getting on with his knots?'

Tabitha looked a little bewildered. 'Very nicely, I imagine. Why is he doing them?'

Mr Raynard darted a quick look at her curious face. 'You'll know—any minute now.' He held his book up for her to see. It was a treatise on coastal navigation and made no sense to her at all.

'Are you both taking a course on sailing?' she hazarded at length.

'You could call it that—and then again, you couldn't,' said her chief obscurely. 'My wife's late, she promised she would be here.'

Tabitha began to walk away from his bed. 'Mrs Raynard's coming through the door now,' she said. 'Good night, sir.'

She paused for a word with Mrs Raynard and went on her way towards the ward door. Another fifteen minutes and the night staff would be on; already the two student nurses were doing a last round of the ward, filling water jugs and collecting papers which their readers had refused to hand over earlier in the evening; there was no one very ill. Tabitha decided to go to the office—it was hot there, but it would be nice to have a few minutes to herself. She was at the door when it was swung open from the other side and Marius came in; when she would have passed him with a civil good evening he caught her arm with a 'No—we want you by Mr Raynard's bed for a few minutes.'

He spoke without urgency, but there was no escaping the gentle grip on her elbow. She would have liked to have asked why as they went back down the ward, but there was no time, only, as they approached Mr Raynard's bed, she was able to observe that neither he nor his wife looked in the least surprised at her return.

'Of course,' grunted Mr Raynard, 'I don't like the idea of doing this in public as it were, but Marius has the idea that his suggestion needs our combined support.' He fixed Tabitha with a gimlet eye. 'You'll not be able to disobey me, my girl.'

Tabitha's bewilderment grew, mixed with a vague annoyance as she watched Marius scoop Mr Bow out of his bed and into the wheelchair by it, and trundle him briskly into Mr Raynard's cubicle. She said tartly: 'I shouldn't count on that, sir,' and he roared with laughter before saying:

'Go on, Marius, before Tabby gets cross.'

Marius was facing her across the bed. He said in his usual placid voice: 'It's not fair to tease you, Tabitha. We—that is, all of us here—want you to accompany us on holiday. Mr Bow and Mr Raynard will still be partial invalids even in a couple of weeks' time, but they have a crazy idea that a week or two's sailing is just what they need. They'll neither of them be much use in a boat, but Mrs Raynard crews and you have done some sailing, haven't you? It seems to all of us ideal if you would help us out by coming along as well, to keep an eye on them both and be company for Mrs Raynard. There's plenty of room in my house for all of us and the boat will take us easily enough, though heaven alone knows where we shall stow two plastered legs.' He paused and then said with a smile: 'The whole thing's a little mad, isn't it, but if anything goes wrong they'll at least be in good hands. There's just one other thing— do you suppose Meg would mind looking after Podger for a few more weeks? I promise you it won't be much longer than that. I've another lecture tour in about two months' time, after that Mr Bow will be permanently settled and Podger can rejoin him.'

The silence almost shouted at her when he finished speaking. Not only were those around the bed waiting on her answer, she was aware too that those nearest them in the ward were straining their ears, and that the two student nurses had been tidying the same bed on the opposite side of the ward since Marius had begun to speak; all the same, she had to stop and think. She recognized the fact that it was a matter of convenience that Marius should have asked her to go with them. Both gentlemen would need help to a limited extent and some restraining influence; not by the wildest stretch of the imagination could she suppose that Marius's invitation had been offered for any other reason. She asked at length:

'How long should we be gone?' and saw the sudden gleam in Marius's eyes. 'If I should go,' she added hastily, and he laughed.

'Three weeks at the outside.'

It sounded wonderful, but there were still several things she had thought of. 'I'm not booked for a holiday until September—and who will do your work, Mr Raynard?'

The Old Man's face assumed a cunning expression. 'Ah, this is where we have used our undoubtedly intelligent brains. Provided—I say provided Tabby, you agree to come—we have persuaded the powers that be, to allow the ward to be emptied so that it may be brought up to date and redecorated—heaven knows it's long overdue. It will take about ten days, that leaves George a few days to get the patients transferred; the rest he can cope with in the surgical annexe and then fill this place up again ready for Marius when we come back.'

'And when are you going to start work, Mr Raynard?' Tabitha wanted to know. 'You won't be able to manage the theatre...' Mr Raynard showed his splendid teeth. 'Quiet, girl! I shall do very well. George will be here to do most of the work when Marius goes. I've got it all thought out, so don't distract my thoughts.'

So Marius wouldn't be coming back; at least, only for a very short time. Then presumably he would go to Chidlake, to Lilith. One of Meg's endless fund of quotations came into her head, quite unbidden. 'A bird in the hand...' Marius was hardly a bird, but it seemed to Tabitha that for once there was some point in the saying. She looked around at their faces; Mr Bow, bearing the satisfied look of a Father Christmas who had successfully weathered yet another Christmas Eve; Mr Raynard looking like a thunder cloud—which meant nothing at all; his wife, who caught Tabby's eye and smiled as though she meant it, and Marius, seemingly placid and unworried as to what she would say. But the look he gave her, although it was both these things, also contained the certainty that she wouldn't disappoint either Mr Raynard or Knotty. She said, looking at him: 'I should like to come very much.'

Later, sitting in the flat, talking it over with Meg, she wondered if she had been wise to accept. After all, there were other nurses—she said so out loud to Meg, who pointed out in a practical voice that there wouldn't be much sense in taking a stranger with them—someone they wouldn't know and probably wouldn't like either. Meg knew all about Mr Raynard's peculiar temperament and she knew about Mr Bow too.

'Poor old man,' she said kindly, 'you can't expect him to take to someone he's never met before—why, it would spoil his holiday.' She looked at Tabitha's downbent head. 'That's why they asked you, Miss Tabby. They know you'll put up with Mr Raynard's tantrums, and his wife likes you.'

She didn't mention Marius at all, and neither did Tabitha.

A couple of days later when she had the opportunity to speak to Marius she asked what arrangements she should make. She had already been to Matron, to be told that Mr Raynard had already spoken personally to that lady, who said with an unwonted degree of friendliness:

'Of course I agreed at once, Sister Crawley, provided you yourself wish to accompany the party. It seems to me to be a very good idea, and an excellent opportunity to have the ward redecorated and modernized while you are away. I shall come down to see you in a day or so; I daresay you may have some ideas about colour schemes and so forth.'

She nodded gracious dismissal and Tabitha went back to the ward where she found Marius and George drinking coffee in her office. It was then that she asked what she was expected to do next.

'Nothing,' said Marius lazily. 'At least, get your passport up to date if it isn't, and I suppose women buy clothes.' He looked at George. 'Do they, George?'

George, being a married man, said that yes, they did and he couldn't think why, for old clothes were the only possible wear on holiday. This remark naturally led to a discussion as to the best type of holiday, and Tabitha, seeing that she wasn't going to get anywhere at all with her own affairs, excused herself, saying with a tinge of sarcasm that there were those who worked; a remark which was quite lost upon her hearers, deep as they were in the joys of fly fishing.

She had better luck with Mrs Raynard, who happened to visit her husband that afternoon. The two of them spent ten minutes comparing notes about what they should take with them so that Tabitha's mind was set at rest upon that important point at least, although no one had, as yet, told her how they were going. When she had asked Mr Raynard all he said was:

'Good grief, girl, Marius will see to everything—why do you fuss? You're all alike!'

'In which case,' said Tabitha, thoroughly put out by this unfair remark, 'you can quite well do without me, and I certainly don't care to come if I'm to be bawled at every time I open my mouth!'

The last word came out as a small scream, for she was firmly caught round the waist from behind. She didn't need to ask who it was and her first thought was that it was lucky that they were in the cubicle and not out in the ward. 'My solemn promise,' said Marius's voice in her ear, 'that if the chief puts you out I shall personally take him out into deep water and drop him overboard. I shan't need weight—that plaster will do very well.'

They all laughed and he let her go, whereupon she turned smartly on her heel and made for the door, where she paused to say: 'There are two new cases in, sir—would you like to see them, or shall I ring for Mr Steele?'

He didn't answer this but asked instead: 'When are you off, Tabby?'

'At six.'

'I've had no opportunity to talk to you about the journey to Veere—perhaps this evening?'

'No,' said Tabitha too quickly. 'I—I've a previous engagement!' She gave him a direct look, for after all it wasn't really a lie; she had promised Meg that she would help her make jam. Marius returned the look with one of his own and although his expression was politely regretful, she was fairly sure that he was laughing at her. 'Some other time,' he murmured gently. 'And now what about these patients?'

Some other time was a vague term rendered useless by a sudden avalanche of work, for a local building site sent in two men, one with a fractured spine and the other with a crushed pelvis; then there was the postman whose brakes had failed on a steep hill just outside the city, and the retired naval officer who, like Mr Raynard, had come a cropper in his garden and fractured his patella into so many pieces that all Marius could do was to remove them—the old gentleman would be a little stiff in the knee, but as he was well over seventy, this drawback wasn't too severe. There was a little lull after that so that there was time to catch up on the paper work—time for Marius to seek her out too.

Which he did one afternoon as she sat making out the papers of the patients who had been admitted for operation in two days' time. He asked from the door: 'May I come in?', and then, before she could do more than nod: 'You have a day off tomorrow, haven't you—unless you're going to put it off again?'

She had done just that earlier in the week because Rogers' young man had had a birthday and wanted to take her out to celebrate. 'No,' she said sedately.

'Good. I'm going to Chidlake, come with me—we can talk on the way.' He came a little further into the room. 'You can give Mrs Crawley and Lilith a surprise.'

A fine surprise, thought Tabitha, feeling sick at the thought of the fun they would have at her expense. She drew a breath. 'I—I don't suppose you know that I—we don't get on, that is we haven't many interests in common. I don't go home often.' She was drawing a cat with enormous whiskers and a curly tail on the blotting paper and didn't look up.

'Of course I know,' said Marius quietly. 'I've been—er—told. But my dear good girl, even if that is the case, surely you can be civil to each other at least on the surface—think how much easier it would be when you went home.'

Tabitha drew a kitten beside the cat, concentrating fiercely upon it. There was a great deal she would have liked to say, but her thoughts couldn't be put into coherent words—besides, Lilith would have said all there was to say and he would be biased already. She muttered: 'I daresay,' and started on another kitten. Marius sat down and she listened to the chair's protesting squeak—one day it would give way under him and she would have to explain to Matron…no, he wouldn't be here long enough for that. She sighed and gave the mother cat a bonnet with a feather.

'You're afraid,' said Marius very softly.

She put her pen down and sat up straight and faced him squarely, her plain face animated into near beauty by her rage. 'How dare you?' Her pleasant voice was a little shrill but well under control. 'Until you came I had my life planned and everything was…you've done nothing but…I was safe…'

'In a rut, with your hair sleeked back and your nose buried in your work, just because a long time ago somebody called you a plain girl.'

'Oh, but she meant it,' Tabitha gabbled wildly, 'and I am.'

She went on furiously: 'Can't you see you've stirred me up? I was happy before.'

'Happy? With your broom and no chance of a glass slipper?'

He got up and pulled her out of her chair and held her hands in his.

'Tabitha, shall we not be friends? After all, I expect to see a great deal of you in the future and we can't go on like this, at loggerheads, for ever and ever.'

Tabitha stared ahead of her at his white drill coat; it was stiff and spotless, showing a glimpse of a silk tie. If she raised her eyes just an inch or so, she could see his face, but she had no intention of doing that; she was thinking that when he married Lilith it would be so much more comfortable if they all got on well together. She imagined herself in five or six years' time, spending her holidays in London, or wherever Lilith decided to live, looking after the children while Marius took Lilith on some splendid trip. She said in a bewildered voice: 'Could we be friends?'

She felt his hands tighten on her own. 'Yes, Tabby.' He let go of one hand and lifted her chin and gave her a long look, then kissed her on the cheek—a nice brotherly kiss, thought Tabitha, even in her limited experience. He smiled suddenly and with such charm that she closed her eyes for a second. 'You'll come with me tomorrow, Tabitha. I promise you it will be all right. Will you trust me?'

'Yes.' She moved away so that he let go her other hand too, and swallowed the lump in her throat which threatened to choke her. 'What time do you want me to be ready?'

'About ten or thereabouts, if that suits you. What about Meg? Can we give her a lift somewhere?'

'I don't know. I'll ask her. She might like to visit her sister, only there's Podger—we try not to leave him alone too much.'

He didn't seem to find this ridiculous. 'Supposing we come back directly after tea, that wouldn't be too long for him to be on his own, would it?'

Tabitha thought not and added diffidently: 'You know, unexpected people for lunch aren't always welcome— shouldn't I...?'

Marius said positively: 'No, you shouldn't.' He got up again and went to the door. 'I'll see you tomorrow.' He smiled very kindly as he went.

Tabitha told Meg all about it when she got home later that evening and was surprised when she said: 'And a better friend you couldn't have, Miss Tabby. You be glad of his friendship, love, it's not what you want, I know, but mark my words, nothing but good will come of it.' She looked at Tabitha with affection. 'You're a spirited girl, your father always said you had pluck—now's the chance to show it. You be thankful he wants you for a friend, Miss Tabby.'

But Tabby, doing her best to be thankful, only succeeded in being very miserable indeed, but Meg, asleep in her own small room, wasn't to know that.

It was a heavenly morning. Tabitha got up early, took Meg a cup of tea and then started to tidy the house because Meg had said that she would like to visit her sister at Ottery. She came downstairs presently and cooked their breakfast, and they ate it together in the kitchen while Podger emptied his saucer under the table, then presently when they had washed up together, Tabitha went back upstairs to finish dressing. She put on the dress she had worn the last time she had gone to Chidlake—the one her stepmother had considered wasted upon her. Tabitha looked at herself in the mirror with a touch of defiance; it was a pretty dress and despite Mrs Crawley's opinion, she intended to wear it. It was a soft shade of apricot, sleeveless and round-necked, exactly the right kind of dress for such a lovely day, and as if he had known she needed reassuring about it, when she went downstairs Marius, who had just arrived, said 'Hullo, Tabitha, that's a pretty dress, and it suits you,' which remark caused her to smile with relief and pleasure, for Marius wasn't a man to flatter—at least, she amended to herself, she didn't think that he would flatter her, so that his remark was all the more to be appreciated.

They stopped at Meg's insistence and had coffee at her sister's house and by the time they had walked round the garden, admired the pet rabbits, the goat and a great many hens and chicks who lived in the paddock at the back of the cottage, it was almost midday.

'What time did you say you would arrive?' asked Tabitha anxiously.

'Twelvish—my dear girl, do relax, we're almost there.'

It was true, they were—they flashed past All Hallows school and very shortly afterwards Marius turned the Bentley down the familiar lane which led to Chidlake. When they came to the bend at the top of the hill, Tabitha said: 'Please will you stop for a moment, Marius—it's such a lovely view.' It was; the sun sparkled over Lyme Bay highlighting the cliffs until they faded, miles away, into distant Portland Bill. Nearer, the village lay half hidden below them with Chidlake a little above it, old and tranquil in the sun. Tabitha sighed without knowing it and Marius said quickly: 'It's beautiful, isn't it? I miss this in Holland—it's lovely there too, but in quite a different way.' He talked casually about his own country as they slipped down the hill and through the gates, giving her time to collect herself, and when he helped her out of the car he kept a hand tucked beneath her elbow, and that was how Lilith, running out of the house, saw them. Before she could speak he said cheerfully: 'Hullo, you beautiful girl—I've brought Tabitha with me. She's been working much too hard and she needs a little of your sea air.'

Tabitha watched Lilith's face crumble into sheer rage and then quickly rearrange itself into a welcoming smile as she slipped an arm into Marius's, looking up into his face with a charmingly proprietorial air.

'Marius, how lovely to see you!' She turned to Tabitha, the smile still upon her lips but temper still blazing in her beautiful eyes.

'You too, Tabby—such a surprise to see you. You come so seldom, and then only after we've begged and begged.'

Tabitha thought of several retorts to this remark; they were all quite unsuitable, so she kept silent, contenting herself by freeing her arm from Marius's grasp; it was like trying to prise herself loose from an iron vice and just as impossible, for his hand tightened its gentle grip as they walked, the three of them, into the house.

Mrs Crawley came out of the drawing room as they went in, a welcoming smile already upon her face. Like her daughter she kept the smile there even when she saw Tabitha and said lightly: 'Marius, how very nice—and Tabby too.' She looked at her then, and Tabitha saw how cold her stepmother's eyes had become. 'A pity you didn't let me know you were coming—so awkward for lunch....'

'My fault,' declared Marius instantly. He still had hold of Tabitha's arm and now she was glad of its reassuring grip. 'Tabitha didn't like the idea of taking you by surprise, but I overruled her—after all, she is one of the family.' He smiled as he spoke and looked placidly at the three of them. 'Besides, she has some news for you—it seemed a good opportunity to tell you.'

'News?' queried Mrs Crawley sharply, and looked so apprehensive that Tabitha had a moment of wicked delight. 'Well, do come in, and you shall tell us over drinks.'

She led the way into the drawing room, but before Tabitha could sit down she was sent off to the kitchen to tell the cook that there would be one more for lunch, and when she got back the drinks had been poured and Lilith was sitting with Marius on a settee at the far end of the room, and her stepmother was in her usual chair by the French windows. She said at once: 'Come over here, Tabitha, and tell me your news. Your drink is on the table, bring it with you.'

Tabitha started across the room, wishing with all her heart that she had never come. Lilith and Marius were too far away to join in any conversation she might have with Mrs Crawley; she would have to tell her without any help from Marius, and she could imagine just what her stepmother would say. She had reached the table when Marius spoke.

'As it is I who persuaded you in the first place, Tabitha, I think I should have a share in the telling.' He had got up as he spoke and she found him beside her. As he piloted her across to where Mrs Crawley was sitting he looked over his shoulder and said: 'Come on, Lilith,' and she got up reluctantly and joined them too. Presently when everyone was settled again, Mrs Crawley asked: 'Well?'

Marius was at his most casual. 'There are two old friends of mine in Tabitha's ward, on the mend with broken legs. They are coming to stay with me for a week or so in Holland. Mr Raynard's wife will accompany us and we have persuaded Tabitha to come too and keep an eye on the two invalids.'

Lilith, who had arranged herself gracefully on a chair close to Marius, sat up. 'What? But she can't—she's got her ward to look after.'

If Marius found her remark strange he gave no sign but said merely:

'That is all arranged. Tabby is due for a holiday anyway— it won't be all work, you know.'

Lilith rounded on Tabitha. 'Why didn't you tell us?' she wanted to know, and Tabitha, who had been sitting as still as a mouse, holding her tongue because she thought that Marius would deal with the situation far better than she could, thought she had better answer.

'I've only known for a short time and I didn't think you would be interested.'

Mrs Crawley gave a tinkling laugh. 'Tabby, how sly of you!' She said it nastily, and Tabitha went pink and bit her lip for fear her mounting temper should escape and spoil everything. Marius came to her rescue.

'Not sly,' his voice was bland. 'We saw no point in telling anyone until we had settled everything—anyway, she made the journey here today especially to tell you.' He smiled across at Lilith, apparently unnoticing of her sulky face. 'I knew you'd be delighted, Lilith—I seem to remember you saying how you hoped that Tabitha would have some fun this summer.' He got up and went and sat on the arm of her chair. 'After all, you get more than your fair share of that, don't you? But I suppose that's natural with a face like yours. It seems to me that there is always a queue of eager young men waiting to fulfil your lightest wish. A mere middle-aged bachelor like myself doesn't stand a chance.'

Tabitha watched Lilith's good humour return under Marius's

skilful flattery while she attempted to deal with her own very
mixed feelings. To begin with she was sure that Marius's remarks about Lilith's concern for her fun were pure fiction and
she didn't much like being designated as a hard-working
woman in need of a holiday, and did he have to flatter Lilith
quite so outrageously? She looked up and caught his eyes on
her and could have sworn that there was a gleam of laughter
in them. But he said nothing more and it seemed as though her
stepmother and Lilith had accepted his explanation, though
grudgingly. She watched while he got to his feet and pulled
Lilith out of her chair, saying: 'Anyway, now I'm here, come
and show me the garden; something must have grown since I
was here last.'

Tabitha watched them go outside, arm-in-arm. Probably the
moment they were out of sight, she thought bitterly, Marius
would kiss her stepsister. A pain which was almost physical
filled her chest so that she caught her breath with its sharpness;
she had been unhappy for a long time, but this was a different
kind of unhappiness; she wanted to get up and run away from
it. Instead, she turned an interested, rather pale face to her
stepmother who was speaking. 'They make a delightful pair,'
she observed complacently, 'Lilith couldn't do better for herself. I hear he's very rich and well connected, and being so
much older than Lilith she will be able to do exactly as she
likes with him.'

Tabitha felt sick. She said carefully: 'Lilith's lucky to have
found someone to love so early in her life.'

Mrs Crawley laughed shortly. 'Love—who said anything
about love?' she wanted to know. 'Lilith has the good sense
to want a rich easy-going husband. Only a fool like you would
start drooling about love.' She frowned. 'I can't say I'm delighted at your news—why should I be? On the other hand,
perhaps it's a good thing. Some other girl might have gone,
but you're just a nurse who works for him and I suppose you'll
be employed as a sort of mother's help. He sees you every day,
so you're quite commonplace to him, and anyway, you aren't
exactly exciting, are you, Tabby? I should hardly call you a
threat to Lilith's future.'

She smiled—the smile Tabitha couldn't bear—so she got up so as not to see it and said: 'Here they come—shall I go and tell Cook she can serve lunch?'

Lunch went very well, though it seemed to Tabitha that everything was a little unreal, for she and Lilith and her stepmother were all playing parts while Marius, entertaining them with casual charm, appeared not to notice their stilted politeness to each other. All the same it was a relief when after the meal her stepmother suggested that she might like to go upstairs and pack any clothes she might need for her holiday. Tabitha, who had no clothes upstairs, nevertheless agreed because she could see that it was a ruse to get her out of the way; she was even more sure of this when Mrs Crawley announced that she would rest for an hour or so. They went upstairs together, and presently Tabitha, standing in her little room by the window, heard the purr of the Bentley's engine, and by craning her neck was able to watch Marius, with Lilith beside him, drive away.

She sat on her bed for quite half an hour, wondering if she should back out of the trip to Veere, but in the end she decided against the idea. It seemed certain that Lilith was going to get Marius, and as he didn't appear to mind being caught, there was nothing to do about that. But there was no reason why she shouldn't have a holiday. She would be able to see Marius every day and whatever happened afterwards, she would have that to remember. She went downstairs and out into the garden and started to weed one of the borders.

They left soon after tea, although she had half expected that Marius would want to stay later, despite his promise. He and Lilith had come back at the end of the afternoon, laughing and talking in the most friendly way, but Tabitha detected a faint uneasiness in Lilith's manner as well as an expression of bewilderment on her face, and her heart leapt with foolish delight because that must mean that Marius hadn't asked her to marry him.

They didn't talk much on the way back; it was only as they were approaching Ottery that Marius said: 'Well, it wasn't so bad, was it? You would have had to have told them sooner or

later, you know—they would have got to hear about it somehow or other, these things get around. It will be easier for you
next time you see them....'

Tabitha interrupted him: 'Is that why you went to all that
trouble—making it easy for me?'

'No trouble, dear girl,' he gave her a sidelong glance. 'I
intended you to tell them yourself, but you looked'—he
paused—'anyway, since I asked you to come in the first place,
it seemed hardly fair.'

He stopped the car outside the cottage in Ottery. 'By the
way, I thought you had some clothes to bring back?'

Tabitha blushed. 'Well—no, I haven't anything at Chidlake.
It was just so that you and Lilith...' She was interrupted by
his laugh, which was one of genuine amusement.

When they got back to the flat he got out of the car to help
Meg and then opened the door for them and Tabitha said uncertainly: 'Well, do come in if you'd like to,' and led the way
to the kitchen where Podger was waiting for them. Tabitha
picked him up and Meg, after a glance at her, said comfortably:
'I've a dozen of the freshest eggs in my bag. How about scram-
bling some of them for supper?'

'If that's an invitation, I accept,' said Marius. 'If someone
will show me where everything is, I'll lay the table.' Which
he did while Tabitha fed the cat and made the coffee and Meg
set to work with the eggs. They sat down presently and ate
their simple meal, and when Meg produced a large jam sponge,
as light as a feather, and a bowl of cream they ate that too.
The talk was of everyday things, and Meg, who could be dis-
creet, asked no questions about Chidlake or its occupants, but
wanted to know about their holiday instead. They all washed
up afterwards and when Tabitha went to the door with Marius,
he said: 'That was the best meal I've had for a long time,' and
then, 'A very nice ending to the day, Tabby, though I can see
that I must have patience for a little longer.'

She thought he was talking about Lilith—who surely hadn't
refused him? She said kindly: 'Don't worry, I'm sure you
won't have to wait.'

He kissed her on the mouth and she guessed that he hadn't

meant to do so. 'I'll remind you of that one day,' he said, and got into the car.

Tabitha went back to the kitchen and helped Meg get ready for the morning. She told her a little of her day at Chidlake, and Meg heard her out with patience and then said: 'There's many a slip, Miss Tabby dear, and don't you worry your head over the things your stepmother says. Hard words break no bones,' she added comfortingly.

Who cares about bones, thought Tabitha, going to her bed, it's my heart that's been broken. She undressed quickly and got into bed, where she lay awake for a very long time wondering why Marius hadn't proposed to Lilith, and alternatively, why Lilith, who had seemed so keen to marry him, hadn't accepted him if he had proposed. It was a question she would dearly have loved to have answered. Unfortunately there was no one to do so. She would have to go on guessing.

# CHAPTER FIVE

DURING the next few days Tabitha saw very little of Marius. Of course there were the rounds and the brief businesslike discussions about the patients' treatments, but that was all. It wasn't until the end of the week that he paused on his way out of the ward after a morning round to tell her that he was going to Chidlake that afternoon and had she any messages. She had said no without any hesitation, and then sought for a few suitable words to soften the baldness of her answer, but he was already on his way down the corridor. He came back that evening, just before she was due to go off duty, and feeling that she should make amends for her abruptness of the morning, she had asked:

'Did you have a pleasant time at Chidlake?'

He had cast down the chart he was reading and given her a thoughtful stare, then said to mystify her: 'I hope so. I shan't know for several weeks.'

Tabitha stared back, trying to make sense of what he had said; it wasn't until later that she was forced to the conclusion that he had gone for the express purpose of asking Lilith to marry him, and for some reason of her own, Lilith had chosen to keep him waiting for the answer. She voiced this opinion out loud to Podger, who had made a sympathetic noise in the back of his throat, blinked at her several times and then curled himself into a tight ball and gone to sleep.

'Oh, well,' said Tabitha, 'I suppose I may as well do the same,' and turned out the light to lie wide awake, and because she didn't want to think about Marius any more that night, she turned her thoughts to the ward. Matron had paid her promised visit and left various samples of material for ward curtains. Tabitha, by concentrating fiercely upon them, and still concentrating, went at last to sleep.

It wasn't until Friday evening while she was speeding round

getting things shipshape before her day off that Marius had anything of a private nature to say to her, and that so unexpected that she stopped counting sheets to listen to him and then said:

'There, now I've forgotten where I was—I'll have to start again.' But before she did so, she said politely: 'Thank you very much, but I planned to drive myself over and I shall take Meg—she dearly loves a wedding, and she can go to the local inn and have lunch while I'm at the reception.'

She started on the sheets once more, counting under her breath. She had got to twelve when Marius took her hand off the pile and said firmly:

'Leave those. If you're offended because I didn't ask you sooner, I'm sorry. I'm afraid I took it for granted that we would be going together. Come off your perch, Tabby, and tell me what time I should pick you and Meg up.'

He sounded very persuasive; Tabitha came off her perch, although she was still a little reluctant. 'The wedding's at half past twelve.' She sounded offhand because she was not sure if he was just being polite or really wanted to take them, and as though he had read her thoughts he said bracingly: 'You really should cultivate a good opinion of yourself, Tabitha. I should like you to come with me.'

She gave him a quick look and saw that he was wearing his kind face and smiling too and her own mouth curved. She said cheerfully:

'It's only about twelve miles to Bradninch—we ought to get there by a quarter past twelve. I'd planned to leave at about a quarter to because I'm not sure about parking the car.'

'We'll use mine, I get claustrophobia in anything smaller. I'll pick you up.'

Tabitha smoothed the top sheet with extreme care and said without looking at him: 'If you like to come a few minutes earlier and have coffee before we go...'

'Half past eleven,' he answered promptly. 'I was hoping you would ask me—one can never be sure of wedding feasts and I might get peckish. What will you wear?'

She gave him a surprised look. 'A—a dress,' and then because he smiled, 'It's a sort of clotted cream colour—silk. I've bought a new hat—a pink one with a big wavy brim.'

'Oh, lord,' said Marius, 'that means every time I want to say something to you I shall have to bend double and peer underneath.'

'Yes.' It wasn't the word but the way she had said it which made him say blandly: 'So that's it—hiding your light under a bushel again, Tabby. You'll oblige me by wearing it well back—I like to see your face.'

Tabitha was so astonished that she dropped some of the sheets. She picked them up, red in the face, and Marius, handing her his own quota of fallen linen, gave her a thoughtful look, although all he said was: 'Well, I must be off. I'll see you in the morning. Good night.'

Tabitha answered a little breathlessly and fell to counting sheets once more, with so little success that she was doing it when the night nurse came to look for her.

There was a fruit cake to go with the coffee. Marius, elegant in a grey suit of impeccable cut, sat on the kitchen table munching a large slice while Tabitha went upstairs to put on her hat, but when she came down he balanced the cake on his saucer and stood up the better to inspect her. She stood selfconsciously in front of him, hoping that the hat would meet with his approval, for she had spent a long time trying it on at different angles, and then, mindful of what he had said, perched it well back, defiantly framing the face she had intended to shade.

He nodded approval. 'Very nice—pink suits you, Tabby, and that's a very pretty dress too. You look elegant—does she not, Meg?' he appealed to the older woman, who said vigorously: 'Miss Tabby always looks smart,' and even though Tabitha wasn't sure if what they said was true at least she felt warmed by their praise.

They arrived in good time at the church, which was a good thing, for most of the village seemed bent on being at the wedding. Fortunately for them an earnest young man in the porch, struggling to sort the guests into His and Hers, recognized them. He had been a frequent visitor to the ward when Jimmy had been a patient there, and although he blinked a little at the unexpected sight of Tabitha without her cap and strings and apron, he ushered them into a seat in the body of the church where they had an excellent view of the bridegroom, very neat in his navy blue suit with its trouser leg cut neatly up its seam to accommodate his leg plaster. He turned round and saw them and waved discreetly and made the thumbs up sign which Tabitha privately thought rather unsuitable to the occasion. She was sitting between Meg and Marius and as the bride came down the aisle she was forced to peer round him in order to see her. It was like looking round a tree trunk.

The reception was in the Town Hall at the top of the hill, and when they had escorted Meg to the hotel and dealt with the question of her lunch, they parked the Bentley amongst the crowd of cars already there and went upstairs to the big room on the first floor where they greeted the happy couple and then passed on to be immediately engulfed in hospitality. Sandwiches, sausages on sticks, little rolls dangerously oozing mustard and cress and large ones filled even more dangerously with chopped egg were offered them from all sides; they found themselves, with their filled plates in one hand and glasses of sweet Spanish wine in the other, in a group of Jimmy's friends, all of whom had been to the hospital to visit him at one time or another. Then they had been a little overawed by their surroundings, but now the boot was on the other foot—they set themselves to entertain their guests, and naturally being friends of Jimmy's they were also Rugger enthusiasts; Tabitha found herself taking part in an animated talk concerning something she knew very little about and it was small comfort to observe that Marius was enjoying himself enormously. But with the advent of the bride and groom and two of the bridesmaids who came to join the group she was able to escape to a corner with Jimmy's new wife and spend a short but pleasant period discussing the wedding gown, the bridesmaids' dresses and the trousseau before the bride was whisked away to change.

'How nice a wedding is,' observed Tabitha as they drove away an hour or more later. 'I mean a wedding where everyone really likes the bride and groom and not the kind where the women go just to be spiteful about each other's hats.'

Meg and Marius agreed and then lapsed into silence while Tabitha, for Meg's benefit, described exactly what the bride wore—she went on to detail the bridesmaids' dresses too as well as the bride's mother's and several more of the most striking outfits there, pausing in midsentence to point out to Marius that he had taken the wrong fork at Silverton, where they joined the main road, but Marius said with calm: 'The wrong fork for home, you mean? There's a nice tea place along here somewhere—the Fisherman's Cot—I thought we might sit a while. I still have to hear what the bridegroom's mother wore.'

Tabitha went a bright pink. 'Oh—have I been boring you?' She looked contrite. 'I'm so sorry.'

'Don't be. I'm vastly entertained, though how you contrive to remember who was wearing what is beyond me.'

He turned the car off the road as he spoke and parked by a picturesque thatched house with a small river running through its pretty garden. They had tea sitting at one of the open windows with the scent of the flowers vying with the delicious aroma of fresh baked scones.

'I'm hungry,' said Tabitha simply, eyeing the big dishes of jam and cream which accompanied the scones, and Meg who was pouring the tea, said:

'Probably you are, Miss Tabby. However good the food is at a wedding reception you can never get enough of it. I,' she added, 'had an excellent lunch.' She beamed at them both and asked Marius: 'Well, Mr van Beek, what do you think of our nice country village weddings?'

He split a scone with masterly precision. 'Delightful, Meg— I intend to have a village wedding myself.'

There was silence, broken by Meg who asked hastily: 'Are they the same in Holland?'

Tabitha didn't give him the chance to answer; she felt numb with shock, but she had to speak. 'She might not like it,' she managed.

Marius eyed her across the table; he looked as though he was enjoying a private joke although he wasn't even smiling. He said silkily:

'I am aware that it is usual for the bride to choose; it just so happens that I already know her inclination.' He turned away from her and addressed Meg, just as though Tabitha had never interrupted him. He described a Dutch wedding with a wealth of detail and a good deal of humour and presently, without her realizing it, drew Tabitha back into the conversation.

It was well after six when they arrived back at the flat and as Marius opened the door and handed her back the key, Tabitha asked a little uncertainly: 'Would you like to come in? I daresay we shall be making some coffee…'

He cut her short in the nicest possible way. 'That would have been delightful, but I've an engagement in an hour.'

Tabitha longed to ask where and with whom; instead she said: 'Then we must thank you now for taking us—we enjoyed it, didn't we, Meg?'

'That I did, Mr van Beek, and thank you. Now I'll go and see to Podger.'

Meg shut the door behind her leaving Tabitha, feeling awkward, outside on the step. She put out a hand and said: 'Well, goodbye and thank you again, Marius.'

He took the hand and didn't let it go. She could feel its cool firmness engulfing her own, sending a tingling shock up her arm. He said slowly: 'You never ask questions, Tabby. Perhaps you are afraid of the answers.'

She gave him a steady look. 'Yes, I daresay—anyway it's not my business, is it—what you do, I mean.'

His hand tightened a little. 'I'm not secretive, Tabby, though I believe you think I am. When I marry I shall share every moment of my life with my wife, whether we're together or not.'

Tabitha looked at him thoughtfully, wondering what Lilith would have to say to that, for presumably he would expect his wife to feel the same way. 'Yes, I imagine you would,' she said soberly. 'Married people shouldn't have secrets.'

He gave her back her hand. 'I'm glad we agree about that.' He smiled briefly. 'I'll see you on Monday.'

He got into the Bentley and drove away and she went indoors and upstairs to take off the pink hat. It was a considerable

time later that she remembered that he had said nothing at all
about their journey, now only seven days away.

As it turned out, the week wasn't very busy, for the beds as
they emptied were kept that way; the hard core of patients who
were left and the emergencies would go to the surgical annexe.
But Tabitha was kept busy with the domestic side of the ward,
for beds had to be taken down and stored away and everything
that could be moved out of the way of the workmen, had to
be moved. It was tiring work and a little boring too, although
Mr Raynard and Mr Bow kept her busy between them, for Mr
Raynard was now promoted to gutter crutches and Mr Bow
had a walking iron fixed and although he had crutches too, he
had a great objection to using them. She wondered from time
to time just how they would manage in the boat. They apparently had no such qualms, nor had Marius.

It wasn't until the week was half over that he sought her
out. She was in the linen room again, attacking the piles of
pillows which had to be stacked on the shelves. It was a warm
day and the pillows were filled with feathers—there was a good
deal of fluff in her hair and she had become hot and untidy
and her nose shone. She pushed her cap further back on her
head as Marius opened the door and gave him an unwelcoming
look, although her heart leapt to see him.

He sounded cheerful. 'Can you stop what you're doing for
a moment, or shall I talk while you fuss round with those pillows?'

'If I had known,' began Tabitha forcefully, 'just what an
upheaval having the ward painted was going to be, I should
have done everything in my power to have stopped it. I'm fed
up with these wretched things.' She sat herself down on a pile
of blankets, folded her hands in her aproned lap and said: 'I'm
ready.'

Marius settled himself amongst the pillows and began. 'I did
tell you we were travelling on Sunday?' and she replied patiently: 'Oh, yes—I know the day. I don't know at what time,
or how, or how much luggage I may bring or whether I should
provide my own sandwiches...'

'Oh, lord, Tabby, forgive me. I quite intended to tell you—

when was it? last week some time—and it went right out of my mind.'

He had gone to Chidlake, that was why it had gone out of his mind. She gave him a fleeting look and said nicely: 'It's quite all right—there's still a couple of days if there's anything I don't know about.'

He didn't speak, but sat looking at her for such a long time that she ventured: 'Is anything the matter?'

He shook his head. 'On the contrary.' He smiled slowly, his eyes twinkling, making her heart jump pleasantly; a delightful sensation, but it would never do to encourage it. She asked with a composure she didn't feel: 'What time?'

'Ah, yes—will ten o'clock suit you? You'll be travelling with Knotty and me—Muriel Raynard will drive their car. Any luggage within reason. How much have you got?'

'One case and a shoulder bag for odds and ends.'

He looked surprised. 'There's room for more than that if you'd like to take another case.' She shook her head and he went on: 'We'll eat on the way and cross by Hovercraft to Calais—it's the best way with our two invalids. We should be in Veere by early evening, allowing for stops on the way as and when necessary.' He smiled again. 'You will of course be my guest.'

Tabitha said thank you rather stiffly and then became rigid as he continued: 'I think it is only fair to pay you a fee for the period you will be with us; after all, your time won't be your own for a good deal of that period and you may have already planned a holiday which you have had to give up on our account.'

Tabitha gave him a haughty look. 'I shan't come,' she said instantly, her bosom swelling with indignation. 'I just shan't come if you pay me!' She spoke with such vehemence that Marius's rather sleepy eyes opened wide and then narrowed again under lifted brows.

'Why ever not?' His voice was silky.

Tabitha wondered how she could ever explain. How could she tell him that she was doing it because she loved him very much and it was a chance of being with him, even if only one of a party. And how could she explain the humiliation of being paid like the mother's help her stepmother had supposed her to be? Perhaps that was how he thought of her. She sat looking at her hands tidily folded in her lap still, and said nothing.

Marius repeated: 'Well?' his voice mildly impatient.

She looked up briefly and shrugged her shoulders. She couldn't tell him and she wasn't going to embark on a lot of lies. She repeated: 'I shan't go,' and as an afterthought, 'There's a good agency in the city—there's sure to be someone…'

'Oh, Tabby,' his voice was kind and quiet too. 'Something's hurt you and I'm not sure—' he stopped and frowned, his grey eyes suddenly alert. 'Someone has put an idea into your head. No, don't deny it, it's written all over your face. Another *idée fixe.*' He leaned forward and put a large, wellshaped hand over hers. 'Tabby, we're friends, aren't we? Do you suppose I would trade on our friendship in order to get something for nothing?' He cupped his other hand around hers, so that they were both held fast in a firm grip. 'You don't suppose I'm doing Raynard's work for nothing, do you?'

'Well, yes—actually I do,' said Tabitha, and he gave a great shout of laughter.

'Tabby, you're as bad as my young nieces!'

Tabitha looked at him with round eyes. 'Are you an uncle?' she asked, much struck.

'Yes, of course—how can I avoid it with a brother and sister, both married?'

'How many? Nephews and nieces, I mean.'

'Seven, though the youngest is too small to appreciate me yet.'

'Why am I as bad as your nieces?'

'Because you speak your mind with the directness of a child on occasion, and at other times, when it suits you, you are so obscure I can't even pretend to understand you.'

Tabitha digested this in silence; perhaps it was a good thing, he was far too quick at guessing her thoughts as it was. She kept quiet, conscious of his hands on hers.

'Having disposed of that red herring,' he said blandly, 'let

us settle this vexed question of fees. I won't say another word
about them, Tabby, as long as you come—you may make any
conditions you like, for you must see that we can't do without
you.'

And I wish that were true, thought Tabitha. She asked
bleakly: 'Why?'

His voice was still bland, but now it was persuasive too.
'My dear Tabby, surely you can see that for yourself. You
manage them both perfectly—they're at the stage when they
need constant restraint for fear they undo all our hard work;
Knotty is convinced that crutches are an affront to his dignity
and Bill Raynard has only to get his hands on a gouge and
chisel to go hobbling up to theatre and get started on the next
case. I know they'll be under our eyes in Veere, but I fancy
we shall still have our work cut out.' He squeezed her hands
and it was as though he squeezed her heart. 'Please, Tabby,'
his voice wasn't bland any more, just friendly.

'Well—of course I want to come, it was only…'

He didn't let her finish. 'Good girl! I think that, despite our
two patients, we shall have a very good holiday. The weather
promises fine; we can sail every day if we wish and there's
plenty of room for us all in the house. Hans is a splendid cook,
he'll enjoy himself.'

'Hans?'

He let go of her hands and got to his feet. 'Hans is to me
what Meg is to you—he's been my friend since I was a very
small boy; he taught me to sail and drive a car. He taught me
to skate too, and a great many other things besides, and when
my parents died and I went to live in the house in Veere he
was there, and he's been there ever since. You'll like him.'

'I can't speak Dutch.'

'Hans speaks a peculiar English which you will have no
difficulty in understanding. I must go, I've several things to
do. I'll be on the ward in the morning—our last operating day,
is it not?'

He smiled at her briefly and had gone so quickly that her
own goodbye was still on her lips as the door shut behind him.

Tabitha was awake early on Sunday morning. She got up,

made tea for Meg and herself and went into the sliver of garden
behind the flat. The dawn mist had rolled away, leaving a blue
sky which looked as though it had been freshly painted. The
sun was already warm, even for a July morning, the gay little
border of flowers Tabitha had so assiduously cultivated appeared to be embroidered along the edges of the grass plot upon
which she stood, although Podger knew better; for he wandered
amongst them sniffing delicately. But when she went back indoors he went with her and sat on the end of her bed while
she dressed and then accompanied her to the kitchen to share
the breakfast Meg had got ready.

Tabitha had decided on a French navy dress, banded with
white, in which to travel, it was cool and uncrushable and
plainly cut; she matched it with flat-heeled sandals and a bright
scarf of coral patterned with blue and white, just in case her
hair became unmanageable, and when Marius arrived she was
glad that she had taken pains with her appearance, for he said
at once: 'You look stunning, Tabby, and exactly right.' It was
only a pity that he himself wasn't stunned but went on to suggest that he might get Mr Bow out of the car and bring him in
to have a cup of Meg's coffee.

Old Knotty, he explained, was very anxious to meet Meg
and see his friend Podger again. So Mr Bow was helped into
the sitting room and sat in a Windsor chair by the window
because it was high enough for him to get up again without
too much heaving and pulling, and Meg came in with the coffee while Tabitha fetched Podger and they all sat for half an
hour talking pleasantly, just as if they weren't going anywhere
at all. Tabitha felt quite relieved when Marius suggested they
should go.

'Well, I suppose we had better make a start,' he said. 'We're
meeting the others at Funtingdon for lunch.'

'Where's that?' asked Tabitha.

'A mile or so this side of Chichester. We have to turn off
the main road to reach it.' He looked at his watch. 'I suggested
half past twelve—we've plenty of time.'

'How far is it?' Tabitha liked to know things and it was
already half past ten.

'A hundred miles or so—we can put on a bit of speed after lunch. I've booked on the five o'clock Hovercraft from Dover. It's roughly another hundred miles once we're on the other side, allowing for stops and the ferry at Breskens. We should be home in good time to enjoy supper, but there's no hurry; if Knotty gets tired or the Raynards feel it's too much of a trip, we can rack up for the night wherever we happen to be.'

It was evident that he had the whole journey planned; Tabitha, being handed into the front seat of the Bentley, decided not to bother about it any more; there was no need. She looked in her handbag to make sure that she had her passport and then leaned through the window to give Meg a parting kiss while Mr Bow took a dignified farewell of Podger, who showed a tendency to join the party. Marius finally laid him in Meg's arms, where he lay with his eyes shut, until they drove away.

They arrived at Funtingdon before the others, parked the car and set about the slow business of getting Knotty inside to the table Marius had reserved, but they had barely sat down when the Raynards' big Rover drew up beside the Bentley and Marius went out to help Bill Raynard. When they were all sitting round the table Marius suggested drinks while they ordered food. They ate lobster Thermidor and fresh fruit salad with lashings of cream and drank a light white wine and that sparingly because of the drivers, and presently, after coffee, Tabitha and Muriel Raynard went away to do their hair and faces again. Sitting before the mirror in the comfortable powder room, Tabitha felt a small glow of content. It had been fun coming up from the flat; Marius had been an excellent companion and so had Mr Bow, who from the comfort of the back seat had had quite a lot to say for himself. Besides which, when the Raynards had arrived, they had seemed really glad to see her. She heaved a sigh and powdered her nose with care.

'Happy?' asked Mrs Raynard. 'I'm looking forward to this holiday, aren't you? Even with a couple of stiff legs in the party it should be great fun.' She turned to smile at Tabitha. 'And do call me Muriel, and I know Bill wants you to call him Bill.'

'Oh, I couldn't possibly—I mean, he's a senior surgeon...'

'He calls you Tabby,' observed Muriel reasonably.

'Yes, I know. But so does everyone—even the patients behind my back.'

Muriel gave her a shrewd look. 'What about Marius—you don't call him Mr van Beek, do you? Though I suppose you do on the ward, or do you say sir?'

Tabitha smiled. 'Well, yes—actually, I do.'

'Then you can do the same with Bill, can't you? We're out of hospital now. I suppose the men will talk bones some of the time, but we can always go away and leave them to it. I wonder if there are any good dress shops in Veere?'

They walked back, still talking, to the table and found that Marius had got his companions into the cars again and was leaning over the Bentley's bonnet, studying a map. 'If we've kept you waiting we're sorry,' said Tabitha quickly for both of them, and hopped into the car as he opened the door.

'Don't you know by now that I'm a patient man?' he wanted to know as he got in beside her and started the engine.

They arrived in Dover with time to spare even though they had stopped for tea in Hawkhurst, and Tabitha had been impressed at the way in which Marius, without once lifting his voice or appearing in the least impatient, had contrived to get his party attended to in the shortest possible space of time; he had merely smiled charmingly, inviting co-operation from whoever it was attending to his wants. He was, she reflected, rather like that on the ward; she herself had run willingly at his bidding without being aware of it. It was the same on the Hovercraft; sitting beside him as they drove out of Calais, she decided it was either a gift or a lifelong habit of expecting those around him to do as he wished. A little of both, perhaps.

The late afternoon was very warm. Mr Bow was snoring gently behind them and Tabitha, looking through the back window of the Bentley, could see the Rover on their tail and Mr Raynard asleep beside his wife. She said, thinking aloud: 'I daresay they'll both be all the better for a quiet day tomorrow.'

'Now you know why we were so insistent that you should come,' said Marius blandly. 'I agree with you wholeheartedly and I shall leave it to you to see that they do.'

'Has your house a garden? They could lie in chairs...'

'There's a small garden. It's walled—we'd have them climbing over it the moment we left them alone! They came to sail, remember, and sail they will, even if they're half dead.' He turned a laughing face to hers. 'The water is just across the street from the house. If you could persuade them to sit near the boat clubhouse—it's only a stone's throw away from the house—we could get on with making ready to sail and you'd be near enough to see what they were up to.'

It sounded wonderful. Tabitha said so, her pretty voice high with excitement. 'How far can we sail?' she wanted to know.

'All over the Veerse Meer. We'll take food with us and spend the whole day—there are any number of places where we can tie up.' He gave her a smiling look, his grey eyes twinkling down at her so that her happiness threatened to choke her. 'Glad you came?' he asked.

She nodded and smiled at him and then looked away quickly for fear she should let him see just how happy she was, but he didn't look at her again, for there was, for the moment, no speed limit and he gave his attention to getting as much out of the big car as he could, only slowing down from time to time when the Rover fell too far behind.

They passed through Dunkirk and on to Ostend where the road became a vilely surfaced one of cobblestones so that Marius slowed down to avoid shaking Mr Bow too much, but once they were through the town and had left the trams and shops and hotels and the little gay villas behind, he put his foot down once more as they drove on to Knokke and Breskens, pausing only briefly at the Customs at Sluis.

'Now we're in Holland,' said Marius as they left the Customs post behind them and drove on up the straight road to the bustling little town, where he dropped to a crawl to enable Muriel to keep just behind him, for although the town was small it was full of people and cars and stalls and shops doing a roaring trade.

'But it's Sunday,' said Tabitha, astonished, 'and almost seven o'clock.'

'It's also the first town over the border,' Marius explained.

'The Belgians come over to shop because it's cheaper, and the shops open on Sunday and stay open until late to catch as many customers as possible. So everyone is pleased.'

'I see the windmill's still standing,' said Mr Bow from the back seat.

Marius glanced briefly over his shoulder and smiled. 'Yes—but it's been turned into a restaurant. Do you find the town altered much, Knotty?'

'A great deal, but then it's many years since I was last here. It will be interesting to see how rusty my Dutch has become.'

'You shall try it out on Hans.'

Tabitha twisted round in her seat the better to address Mr Bow. 'Is it hard to learn—Dutch? I've always imagined it was, because people talk about double Dutch.'

They both laughed and Mr Bow said in his pendantic way: 'Yes, it is hard, my dear young lady; not only is it spoken in the back of the throat, but the verbs are kept until the end of a sentence, which makes for incredible misunderstandings when first learning the language.'

'All the same,' she said robustly, 'I'd like to have a try, though I suppose everyone speaks English.'

'No, they don't,' Marius remarked. 'Veere isn't a tourist centre for foreigners—the Dutch go there for the sailing, but it's too quiet for more than a fleeting visitor's tour. We get boats from England, of course, as well as France and Belgium, and although a number of people speak English or at least make themselves understood, there are any number who don't—you should be able to put in quite a lot of practice.'

'By all means,' chimed in Mr Bow. 'You never know how useful the knowledge might be to you in future years.'

Tabitha smiled and said nothing, for it wasn't much use saying that she envisaged a future in which the speaking of the Dutch language, however rudimentary, would be superfluous. It was fortunate that they were approaching Breskens and in watching the long queues of cars and road freighters waiting for the ferry, the conversation was channeled into another subject. They had to wait a little while, so Tabitha got out of the car and went to talk to Muriel behind them until at last they

saw the funnel of the ferry sliding along behind the dyke and
they were able to go aboard, where the two less active members
of the party were left below while Marius escorted Muriel and
Tabitha up to the deck. The river was wide and the water calm.
Flushing, still in the distance, looked pleasant in the evening
sun. Tabitha leaned over the rail and watched the blue-grey
water and listened to Marius telling Muriel the town's history,
but it was his deep quiet voice to which she listened so that
she didn't hear a word of what he was saying.

They didn't go into Flushing but drove past the naval base
and the shipyards and turned away towards Middelburg, a mile
or two away and almost at the end of their journey. They didn't
go through that city either, rather to Tabitha's regret, for it
looked intriguingly old-fashioned. She was forced to be content
with Marius's assurance that they would spend the day there
before their return. They were in the country again by now, on
a good road running between flat green fields and clusters of
trees, and ahead, on the near horizon, she could see a huge
church dome and beyond it a slender steeple, fairylike in its
delicate tracery even at that distance. 'That is Veere,' said Marius. His voice sounded happy.

They seemed to come upon the little town quite suddenly,
first over a little bridge spanning a little water, very quiet and
peaceful, and then passing the great church with its massive
dome. 'It's got an interesting history,' explained Marius. 'It's
not used any more, though it's kept in repair.'

He had slowed the car so that Tabitha could look about her.
The road had become quite narrow and countrylike, with small
cottages on either side, and she was quite unprepared for the
sudden right turn into a broad cobbled street running alongside
a narrow stretch of water crammed with boats of all kinds, and
lined on its other tree-shaded side by lovely old houses. There
was another road, running off at right angles, away from the
water, but they passed that and she barely had time to take a
quick glimpse up it before Marius brought the car to a stop.
'Here we are,' he said.

He had stopped about two-thirds of the way down the quayside and as he got out he said over his shoulder to Mr Bow:

'Remember, Knotty?' and Mr Bow said in a pleased voice: 'Indeed, dear boy, I remember. While you are helping our dear Tabby out of the car I shall have a few minutes' contemplation.' He fixed his former pupil with a bright blue eye, then closed them both, as though to lend force to his statement. Tabitha, watching Marius walk round the bonnet to open the door for her, wondered why he was smiling, but she forgot about it immediately as she got out and the beauty of her surroundings burst upon her. For the moment, however, she had no eyes for anything else but Marius's house, and with him silent beside her, she stood studying it.

It was a tall house, taller than its neighbours, and she noticed that each of the old houses was different from its neighbours, too, even though there was no space between them. The house she was looking at had two large windows downstairs and an important street door with a square fanlight, very much ornamented, above it, the whole framed with white painted woodwork. Above these were three more windows, a little smaller, and above those again, three more, even smaller, crowned by a tiled, pointed roof which also contained a miniature window, flanked by shutters. The house shone with its fresh paintwork and plaster front and its windows twinkled in the evening light. She said on a breath: 'It's lovely, Marius!' and longed to go inside, and as if in answer to her wish, the door swung open and Hans—for it could be no one else—stood on its step.

She said: 'That's Hans, isn't it?' and turned to look at Marius, to find him staring down at her, his look so searching that she asked sharply: 'What is it?'

But he didn't answer, only laughed softly and turned away to speak to Muriel getting out of their car, so that the lovely moment was gone in a little whirl of greetings from Hans, comments on the journey from everyone and the unloading of the invalids and the luggage. The invalids were a little stiff and Mr Bow admitted to some pain, and Tabitha suspected that Mr Raynard wasn't sorry the trip was over either. Once indoors, she decided, she would make them comfortable in the living room, give them each some Panadol and allow them to rest for a few minutes before the supper Marius had mentioned. She gathered up some of the smaller luggage and followed the others into the house, where Hans, hovering in the hall, removed it from her grasp and ushered her through a door on the left. It opened into a room which extended from the front to the back of the house, which hadn't looked all that big from the outside, but the room was surprisingly large and it was obvious that the house extended back to a great depth.

As in the hall, the walls were oak-panelled to head height, above which they were ornamented with some quite beautiful plasterwork, as was the ceiling. The floor was close-carpeted in a deeply piled carpet of a dim terra-cotta shade and the furniture was, as far as she could judge in one brief glimpse, a happy mixture of the very comfortable and the antique. A room to be explored at her leisure, but now there was no time, for Marius was standing before her, saying in his calm way: 'Welcome to my home, Tabitha.'

'Thank you,' said Tabitha gravely. 'It's beautiful—how can you bear to leave it?' She was so earnest about it that he laughed.

'You shall have a good look round at your leisure. Now I'm going to leave you to deal with our invalids while Hans takes the luggage up to our rooms. We can settle them in later, after supper—their rooms are upstairs, but that will be splendid exercise for them both just as long as you and I are there to make sure they don't lean too heavily on their plasters.'

He was interrupted by the entry of a dog, a black Keeshond who greeted his master with a great show of affection before submitting to being introduced to the company as Smith, and presently when Marius went away, the dog went with him, leaving Tabitha to arrange the two invalids in comfortable chairs with suitable support for their injured legs, and as she had had the forethought to provide them with a pile of charts and maps, and Hans had arrived at exactly the right moment with a tray of drinks, there was no fault to find with their comfort; they settled down happily to con the charts just as Marius returned, accompanied by a plump fair-haired girl whom he introduced as Anneke. 'She doesn't speak a word of English,' he explained, 'but if you two girls like to go upstairs with her, she will show you your rooms and so forth. Supper will be about ten minutes if you're agreeable.'

They followed Anneke into the hall which had a door at its end and an arched opening beside it, which, Tabitha discovered, led directly to a staircase. It had shallow oak treads and curved into the wall and had rails on either side of it, most beautifully carved. The staircase led on to a landing which meandered off in all directions into short cul-de-sacs, each of which ended in a door. Anneke chose the first of these, flung open its door, and stood aside for them to go in. The room was large with two old-fashioned sash windows overlooking the garden—the walled garden, Tabitha decided after a quick peep. It was furnished with solid mahogany of the late Empire period, polished to an exquisite patina, the curtains were of blue and green chintz, as was the bedspread. The walls were covered in the palest pink which was repeated exactly in the shades of the bedside lamps and the wall lamp convenient to the comfortable chairs drawn up to the table set between the windows. It was a charming room, warm from the sun and fragrant with the bowl of roses on the dressing table.

'Ours,' said Muriel with satisfaction. 'Here's our luggage.' She looked at Anneke, who smiled and nodded and crossed the room to open what appeared to be a cupboard door, revealing a shower room with the satisfied air of a magician carrying out a successful trick. Muriel sat down in one of the chairs. 'I'm going to sit and admire my surroundings for five minutes,' she announced. 'I'll find you presently, Tabby.'

Outside on the landing again Tabitha resisted a desire to linger over the paintings on the walls and asked experimentally: 'Mr Bow's room?'

She was understood—another door was opened on to a smaller room, but just as delightfully furnished. It had a view of the harbour and Tabitha would have liked to spend a few minutes at the window, but instead she obeyed Anneke's beckoning hand and peered into another shower room, tiny but beautifully equipped. Marius certainly had a well appointed house.

She was a little disappointed when Anneke started up a

smaller staircase in one corner of the landing—there were still three doors, all shut; she dearly wanted to see what was behind them. The next landing was the same size as the one below and had the same little passages. Her bedroom was presumably down one of them. It was—facing the harbour just as Mr Bow's did, but a far larger room, all pink and cream and slender Hepplewhite furniture. It too had its bowl of roses and a little pile of books and magazines on the bedside table, and for her comfort, a small velvet-covered armchair by the window so that she could sit at ease, watching the ever-changing scene below. This time she knew what to expect when Anneke opened one of the doors in its walls, although this time it wasn't a shower room but a miniature bathroom, pink-tiled and its floor covered with a thick pile carpet. She followed Anneke out on to the landing again and called down the stairs. 'Muriel, I'm up here when you're ready,' and went back again to examine her room more thoroughly before tidying herself. She was just ready when Mrs Raynard arrived to look round with a good deal of interest and approval. 'It's a lovely house,' she commented, 'quite perfect and with every conceivable modern comfort one could wish for. I'm dying to see all over it, aren't you, Tabitha?'

Marius came to meet them when they went downstairs. He gave them each a glass and asked: 'Everything all right, I hope? Ask for anything you want.'

'It's perfect,' said Tabitha. 'I can't think of the right words.'

He nodded in a satisfied way and she went and sat by Mr Bow until it was time for them to go in to supper, which they ate in an atmosphere of great conviviality, with Anneke looking after them and Hans appearing from time to time to make sure they were eating sufficient of his delicious cutlets and accompanying dishes of vegetables, which he followed with fresh peaches poached in brandy and a great deal of whipped cream. They drank their coffee round the dining table so that Mr Bow and Mr Raynard did not have to make the journey back to the sitting room, and under cover of the general conversation Tabitha found the opportunity to look about her. The dining room was at the end of the hall, by the staircase; a small room furnished with an oval table and straight-backed chairs which she thought might be William and Mary. There was an oval-fronted sideboard along one wall and a glass-fronted corner cupboard which was full of china and glass. The window looked out on to the garden at the back of the house and was draped with mulberry damask curtains; a carpet of the same colour covered the floor. Above the table hung a crystal chandelier, small replicas of which hung around the walls. It seemed to her to be a cosy room despite its richness. It would be pleasant to dine there on a dark winter's day—with Marius, of course, after he had got home from a hard day's work. She smiled at the thought and jumped visibly when he said: 'Tabby's a long way away,' and when she looked round her they were all smiling. She said, stammering a little: 'I'm so sorry—it's such a pleasant room—I was thinking about it…'

'I'm flattered that it has such an effect upon you.' Marius's voice was casual and friendly. 'I know how you feel—each time I leave home I'm positively homesick.'

It was nice that he understood; she gave him a wide smile and joined with enthusiasm in the spirited discussion as to what they should do the next day, and could not but admire the tact with which Marius put forward the suggestion that his two friends might like to take things easy. Mindful of what he had said, Tabitha added her gentle persuasion to his, adding the artful rider that someone would have to make a list of provisions for the trips they intended making. This apparently satisfied the two invalids, who shortly afterwards consented to go to bed—an undertaking which took some time and caused a good deal of merriment before they were safely in their respective rooms. It was while Tabitha was helping Mr Bow into bed and putting the cradle thoughtfully provided in position under the bedclothes that the old man said:

'I fancy this holiday will do us all a good deal of good, my dear Tabitha. I for one feel a different man already, for it is surprising how everything takes on a better colour when there is once more a future to look forward to.'

Tabitha was putting a bedsock over his toes, because he got cold feet and he was, after all, an old man, and she didn't look up. 'I'm sure you're right,' she agreed cheerfully, her bright voice concealing the cheerless thoughts she harboured concerning her own future.

But it was impossible to be low-spirited when she wakened the following morning to find Anneke standing by her bed with morning tea. There was a note on the tray—she recognized Marius's hieroglyphic writing and opened it to decipher it with the ease of one used to reading the almost unintelligible scrawl of the medical profession. 'It's early,' he had written, 'but come down as soon as you are dressed. I want to talk to you.'

Tabitha's heart sang; not only was it a glorious morning but Marius wanted to talk to her. As she dressed she sensibly told herself that it was probably about Mr Bow and Mr Raynard, which sober thought did nothing to steady her pulse. Ten minutes later, in navy slacks and a white cotton sweater, her hair tied back and hanging to her waist, she went downstairs.

There was no sign of Marius in the hall, nor was he in the vast sitting room. She went back along the hall and into the dining room. That was empty too, but there were several doors in it. She tried two and found cupboards, but the third revealed a small room, its walls lined with books, its French window opening on to the garden. There was a large desk bearing a powerful reading lamp and a great many papers on it. Marius was sitting behind it, writing. He looked up as she went in with the air of a man who hadn't expected to be disturbed, and she said hastily:

'I couldn't find you—I didn't mean to trespass, only you said come down as soon as I could be dressed.'

He got up and came round the desk to stand before her, studying her with a laughing leisurely gaze. 'You may go where you like in my house, Tabitha—if I had known that you would be so quick I would have been waiting for you. What did you do? Wave a wand?'

She laughed. 'No—but I didn't bother with my hair.'

He put a hand behind her and gave its brown silkiness a gentle tug.

'Well, don't bother while you're here—it looks nice.' He grinned suddenly: 'Good morning, Tabitha,' and when she looked up, kissed her and said immediately: 'Come and see the boat,' and led her through the house and out into the bright morning where they were joined by Smith. There weren't many people about yet; a paper boy with his load of news, the postman, a waiter stacking chairs outside a café—there was more movement on the boats though, a leisurely coming and going which fitted in very well with the summer morning's gentle warmth.

'You wanted to talk to me,' reminded Tabitha as they went along, and when he slipped an arm through hers and said: 'Presently, dear girl,' she was content to let it rest there because she wanted to look about her as they crossed the street to the water's edge. Just below them lay the boats—yachts, motor cruisers, dinghies, catamarans, yawls, rowing boats and a great number of inflatables. To their right lay a low brick building which she guessed to be the yacht club. They strolled towards it and as they went she asked: 'Which one is yours?'

He walked on for a few paces and stopped by a roomy yacht moored to the bank. 'This one,' he said. It was very smart as to paintwork and carried plenty of sail and there was a diesel engine as well. It looked large enough to take all of them with room to spare. She asked:

'How many berths?'

'Six—there's plenty of space aboard and she's a dream to handle. Come aboard.' He stepped on to the deck and stretched out a hand to help her down beside him.

Tabitha was full of questions. 'Is she Dutch?'

'Yes—van Essen designed her. Come below.'

She looked at everything, still asking questions and listening carefully to his answers. 'It's rather different from a dinghy,' she observed finally as they went back on deck. 'I hope I shall be useful crewing.'

'You will,' he said cheerfully. 'She's the easiest thing in the world to handle.' He caught her by the hand and helped her back on to the duckboards. 'Come to the end of the harbour and get a view of the lake.'

She admired the houses as they went the few hundred yards. 'And what's this tower?' she wanted to know.

'The oldest inn in Holland,' he explained, 'although it's now an hotel and restaurant. William of Orange held his wedding feast here—you can see a copy of the bill if you've a mind. We'll go there for dinner one evening—it's quaint inside and the food's good.'

He led her under the archway beside the hotel and leant against the brick wall overlooking the water. The lake spread before them, disappearing into the early morning haze of a warmth to come. Tabitha could see the further shore quite clearly as well as a great many small islands.

Marius waved an arm in their general direction. 'We can go out into the Oosterschelde from here, but if we only want to potter there are a hundred places along the shore where we can tie up and swim and lie in the sun. We'll take Hans with us, I think, he'll be useful getting our two invalids ashore.'

His words reminded her. 'You wanted to talk to me,' she said again. 'Was it about them?'

He smiled down at her and flung an arm around her shoulders. 'What a girl you are!' he commented, although he didn't say what kind of a girl. 'Yes, it was. Could you persuade Knotty to have breakfast in bed, do you think? He's getting on, and although he's as strong as a horse for his age, he's going to be too active. And Billi?'

Tabitha thought. 'Well, I think I can persuade them both. That'll give me time to get their chairs ready before they come down; if they see them there they're less likely to want to do something else.'

'Perceptive girl!' His voice sounded amused. 'That's my idea too.' He looked at his watch. 'It's almost time for breakfast and I told Anneke not to take up their morning tea until eight, which gives you plenty of time to work on them.'

Which she did, to such good effect that it was midmorning by the time the two well-rested gentlemen, amenable as to any suggestion made as to their comfort, were helped across the street to where their chairs had been arranged within hailing distance of the yacht. On board, Tabitha and Muriel, under Marius's casual direction, made ready for their first trip, a de-lightful task which took the rest of the morning with an interval

for iced lemonade which an obliging waiter from the Struys-
kelder, just across the street, brought them. He stood a little
while talking to Marius, and Mr Bow tried out some of his
Dutch on him and was elated to find that it wasn't so rusty
after all.

That afternoon they went for a short sail, just to get their
hand in, as Marius put it, and Tabitha was surprised and
amused to see of what little consequence a leg in plaster could
be when its wearer was enjoying himself. They took their tea
with them and she and Muriel boiled the kettle in the galley
and took the tea tray up on deck. They didn't turn back until
the sun was beginning to drop in the still blue sky, and as they
neared the harbour Tabitha thought there had never been anything as beautiful as the little town, its gabled roofs and fairy-
tale spire silhouetted against the early evening light. As they
passed the walls of the Campveerse Toren, she looked up and
saw that the restaurant was candlelit ready for its diners. Marius
caught her glance and said mildly:

'Romantic, isn't it? Couples come from all over Holland to
be married here and have their reception at the hotel for that
very reason.'

A remark which Tabitha found difficult to answer except
with a polite: 'Oh, really?'

The next three days passed with the speed of complete happiness. They sailed and talked, picnicked and swam and just
lay in the sun, and in the evenings they ate Hans's beautifully
cooked dinners and talked again. It was amazing what a lot
they all had to say to each other, and although Tabitha wasn't
much alone with Marius she knew that their friendship had
deepened even in those few days. She comforted herself with
the thought that he liked her as a friend and tried to be thankful
as Meg had told her she should.

# CHAPTER SIX

THE MORNING had begun for Tabitha with no inkling of the shattering blow she was to be dealt later in the day. True, it was raining, but that hadn't mattered in the least, for once the invalids were attended to and helped downstairs, they were left to plan the following day's outing, and Marius was free to fulfil his promise to show Muriel and Tabitha over his home. They had explored it thoroughly and lightheartedly, peeping into his own rather austere room and then into the room below Tabitha's—a very splendid room indeed with a walnut four-poster bed hung with muted pinks and blues and a carpet as deep and soft as moss under their feet. It had a vast fitted wardrobe along one wall and several very comfortable chairs. The dressing table, between the windows, was inlaid with Dutch marquetry and held a silver-framed winged mirror; Tabitha could imagine how delightful it would be to sit before it, brushing her hair with a silver-backed brush to match the mirror…There was a very modern bathroom too, hidden behind another door so that its streamlined perfection did nothing to detract from the old-world charm of the bedroom. Across the landing was the one-time nursery, small and cosy and as Marius laughingly explained, quite inadequate. 'This was used by my youngest sister, she was born several years after us—we had your room, Muriel.'

'Which you plan to use, Marius?' Muriel had asked the question which Tabitha had longed to put herself; she waited for his answer, wondering if he had minded.

'That question's a little previous, isn't it?' He was laughing and not in the least annoyed. 'But yes, since I should hope for a large family I suppose the room you are in now would be converted into a nursery again. Come up and see the attic,' he went on easily, 'we used it as a playroom and later on as a bolthole if we wanted to get away from each other.'

He took them on a leisurely tour of the rest of the house and then rejoined the others, still bent over their maps and charts, and by the time they had had their coffee the weather was clearing a little and the two girls decided to make a more detailed inspection of the few shops in the little town. It was on their return, laughing and very pleased with themselves and their purchases from the boutique on the quay, that they walked into the sitting room and found the men sitting where they had left them, only now Lilith, her golden beauty highlighted by a simple white shift dress, was sitting on the arm of Marius's chair.

Tabitha, who never felt sick, felt sick now. She stood in the doorway staring at her stepsister and listening to the sound of her pathetic little castles in the air tumbling about her ears. She said from a mouth gone dry: 'Hullo, Lilith—what a surprise.'

'Hullo,' said Lilith airily, and got up as Marius rose to introduce her to Mrs Raynard. 'It was such heavenly weather and I said to Mummy, do let's go and see Marius—I knew he'd love it, because he must be finding it a bit dull—I mean you, Mrs Raynard, have your husband and Mr Bow has Tabby to look after him, but there's no one to keep Marius company.'

She gave him an angel's smile and he smiled back with lazy good nature and went to pour the drinks. Tabitha, covertly studying his face as he did so, could detect no annoyance in it; indeed, Lilith seemed to be amusing him, just as she was amusing everyone else, excepting Tabitha, who sat quietly, feeling all her newfound confidence and happiness draining away, just as though Lilith were sucking her dry.

'May I stay to lunch?' Lilith smiled enchantingly at Marius and made play with her long eyelashes, causing Tabitha to seethe with hopeless rage; it hardly helped when Marius said laughingly: 'No, you may not. Your mother will be expecting you and it's hardly fair to leave her alone—besides, we're going out. But don't worry, you're only a stone's throw away. I daresay we shall see a great deal more of you.'

Lilith pouted and got to her feet. 'You old bear! At least walk me to the hotel.' Which he did with a show of willingness which turned Tabitha's rage into icy misery. They passed her with a smile; Marius's was absentminded, Lilith's openly triumphant.

The conversation at lunch, naturally enough, was largely of Lilith's visit, although Marius said nothing which could be construed into a romantic interest in her, at the same time agreeing readily enough that she was a beautiful girl with most engaging ways. Tabitha, a little pale, joined in the talk with a kind of desperate cheerfulness and even steeled herself to tell the company just how popular her stepsister was. 'She's clever too,' she went on, determined to turn the knife in the wound while she was about it. 'She has three A levels and she could easily have gone on to university.'

'Why didn't she?' Muriel's voice was dry.

'I—I think my stepmother wanted her at home,' said Tabitha a little wildly. 'She's such good company.' She looked up and found Marius's eyes upon her; he looked slightly mocking and whatever it was she had intended saying flew out of her head so that there was a little silence, covered by Muriel saying: 'It's unusual these days to find a girl who doesn't want a job of some sort.'

As if she had given him a cue, her husband said: 'Perhaps she wants to get married.'

Mrs Raynard gave him a wifely look. 'Darling, you must be joking—she's eighteen, and if I might venture to say so without being offensive, not the domesticated kind.'

Mr Bow, who had been sitting silent, not missing a word, now made a pronouncement of his own. 'It seems to me that this young woman is absorbing far too much of our interest. No one has mentioned our trip tomorrow; Bill and I have worked out a magnificent day for us all and nobody has even asked…' He sounded aggrieved, and Marius said at once:

'Forgive us, Knotty. Bring out your maps and tell us all about it.' Which the old gentleman did, with a good deal of interruption from Bill Raynard. Finally, when they had both had their say, Marius remarked cheerfully: 'It sounds great— let's get away early. I'll tell Hans to get the food packed— he'd better come with us, and Smith, of course. Now, who's for a run to Middelburg?'

The afternoon was spent pleasantly enough, driving slowly round the old city and then parking the car. And after assisting Mr Bow and Mr Raynard on to chairs outside De Nederlands Koffiehuis, going to get a closer view of the St Nicholas Abbey, the magnificent Town Hall and the museum attached to it, and Tabitha, during their sight-seeing tour, couldn't but notice that although he was his usual placid self and very attentive to their wishes, Marius was undoubtedly, behind the façade of his calm good looks, very busy with his own thoughts.

She half expected that Lilith and her stepmother, or at least Lilith, would pay them another visit that evening, but when she thought about it she was forced to concede that her stepmother was far too clever for that. She went to bed uneasily wondering what exactly Lilith planned to do, for it was inconceivable that she had come to a place as alien to her tastes as Veere unless she had some very good reason. Tabitha, unable to sleep, got out of bed and went and sat by the open window. The reason, of course, would be Marius, and the knowledge of this was hardly conducive to sleep; she fetched her dressing gown and a pillow from the bed and sat staring out at the quiet night sky, trying to guess what would happen.

Nothing happened—at least, not in the morning. They were on board and casting off soon after eight o'clock, calling good mornings to other boat owners doing the same thing, exchanging opinions on wind and weather in the cheerful early morning bustle echoed by the early risers going about their business around the little harbour. They glided past the hotel, the diesel chugging softly to itself, and Tabitha couldn't refrain from a quick peep at the windows, half expecting to see Lilith looking out of one of them.

'Not up yet,' observed Marius, seeing her glance. 'People who lie in bed don't know what they're missing.'

He smiled at her, his eyes half shut in their web of laughter lines. 'Let's have some sail—there's a good breeze and we can cut the engine.'

They were all kept busy according to their various capabilities, and Tabitha, doing as she was bid, forgot her worries in the splendour of the morning and the delight of being on the smooth blue water. It promised to be hot; by the time they had reached their objective—one of the islands which dotted the lake, it would be just right for a swim. She went below to help Muriel with the coffee, feeling almost happy. At least here, in the middle of the Veerse Meer, there was no chance of meeting Lilith.

The island was everything it should have been. The invalids were helped ashore by Marius and Hans while Tabitha and Muriel set out the picnic. They had almost finished when Marius asked: 'What about a swim first?' The owners of the plastered legs refused for obvious reasons, Hans said he would swim later, Muriel, without hesitation, said that she couldn't possibly until she had recovered from her crewing.

'Come on, Tabby,' Marius's voice was off-hand. 'It's safe enough.'

She cast him an indignant look, caught up her beach bag and disappeared behind the trees behind them. She put on the bikini; after all, she had to start wearing it some time and it was very hot. When she emerged Mr Bow looked her over. 'If I were younger,' he said, 'I should whistle; as it is I will content myself by saying that you look extremely eye-catching, my dear Tabitha.'

'I *shall* whistle,' declared Bill Raynard, and did while Muriel laughed and called out to her that she looked simply super, and Hans, not to be outdone, murmured in his turn: 'Most super, Miss Tabitha.'

But Marius said nothing. He was standing by the water's edge, waiting for her, and when she was close enough he said:

'Come on, Tabby,' and started to wade purposefully out to deep water. She followed him, smiling for the benefit of the rest of the party while she suppressed a childish desire to cry with disappointment. Everyone had noticed, and even if they had exaggerated a little, she knew that she really looked quite nice. Perhaps he just hadn't noticed, but she scotched this idea at once as being silly; he had a normal man's eye for such things and he was surely no monk.

She began to swim away from the shore without bothering to see where he was, and presently changed to a crawl, cleaving her way through the water as though it were so much glass to be splintered into fragments by her arms. When she was tired she rolled over on to her back and found him beside her, moving through the water without effort. 'Well, that's one way of getting rid of your temper,' he observed.

She tossed her hair out of her eyes. 'Temper?' she spluttered. 'Why should I be in a temper?' She turned over again and began to swim lazily towards the shore and he turned with her.

'I can think of several reasons, dear girl.' He grinned at her. 'I'll race you.'

He allowed her to win by an inch or so and then walked beside her up the beach. By then the sun was so warm that they were almost dry by the time they reached the little group waiting patiently round the spread cloth.

They swam again later in the afternoon, this time with Muriel and Hans and Smith barking at them from shallow water where he occasionally made a sortie to paddle alongside anyone who came near enough. They ate a vast tea after that, and then because the wind was right, set sail for Veere. They were edging their way in amongst the other boats when Tabitha saw Lilith and her stepmother watching them from the hotel wall. They waved gaily and Marius waved back, his gesture followed more slowly by the Raynards. Mr Bow had his eyes closed, although Tabitha could have sworn that they had been open a few seconds earlier. She herself was too busy preparing to make fast to do more than smile vaguely in their direction; she doubted if they noticed anyway.

In a kind of hopeless defiance, Tabitha put on the ivory silk dress she had worn to the wedding, that evening. She had become very brown during the last few days and the contrast between the dress and her tanned skin was very effective. She put on some small old-fashioned coral earrings she had had from her mother, and a coral bracelet. She had found time to wash her hair too and had piled it with all the skill she could muster into the coils and rolls she had first tried out at Lilith's party. She looked passable, she thought, studying herself in the big mirror in her bedroom before she went downstairs with the dull certainty deep inside her that Lilith and her stepmother would call during the evening.

They came after dinner, just as everyone had settled down to an uproarious game of Canasta, which had, perforce, to be abandoned. Tabitha, who had been feeling nervous all the evening, felt the familiar thrill of apprehension and dislike as her stepmother came into the room. Mrs Crawley was still a pretty woman and a charming one when she chose to be. Now she smiled and talked her way gracefully through the introductions before she sought out Tabitha.

'Well, Tabitha, I must say you don't look much like the hired help.' She gave her a thinly veiled look of contempt. 'My dear girl, you look more like a gypsy! Your skin's ruined—too much sea air, I suppose, and what on earth possessed you to do your hair in that ridiculous fashion? It looks as though this holiday, or whatever you choose to call it, has gone to your head. It's a good thing I shall be here for a week or so to advise you.'

Tabitha listened to this speech without comment while she digested the awful news that Lilith and her stepmother would be in Veere for the next week—a whole week out of the twelve days left of her holiday! When she didn't reply, Mrs Crawley said impatiently: 'Well, have you lost your tongue? Though God knows when you do talk you never have anything to say that's worth listening to.'

'In that case,' said Tabitha quickly, 'do come and talk to Mr Bow. He's a most interesting man and a lifelong friend of Marius's.'

She went away after that to the other end of the room, and sat down by Bill Raynard, who said in a grumbling voice:

'Oh, hullo—it's you come to plague the life out of me,' but he pulled her down on to the sofa, giving her hand a comforting squeeze as he did so, and contrived to keep her with him for the rest of the evening. They were deep in a discussion on gardens when Marius crossed the room, pulled up a chair and sat down beside them.

'There's a plan afoot,' he began pleasantly, 'that we should join forces with young van Steen—remember we met him the other day?—he's staying at the hotel too and has his yacht here and proposes to take Mrs Crawley and Lilith for a trip tomorrow. Lilith thinks it would be a splendid idea if we take the *Piet Hein* out too and meet up for a picnic. What do you think of it?'

What Tabitha thought she kept to herself; clearly it would best be left unsaid, but Bill Raynard replied with a heartiness which didn't ring quite true: 'My dear chap, do what you like—it sounds splendid, and after all you're the boss, none of us would dream of opposing your wishes.'

Marius gave him a measured look from suddenly bright eyes. 'Yes?' he looked at Tabitha. 'And what about you, Tabby?'

She had expurged her wicked thoughts; she even felt a little ashamed of them. 'It sounds wonderful.' Her enthusiasm sounded just like Mr Raynard's heartiness, but Marius must have felt satisfied, for he got up. 'Good, then we'll go ahead with our planning.'

Tabitha watched him sit down by Lilith again on the big velvet sofa at the other end of the room; he was too far away for her to hear what he was saying, but she saw Lilith put a hand on his arm and look up into his face. She looked away then and encountered Mr Raynard's eye glaring at her. He spoke grumpily.

'I'm tired—I shall go to bed, and I want my leg rubbed, it's aching. You can help me upstairs and give me some massage—I think I'll have a Panadol too.'

Tabitha got him to his feet with a relief which showed in her face. It was blissful to leave the hubbub of cheerful voices and allow her stiff little smile to relax. Mr Raynard hardly spoke except to grumble, but he had said he was tired and she took no heed of his silence. She was bending over his injured leg, gently kneading its muscles when he snarled:

'Why in the name of heaven I should come to bed early just to make things easy for you, I don't know.' Which remark sent her upright, staring at him. 'You what?' she repeated, and felt her cheeks paling.

'Well, you were hardly surging along on the crest of a wave, were you?' he demanded.

She gave him an agonized look and he went on rapidly: 'Oh, don't worry, everyone else was far too busy being the life and soul of the party—excepting old Knotty—Muriel too, I suspect, though you never can tell with women.' His voice was testy. 'What made you look like that anyway? What was that step-mother of yours saying to you? Or was it the sight of Lilith showing us all how to get your man?'

Tabitha's pale cheeks took fire as she bent over her massaging once more. She had no intention of answering him, but instead asked almost humbly, because she had a great respect for Mr Raynard even though he was so short-tempered: 'Do you think I should leave—go home?'

'Don't be a fool, girl—you're clever enough at hiding your feelings, don't worry on that score.'

Tabitha arranged his injured leg gently beside the sound one and adjusted the cradle over it. She said without much spirit: 'You see, she's so pretty, and—she makes h—people laugh. I feel like dough.'

'Bread is the staff of life,' said Mr Raynard ponderously. 'No man wants a diet of meringues. I know—I'm married.'

The conversation was getting a little out of hand. She said soberly: 'Muriel is a wonderful person, Mr Raynard. I'll fetch the Panadol for you.'

He let her go, merely beseeching her on her return to remember to call him Bill.

She didn't like the idea of going downstairs again, but she did, going into the room quietly, to be accosted almost at once by Mr Bow, who asked her with his usual old-fashioned courtesy if he might go to bed as it had been a long, although delightful day. Getting him to bed took even longer than Bill Raynard, for he was old and slow and forgetful—besides, he liked to talk, but it wasn't until she at last had him between the sheets that he observed in his mild, elderly voice: 'Am I right in supposing that you and your relations have little in common? It seemed to me...would it be a good idea if I were to rest here tomorrow? It would, of course, mean that I should have to ask you to remain with me.'

Tabitha bent down and gave him a quick hug. 'You are a

dear,' she pronounced, 'making a loophole so that I can run
away and hide—but I won't.'

His blue eyes brightened. 'Ah, I thought you wouldn't, but
I felt that I should ask. I see that you have a militant spirit
hidden away somewhere and I must say that I am glad, for I
should very much like to go—I do so enjoy the role of spec-
tator, Tabitha.' He gave her a shrewd glance. 'But you do not,
my dear.'

Tabitha said 'No,' baldly, and then because her stretched
nerves were in tatters: 'Don't you dare pity me!'

Mr Bow, quite undaunted by this show of ill-humour, patted
her hand. 'Pity,' he stated, 'is for those who can no longer help
themselves. I have no pity for you, Tabitha, but I must confess
that I have grown very fond of you. I have fancied from what
I have heard—and forgive an old man his liking for gossip—
that you could be compared with Cinderella, but I think that
you are rather more—er—mettlesome than she was.' He lay
back on his pillows and closed his eyes. 'Good night, my dear
Tabitha.'

When she went downstairs for the second time it was to find
her stepmother and Lilith gone, and Marius with them. She
received this news from Muriel in silence before stating her
intention of going to bed. 'Because,' she declared with a most
realistic yawn, 'it was a long day in the fresh air, wasn't it?
I'm half asleep.'

'I'll come with you,' said Muriel, 'for there's no point in
staying up; If Marius stays for a drink, he's bound to be late.
We leave at nine in the morning, by the way. It's settled that
we should sail across to the other shore where there are some
woods—it sounded very remote and much further than we went
today. But it seems that the wind will be right. We're to take
lunch and have a late tea and leave about six, joining the rest
of the party at the hotel for dinner.'

'What fun,' Tabitha murmured in a hollow voice; perhaps
she could sicken for something meanwhile. She and Muriel
parted on the landing and she went up to her room, to sit by
the window in the dark until she saw Marius's tall figure strolling back from the hotel. He had his head bent, deep in thought;

even if he had looked up he couldn't have seen her, all the same she drew back from the window. It wasn't until she heard his quiet footfall on the stairs below and the shutting of his bedroom door that she went to bed.

On the surface at any rate the two parties set off in the highest spirits the next morning. Tabitha, scorning competition and aware that it wouldn't be of much use anyway, wore her slacks and a matching sleeveless sweater, its collar unbuttoned; her hair she had tied back with a scarf the colour of the water; her bikini was in her beach bag, the only defiant gesture she had made. As it turned out, it wouldn't have mattered what she was wearing, for when they reached the *Piet Hein* it was to find Lilith waiting for them in white short pants and a thin silk shirt, her bright hair tied by a scarf which exactly matched her eyes. Tabitha couldn't blame any man for staring at her; she looked as though she had stepped straight out of a glossy magazine and she was in tearing spirits. Tabitha wished her stepsister good morning and wasn't in the least surprised when she received no answer. Lilith wasn't likely to waste her charm upon her. Even as Tabitha turned to take the picnic basket from Hans, she had hooked her arm in Marius's and stood looking up at him like some beautiful beseeching child. But whatever it was she wanted, she didn't get her way, for Tabitha saw her turn away frowning until Marius called to her as she was leaving the boat. She couldn't hear what it was he said, but it transformed the frown into a smile as she ran off to where Jan van Steen's yacht was moored. Tabitha had met the young man briefly and had liked him. He had been, Marius had told her, a friend of his sister's and still was. 'More money than sense,' Marius had said, 'but a nice enough chap.'

Tabitha stood idly watching Lilith skip aboard the other yacht. Her stepsister would find it useful to have a young man handy with a boat and certainly a car as well. She watched Lilith talking to Jan, knowing that he stood no chance against Marius in Lilith's clever scheming head.

The wind was fresh; the yacht flew over the water with Marius at the helm and the two girls making coffee while Hans, closely followed by Smith and advised by Mr Bow and Bill

Raynard, attended to the sails. After a time they drew away from the other boat and were well ahead of them when at length they tied up at a convenient jetty. There was time to get Mr Bow and Mr Raynard comfortably installed in their canvas chairs under the trees which grew down to meet the sand, and unpack the baskets before Jan hailed them. Tabitha slipped away then, changed into her bikini and went down to the water, surprised to find Muriel already there.

Muriel wasn't a strong swimmer; it seemed unfriendly to leave her pottering about on the edge by herself. Tabitha lay on her back, paddling along gently to keep pace with Muriel's earnest efforts at the breast-stroke. Their conversation was spasmodic and unimportant, enabling Tabitha to keep a sharp eye on what was going on on the beach. Marius, she saw with a sorrowful resentment, had strolled down to meet Lilith, to talk for a few moments and then part again. Presently Lilith, looking stunning in a white bikini of minuscule cut, sauntered down to the water's edge, followed almost at once by Marius. Tabitha heard him ask: 'Are you a good swimmer, Lilith?' and was annoyed to miss her answer. Lilith swam quite well, Tabitha acknowledged to herself, by now in a nasty temper, but she had no staying power; she hoped that Marius would take her out a long, long way so that she would get so fed up that her smiling mask would drop and he would be able to see the real Lilith.

She was sorry for the thought almost before it had crystallised in her mind; to punish herself she turned her back on the pair of them and offered to show Muriel how to do the crawl. She was still engrossed in this task when she heard them swimming towards the beach again. She heard Lilith's laugh, a little strained and apologetic, and Marius didn't laugh at all. She longed to look round but instead invited Muriel to swim to the nearest breakwater. They were half way there when they were overtaken by Marius. He said without preamble: 'Lilith's tired—I've left her on the beach to get her breath. Muriel, be an angel and keep her company. Tabby, come for a swim—it's far too good to go in yet.'

She turned obediently and struck out strongly beside him,

happily aware that she could match his energy if not his strength. They swam side by side, away from the shore and presently, by mutual consent, turned on to their backs. Marius, his head cushioned in his hands, lay supine, his eyes closed. After a minute he spoke.

'You swim as you dance, Tabitha, as though you enjoyed it.'

'Well, I do—I like doing things out of doors, though I simply love dancing.'

He opened his eyes. 'Tabby, will you wear that pretty dress this evening?'

She flipped over and under the calm water in an easy surface dive before she answered. 'It's about all I've got with me,' she said matter-of-factly, 'though I bought a gorgeous dress at that boutique. So did Muriel. We're going to give you all a surprise one evening, so don't tell the others.'

His voice was grave. 'No, I won't—we seldom discuss clothes, you know.'

'Oh, you know what I mean,' she laughed, half exasperated, and then gave a small scream as he caught her by the heels and pulled her under. She came to the surface, her hair, loosed from its pins, hanging in a wet curtain over her face and shoulders. Marius parted it so that she could see, laughing with her, though there was no laughter in his voice.

'Oh, Tabitha, you are such fun to be with—and so different.'

He had his hands on her shoulders as they drifted a little, treading water, and it seemed to her that his eyes had caught its colour as well as its gleam—staring up at him she felt a pleasant tingle run up her spine. She put up a hand to brush the hair away from her face and at the same moment heard her stepmother's voice, very clear in the stillness around them.

'I expect we're wanted for lunch,' said Tabitha, in a voice which shook just a little. She twisted away from him and started for the beach.

She didn't hurry with her dressing and joined the picnic party at length, her hair tied back without any effort at glamour. She had seen her stepmother's face when she and Marius had left the water and the expression upon it hadn't been nice. She sat down between Muriel and Bill Raynard and although she took part in the talk, she said nothing to add to its interest, and when Knotty complained gently after they had finished their lunch that he had an aching ankle, she offered to massage it for him, so that when Marius suggested that they should all go for another swim she was able, in the most natural way imaginable, to decline.

On their own, Knotty, who had appeared to be dozing lightly, became very much awake. 'How thoughtless I am, keeping you from all the fun.' He sounded penitent.

'I had a swim before lunch,' said Tabitha gently, 'and I like being here with you.'

'Yes, I know. Tell me, had you never thought of leaving your job at St Martin's, my dear Tabitha, and going a long way away? London or Scotland or somewhere similar.'

'I couldn't live in London, though it must be fun to stay there with someone to look after you all the time...' She paused, a little pink, but Mr Bow was looking at her with the bland innocence of a child. 'I had thought of going away, but you see I'm near Chidlake at St Martin's, and it was home. I don't think I could bear never to see it again.'

Mr Bow smoothed his beautiful white moustache. 'Tell me about Chidlake,' he invited.

When she had finished, skipping the more unpleasant aspects of her relationship with her stepmother and Lilith, he said gently: 'H'm, yes—you have been dealt a backhander by fate, have you not, Tabitha? A great pity.'

'Yes, but don't think I'm sorry for myself, Mr Bow.'

'I don't, my dear young lady, that is why I like you.' He added, 'Marius is never sorry for himself either—I like him too.'

'He's very nice,' said Tabitha inadequately while she tried to think what Marius could possibly have to be sorry about. 'I think I'll start getting the tea, because Hans and Smith are on board and I daresay they've fallen asleep.'

Tea was a protracted meal. Bill Raynard had slept for most of the afternoon and had wakened refreshed and in a mood to tell amusing stories, of which he had an endless number. Tabitha, sitting beside young van Steen, tried not to watch Lilith, sitting so close to Marius with a charming air of ownership. And once when she looked up, it was to see Marius looking down at his companion with a look of amused tolerance and something else in his face which she was unable to define. Perhaps it was love, she thought miserably; she knew so little of it that she doubted if she would recognize it if she saw it.

They packed up to go shortly after tea, because it was getting on for six o'clock and it would take two hours to get back to Veere. They all stood around, arguing lightheartedly as to who should go with whom. Tabitha took no part in the discussion and when she heard Lilith say: 'But you promised me, Marius,' wasn't in the least surprised when he asked her carelessly if she would mind going back with van Steen. But even as she opened her mouth to agree Mr Bow said forcefully: 'In that case, I shall stay here. I refuse to sail without Tabitha—she's the only one who knows how to deal with my cramp.'

Tabitha succeeded in not looking astonished. To the best of her knowledge Mr Bow had never once complained of the cramp; she remained silent waiting for someone to speak. Muriel solved the problem by saying:

'Bill and I will go in Jan's boat if he'll have us as well as Mrs Crawley, then you can have Hans and Smith and Knotty, and Lilith and Tabby to crew, Marius.'

Marius said lazily: 'Just as you like—it really makes no difference to me.' He turned to Mr Bow. 'Sorry I overlooked the cramp, Knotty.' His voice was dry.

They all made their way to the jetty where the two boats were moored and Tabitha was vaguely surprised to find Lilith beside her, for she had seen her only a few minutes previously, in deep conversation with Muriel. Her stepsister drew close to her and said in an urgent whisper: 'Tabby—Tabby, do help me!'

Tabitha felt surprise and then concern; she asked quietly: 'Are you all right, Lilith?'

'My sunglasses,' said Lilith. 'I've left them where I undressed—you know, behind those trees. There was a little patch of soft grass and I put them down because I thought they'd be safe. Now I've got a simply awful headache, I can't bear it without them—I shall be sick if I don't wear them. If I could just get aboard and sit quiet for a bit. Tabby, will you get them for me?—it'll only take a few minutes and no one's ready to go yet.'

Tabitha said nothing; it was true, no one seemed ready to sail as yet. There would be plenty of time and it was only a short distance. She gave Lilith her beach bag to hold and asked: 'Did you undress to the left or the right of that little patch of grass in the trees where we all were?'

Lilith looked vague. 'Oh, I can't remember. How mean of you to bother me when my head's so bad. You'll find it easily enough and you'll see the glasses—they've got white rims.'

Tabitha turned away and started to walk back to the fringe of trees behind the stretch of sand. She looked round once. No one was looking her way and they were already going aboard; she would have to hurry, although she didn't think Marius would mind waiting for her. She reached the trees and found the little grassy space in their midst where they had dispersed to dress. There were, she saw with faint unease, a great many little mossy patches. She started to search, starting on the left and working round, clockwise, and found nothing. She started once more, for it seemed to her that she had been only a few minutes, going more carefully this time, and drew a blank once more. She was just turning away when it occurred to her that Lilith might have found some other grass patch other than the one she was in. She cast around her and discovered a vague path running deeper into the trees, and presently another stretch of grass. She searched this one too, and because she didn't like to admit defeat, searched again and then went back the way she had come, going slowly in case she had missed the glasses on the path somewhere. She was uneasily aware by now that she was keeping Marius waiting and quickened her steps, at the same time becoming aware of the regular chug-chug of engines. Perhaps Jan van Steen had already gone and Marius was waiting, surely impatient by now.

She came out on to the sand and halted, staring unbelievingly at the two yachts, already well out into the lake, and with the steady thud of their engines and the off-shore wind, she doubted if anyone would hear her. All the same she cupped her hands round her mouth and shouted, and then, when it became obvious that no one had heard her, she waved. She waved and called for a long time, running foolishly down to the end of the jetty in the absurd hope that they would hear her more easily. It was while she was there that she found her beach bag thrown down on the sand beside the jetty and realized that Lilith had sent her back deliberately and had somehow made them believe that she was on board. Her rage gave her added strength—she shouted again, although she knew it was hopeless. The yachts were too far away, and even if anyone looked back she would be but an indistinct figure; besides, it was likely that Lilith had told them that she was in the other boat. She shouted again, her voice a little hoarse, as she watched the boats round the spit of land which took them out of her sight.

And even if she had known, it would have been cold comfort to her that two people had heard her; Marius, busy in the bows of the yacht, had called without turning round: 'I thought I heard someone calling—it sounded like Tabby.' And Lilith, close to him said at once: 'Yes, so did I—she's waving from the other boat,' and waved back just as though Tabitha were really there. Bill Raynard, watching her, said in his wife's ear:

'What's that silly little fool doing? There's no one here worth waving to, unless she's keeping van Steen sweet.'

It was still light when they berthed. They were standing in a little group, talking over the day before they dispersed, the two stiff-legged members of the party accommodated on a convenient wooden seat, when Marius asked sharply: 'Where's Tabitha?'

Muriel and Bill and Jan van Steen answered him in a surprised chorus.

'With you, of course, Marius.' Mrs Crawley said nothing at all because she had just had a glimpse of her daughter's face, and Mr Bow and Hans kept their own counsel—they too had seen Lilith's face.

Marius changed from a casual, easy-going man to one who

was almost frighteningly calm. 'She was to have come with me,' he said, very quietly, 'but you, Lilith, said she had changed her mind and wanted to go with Jan.' He looked with suddenly cold eyes at Lilith. 'You waved to her.'

'But we didn't even see her,' said Muriel, and was interrupted by Marius.

'Somebody must have seen what happened to her—did she go back for anything?'

He looked at each of them in turn and Lilith last of all and when he saw her face he asked: 'You, Lilith?'

She pouted prettily and gave him a laughing look which changed to apprehension. 'It was—well, I thought she was with Jan—how was I to know?'

His voice was silky. 'You sent her back for something?'

'Yes, I had a terrible headache and I didn't want to spoil the party by feeling rotten.' She looked round for sympathy and got none. 'I—I left my sunglasses somewhere in the trees, where we changed. Tabitha went back for them. I couldn't possibly have gone all that way with my head. I suppose she couldn't find them—she was always silly like that...'

Marius stretched out a hand and took her beach bag from her. 'These?' he wanted to know; his voice was soft, almost gentle, and when Lilith began to speak he cut her short, still in that same gentle voice: 'You shall apologise to Tabitha later.' He tossed the bag to her, turned to Mrs Crawley and said with his usual casual charm: 'Mrs Crawley, don't let this upset your dinner party.'

She smiled though her eyes were wary. 'No, I won't. Tabby will be all right—I expect someone's picked her up by now.'

Marius didn't reply, but said over his shoulder to Mr Raynard: 'Bill, you see to things, will you? Hans will run you all up to the hotel in the car.'

Hans was standing at his back, large and solid and as placid-seeming as his master. Marius spoke to him in Dutch and no one knew what he said, except perhaps old Knotty, who, as usual, had his eyes closed.

Marius whistled to Smith and with a careless 'See you later,' went back on board, and Lilith, who had been standing silent, ran forward crying:

'Marius, don't go! Mother said Tabitha will have got a lift by now—but if you must go, take me with you.' She added desperately: 'It was a joke.'

He was bending over the diesel, but he straightened up to look at her. His voice was mild. 'What, and spoil your dinner party? Besides, you should rest and get rid of that headache.' He turned his back and a minute later the *Piet Hein* was edging her way out into the lake once more.

Tabitha sat where the trees and sand merged into each other; very erect, with her back against a tree trunk, her eyes constantly scanning the water. There had been passing boats earlier and she had waved and shouted, but the wind had freshened, carrying her voice with it, and besides, anyone seeing her would very likely think she was a camper going for an evening stroll. But there had been no boat for some time now, although she could still see pale triangles of sail merging into the evening mist. She looked at her watch and made out that it was almost nine o'clock; even if someone came back for her, it would be at least another hour—in the meantime the evening was growing cool as the sky dimmed slowly to a darker blue; only the vivid orange and red of the sun's bedding gave light to the water and a pale gleam to the sands around her. The trees at her back were already in gloom; she glanced over her shoulder and shivered, telling herself not to be silly. She wasn't a nervous girl, but this was a strange country and she was getting hungry and chilled, which somehow made her solitude more obvious.

She searched through her beach bag once more, in the hope that, by some minor miracle, there would be an apple or biscuit tucked in amongst her towel and bikini and other odds and ends, all so useless now. She had even left her cardigan on board when they had first landed. She sighed, and got up and began to walk briskly up and down the beach, stopping to look over the darkening water each time she turned.

It was a good half hour later when she first heard the steady thud of an engine and then saw, silhouetted against the pale sky in the west, the *Piet Hein,* carrying full sail, coming in fast with the inshore wind. She stood watching it, and not until the sails were reefed and the yacht was edging slowly towards the jetty did she go down its rickety length. She knew it was Marius on board, because she had heard Smith's short bark and Marius's voice speaking to the dog, and the fury which had consumed her died a little, swamped in the delight and relief of seeing him. He made the boat fast and the next moment she felt his arms holding her close, while Smith whined softly at their feet. She didn't know what Marius would say; she only knew that she was disappointed when he spoke.

'Poor Tabby—I blame myself for not making certain that you were with Jan.' His voice was quiet and kind and unruffled. 'Were you frightened? You're cold—come aboard quickly.'

He led the way down into the cabin and said cheerfully: 'Coffee in a minute. Here, put this on—it's getting fresh.' He threw her a thick sweater, many sizes too large, and she got into it obediently. She hadn't said a word so far, knowing that once she started she wouldn't be able to stop, and she didn't know what had been said; probably Lilith had managed to lay the blame on her. Marius didn't seem to notice her silence; he gave her a mug of coffee, liberally laced with brandy, before he sat down on a locker opposite her. 'Lilith did it for a joke,' he explained, his voice very even. 'I suppose she thought you would be missed soon after we sailed, but of course I thought you were with Jan...'

Tabitha, her temper stoked by the brandy, interrupted him. 'You said I was to go with you because of Mr Bow's cramp—didn't you notice that I wasn't on board?' Her voice, a little shrill, tailed off—of course he hadn't noticed with Lilith there.

He gave her a thoughtful look. 'I was given to understand that you had decided to go with Jan after all. None of them knew that you had gone back on shore, naturally Jan and I each thought you were on the other boat.' He leaned forward and took the mug from her. 'I'm sorry, Tabitha, it was a dreadful thing to happen. Lilith was upset...'

Tabitha said stonily: 'I was upset too.' She got up. 'Are you ready to go? I'll cast off, shall I?'

She didn't wait for him to answer but went quickly out of the little cabin and went to untie the mooring rope. They didn't speak much as Marius steered the boat away from land; the sails were still reefed and he was using the diesel until they rounded the curve of the shore to take advantage of the wind once more. But once they had done this and the sails were set Marius turned on the automatic steering. 'Hungry?' he asked.

Tabitha was coiling rope neatly on deck. 'Yes—I'll go below and make some sandwiches, shall I?'

He followed her. 'You make the tea, I'll see to the food.'

They had hot bacon sandwiches and great mugs of milky tea, sitting in the stern, side by side. The stars were out by now, and a sliver of moon, and here and there lights twinkled along the shores of the lake. They had finished the sandwiches and had begun on a large wedge of cheese Marius had thoughtfully provided, when he spoke.

'You're furious, aren't you, Tabby? I am too.' She gave him a look of surprise, although his face wasn't easy to see in the dusk. 'I don't look angry, do I, but I believe that I am angrier than you. Our evening has been spoilt.'

'I'm sorry you had to miss the dinner party,' Tabitha rejoined waspishly, and was furious when he laughed.

'I'm happy as I am, Tabby, although you sound as though you're going to scratch out my eyes at any moment! As for the dinner party, we'll have one of our own to make up for it—just us two.'

She thought he was being conciliatory, and she was no child to be coaxed into good humour. 'It's kind of you to suggest it,' she said stiffly, 'but there's no need...' She stopped because her bottled-up feelings and temper and fright exploded inside her, so that the tears cascaded down her cheeks and all she could do was sob. She went on crying for some time, the feel of Marius's arm warm and comforting around her shoulders, but presently she whispered into his shoulder: 'I'm sorry to have been such a fool—I've made you v—very wet.'

She sniffed and sat up and dried her eyes on the sleeve of the sweater she was wearing and he said in a kindly voice:

'Here, have mine,' thrust a large handkerchief into her hands and when she had used it, asked: 'Feel better now?'

She nodded into the dark, thankful that he couldn't see her sodden face. She wasn't in the habit of crying often; when she did, she did it wholeheartedly, just as she danced and swam and ran her ward and, for that matter, fell in love.

Hans was waiting for them. Smith greeted him with a quiet bark as Marius turned on the powerful deck light and slid into the little harbour. Hans' enormous hand steadied Tabitha as she jumped off the boat. 'Not too bad, miss?' he asked anxiously. 'I have food waiting.' He turned to speak to Marius who spoke to him low-voiced before he took Tabitha's arm, whistled to Smith and walked her over to the house. Hans had left the door open and they went through the hall quietly to the kitchen at its end. The light was bright here and Tabitha turned her head away from it sharply because she knew how awful she must be looking—a useless precaution, because Marius stopped under the old-fashioned brass hanging lamp and turned her round to face him, a hand under her chin.

He stared down at her for several moments, his eyes hooded so that she had no idea what he was thinking. Unable to bear it, she muttered: 'Oh, don't—please don't look at me. I'll go straight upstairs.'

He smiled a little. 'Why do you set such store on a pretty face, Tabitha? Perhaps no one has ever told you that a pretty face isn't always a beautiful one, and you, my dear girl, are beautiful at this moment, red nose, puffed eyes, tear-stained cheeks notwithstanding. Now sit down—Hans will be here in a minute and we'll have supper together, the three of us, and don't mind him seeing you like this—he's your devoted slave already.'

He looked as though he was going to say something else, but he didn't, only kissed the top of her head and ruffled her already very ruffled hair.

The day, which had been so disastrous, ended with unexpected satisfaction, at least for Tabitha. Hans, beaming all over his broad, goodnatured face produced a magnificent supper which they ate at the kitchen table, decked with a very white cloth and deep blue pottery plates. They had soup first—*potage Parmentier*, which, Hans told them with some pride, he had made himself, and followed it with a great dish of little fried pancakes stuffed with prawns and oysters and tasting most delicately of cheese and white wine and Pernod. They were so delicious that when Hans got up from the table and returned with a chocolate soufflé Tabitha vowed she couldn't eat another morsel, whereupon he looked so dejected that she rapidly changed her mind and then had a second helping from sheer healthy greed. Marius had gone down the little crooked staircase to the cellar under the kitchen and brought up a bottle of claret, which had the pleasing effect of making her surroundings even more pleasant than they were, a circumstance heightened by her two companions, who, in some way she was too happy to bother about, contrived to make her feel that having supper with her at one o'clock in the morning was the one thing they liked doing most. Moreover, Marius had called her beautiful—a palpable lie, of course, but very soothing to hear after her miserable day.

Warm, sleepy and full of good food and excellent wine, she thanked them both and wished them good night, to sleep the moment her head touched the pillow. She woke once in the night and decided that she would thank them again in the morning, for they had been very kind. She slept again even as she thought it.

# CHAPTER SEVEN

TABITHA wakened early and listened to the faint sounds of the little town stirring, and because it was already a beautiful day, she got up and dressed in pink denim slacks and a pink and white checked shirt, then went downstairs, intent on finding Hans and Marius so that she could thank them once more.

Hans was already in the kitchen, pouring himself a cup of coffee from a blue enamel pot of vast dimensions. He put it down, however, when he saw Tabitha and said: 'Miss Tabitha, good day—you are soon, I make tea.'

Tabitha perched on the table. 'Good morning, Hans. The coffee smells good, may I have a cup, Hans, please?'

He smiled widely. 'Already so Dutch,' he chuckled, 'that is good.' He handed her a blue mug which matched the pot. 'You don't sleep?'

'Yes, very well, thank you, only I woke early and I don't think I thanked you or Mr van Beek nearly enough for being so nice last night. I do thank you, Hans—you were like a fairy godmother...'

'Would that by any chance make me the prince?' asked Marius from the door. She turned to look at him; he had been on the yacht, for he had a handful of tools in one hand and was wearing nothing more than a pair of oil-stained shorts. He saw her look and said mildly: 'Well, perhaps not—I'm hardly dressed for the part, am I?' He smiled and held out a hand for the coffee Hans had poured. 'You're up early, Tabitha, didn't you sleep?'

'Very well. I was explaining to Hans—I wakened early and it seemed to me I hadn't thanked either of you enough for—for last night.'

She looked at him, lounging in a high-backed, painted chair a couple of feet from her, and her heart did a somersault because, despite the shorts and the oil stains, he looked very like

154

a prince should. He stared back at her, a smile curving his mouth, and she said hastily, going pink under his look: 'It was a great nuisance for you having to go back for me—in the dark too,' and stopped because his smile had broadened into a wide grin as Hans said: 'Never worry about the dark, miss. Mister Marius, he lived on the water from when he was a little boy—he sails it blindfold if he must—he knows every square metre.'

Tabitha digested this, then: 'And you let us plan our trips just as though you didn't know your way about—you must have known all the places like the back of your hand.' She frowned, and opened her mouth again to speak her mind when he stopped her.

'Why not, Tabby? Bill loves navigating and planning, even old Knotty, although he remembers it all quite well, enjoyed it, and I've enjoyed it as much as any of you, perhaps more.' He stretched hugely. 'I don't know what's planned for today, but how about a run in the car before breakfast? Give me ten minutes.'

He was gone before she could reply and Hans took the mug from her hand and refilled it, remarking in his placid voice: 'It will be good to drive now—later too hot.'

Tabitha sipped her coffee. 'Hans,' she asked, 'have you always lived in Veere?'

He nodded. 'Thirty-five years, but for a year in Rotterdam. First I was chauffeur and house steward to old Mijnheer van Beek, and friend too for Mister Marius and his brother and sister—we had good times together. I teach them to drive, you understand? But this one, he is best of them. He travels much, but always he comes back to his home which he loves. He is a good man. You like him, Miss Tabitha?'

His question was asked without guile. Tabitha put down her mug.

'Yes, Hans, I like him.' She didn't say any more because she could hear Marius coming down the stairs, and anyway there wasn't much more she could say. She got to her feet and stood waiting for him. He came through the door looking as though he had never held a tool in his life, let alone used it; he had on immaculate slacks, beautifully tailored and an open-necked shirt with a silk scarf tucked inside it. More of a prince than ever, thought Tabitha, wishing she looked more spectacular herself and then reversing the wish when he said idly: 'You look nice, Tabby—you have the happy knack of wearing the right clothes at the right times.'

The car was just across the cobbles, close to the harbour's edge. As they got in Marius asked: 'Shall we just wander— there are some delightful roads.' So they went straight along the shore of the lake to Vrouwenpolder and then turned off to weave a way through the narrow, badly surfaced country lanes running between the flat fields, until they came to Domburg, larger than Veere but not nearly as picturesque, for it had a great many hotels and camping sites, but as Marius pointed out, that was inevitable as it was a popular seaside resort amongst the Dutch. From there the coast road was a good one; Marius followed it for several miles and turned inland again, short of Middelburg, going slowly through the quiet country. Afterwards Tabitha couldn't remember what they had talked about, only that she had enjoyed every moment of it. As they drew up opposite the house once more, Marius turned to look at her.

'That dinner—will you come out tonight?'

She ignored her galloping pulse rate. 'Thank you, I should like that—that is if it doesn't interfere with—with anything.' By anything she had meant Lilith and perhaps he had guessed that, for he said easily:

'Why should it? About eight o'clock at the hotel, I think, don't you?' His smile held faint mockery. 'Leave it to me, Tabby.'

The weather still held, and at breakfast it was decided that they should sail down the canal to Middelburg and Vlissingen and then round the coast and so back to the Veerse Meer from the west. In the excitement of planning this trip there was very little opportunity for much discussion about the previous evening's escapade, or the dinner party. What questions were asked Tabitha left Marius to answer, which he did with a casual good humour which robbed it of all drama, at the same time including her in the conversation with such adroitness that she seemed to be taking a far greater part in the talk than she actually was. As for the dinner party, the Raynards and Mr Bow had enjoyed themselves; the hotel was praised, as was the delicious food, and if rather less was said about their hostess and her daughter, no one saw fit to comment upon it. This led, naturally enough, to Marius observing that perhaps they wouldn't mind too much if he took Tabitha out to dinner that evening, a remark which earned the company's wholehearted approbation, and when Hans, who seemed to know everything going on in the house, came in with the post, remarking that if they were going out that evening they had better make a start on their day's outing or they wouldn't be back in time, everyone made haste to get down to the yacht.

Tabitha, helping Mr Bow as he slowly negotiated the cobbles, couldn't fail to see how much better the old man looked. He had become quite brown, so that his white whiskers looked even whiter and he looked ten years younger, despite the crutches. Bill Raynard too had been revitalized to an astonishing extent. The thought of him returning to St Martin's in a few weeks' time filled Tabitha with unease—he had always been twice as energetic as anyone else; now it looked as though he would be doubling his operation lists and filling the beds faster than she could ever hope to get them made up; he was already beginning to talk with enthusiasm of what he intended to do as soon as he got back to work. She switched her thoughts away from the hospital; time enough to worry about her work when they got back. She heaved a sigh and choked on it when Mr Bow observed gently: 'No sighing today, Tabitha—sighing is wasted breath.'

The day was a success; if it hadn't been for the fact that she was going out to dinner with Marius that evening, Tabitha would have wished it to last for ever. As it was, she felt her heart leap with excitement as they neared Veere, an excitement doused by the expectation of seeing Lilith or her stepmother on the quayside, but there was no sign of either of them—it seemed as though the day was going to end as perfectly as it had begun.

They strolled up to the Campveerse Toren just before eight

o'clock and went up the curving staircase to the restaurant overlooking the water. They had a table in one of the windows and watched the boats coming in for the night while they drank their aperitifs and talked over their day. They were still talking about Chidlake and Veere now as they ate *ratatouille,* which Tabitha had never heard of, followed by roast duckling stuffed with prunes, and finally a dessert of fresh pineapple filled with a delicious concoction of almonds and bananas and whipped cream, lavishly awash with rum, and because Marius said it was a celebration, although he declined to say of what, they drank champagne.

It was while they were sitting over their coffee that Marius said:

'Only a week left—how time flies when one is content.' He gave her a keen glance. 'You are content, Tabitha?'

Tabitha filled their coffee cups for a second time. 'Yes, very—I'm happy too.' Her pretty voice was warm with feeling, for she was happy, or almost; as happy as she would ever be with Lilith, smiling and triumphant, reminding her of a happiness she herself was never likely to have—but she had now, and she had had the whole day with him too. She said slowly:

'St Martin's seems like a dream. I can't imagine myself going back there, making out diet sheets and putting up extensions,' she sighed, and then, for fear he should pity her, said brightly: 'But everyone feels like that after a holiday, don't they? Besides, there's still another week.' She looked out to the dark blue water of the lake. 'Do you think this gorgeous weather will last?'

It was a red herring which he ignored, and that was a pity because she found it so much easier to talk about things and not themselves.

Marius said blandly: 'You won't be putting up extensions for the rest of your life, you know.'

She deliberately misunderstood him. 'Oh, but I couldn't do much else. I've worked on Orthopaedics for several years and I'm hopelessly out of the running with Medical or Surgery—I might manage theatre, I suppose.'

His voice was still bland. 'Ah, yes, when the pretty Sue gets married.'

Which remark, Tabitha thought crossly, he could have better left unsaid. She saw herself in the successive years ahead, taking over from the pretty girls who got married. To rid herself of the unpleasant prospect she said vigorously: 'I shall stay on in Men's Orthopaedic,' and then, not sure that he would choose to answer: 'What are you going to do, Marius?'

Apparently he hadn't minded her question. 'Bill won't be able to do a full day's work for a couple of weeks after we get back. I shall stay a couple of weeks—less, perhaps—then I have a short lecture tour and—er—affairs of my own to settle.'

Tabitha, made reckless by a little too much champagne, opened her mouth to enquire what affairs, but before she could utter he said smoothly:

'No, don't ask, Tabby,' and was about to say more when he looked across the room and saw Lilith and Mrs Crawley and said instead: 'Here are your family. Shall we ask them over for one last drink before we go?'

Tabitha gave him an empty stare. She said dully: 'Yes, of course, it would complete the evening, wouldn't it? You should have invited them for dinner,' and Marius, his eyebrows lifted at her sudden rudeness, said silkily: 'Yes, perhaps I should.'

It was half an hour before they got up to go and even then on the way down the staircase Marius paused, and with a brief murmured excuse went back up again, to reappear after a couple of minutes. Tabitha, studying his face, thought that behind his placid good looks there was quiet satisfaction. They walked back to the house, making conversation while Tabitha thought her own thoughts, knowing that he was thinking his too, and she fancied they were triumphant ones. She said her thank yous and good nights in the hall and went to her room where she went at once to the window without putting on the light. As she had known, with a certainty as strong as though he had told her himself, Marius had already left the house again and was walking briskly back to the hotel.

She slept late the next morning because she hadn't slept very much during the night. She got downstairs just as everyone

was sitting down to breakfast and because of her unusual lateness had to put up with a good deal of mild teasing, which she
answered in a lighthearted manner wholly at variance with her
shadowed eyes, elaborating upon her evening out and even de-
claiming at some length on the pleasure of meeting Lilith and
Mrs Crawley. It was only when she caught Marius's thoughtful
eyes upon her that she realized that she was being far too talkative.

They spent the day sailing and in the afternoon the weather
became overcast, and then suddenly the sky became pitch black
and the storm broke over their heads. Tabitha, who didn't like
thunder and was frightened of lightning, was surprised to discover that neither bothered her overmuch because everyone
else in the party appeared to be enjoying themselves im-
mensely, especially Marius, sitting at the tiller, singing some
song about 'Piet Hein'. The worst of the storm had blown over
as they approached Veere; the sky was blue again and the sun
shone once more. The little town looked delightful with its
quaint roof tops glistening with the recent rain, and everything
looked fresh and green.

They made their way through the crowded little harbour to
their berth, past Jan's boat, but there was no sign of Lilith on
board, nor was she by the harbour. Tabitha heaved a sigh of
relief as she crossed the road with Mr Bow and Marius and
went into the house. There was a note on the side table in the
hall. Tabitha saw that it was in Lilith's handwriting as Marius
picked it up and without reading it, put it in his pocket and led
everyone into the sitting room where there was an instant and
lighthearted discussion as to how they should amuse themselves that evening, which the two girls cut short with the pos-
itive assertion that they refused to discuss anything until they
had bathed and changed.

Half an hour later Tabitha was on her way downstairs again,
her hair piled in its coils and rolls, and wearing a blue and
white patterned dress and flat-heeled blue sandals on her feet.
She made no noise at all on the stairs and none on the thick-
piled hall carpet. The door of the sitting room was half open,

as she neared it she couldn't fail to hear Marius say, his voice urgent:

'Knotty, there's only one thing for it, you'll have to feel ill—just ill enough to stay home. If I know Tabby she'll insist on staying with you. Bill and Muriel can come with me and dine on their own, that will leave me free to dine with Lilith—I'll persuade her to get Mrs Crawley to join us afterwards—if only the woman would make up her mind where she wants to live. I must talk to them, Knotty, they're going in two days. Their coming in the first place has made things a great deal easier, but I must have my answer before they leave. And Tabitha is not to know. You agree to that too, don't you, Bill?'

Tabitha heard Mr Raynard's growling reply as she made her way back to her room. Once there she went to the mirror and stared into it, surprised to see that she looked just the same as she had done before she had gone downstairs. She was a little pale perhaps, but she could always plead a headache after the storm. She went on staring at her reflection, no longer seeing it, conscious only of the pain somewhere deep inside her because Marius, who had wanted to be her friend, was making a mockery of friendship. What was it he didn't want her to know, and why had he told Mr Bow and Bill Raynard? Did he think her such a fool that she was incapable of seeing for herself that he and Lilith…? She turned away from the mirror. It would have given her a great deal of satisfaction to have gone downstairs and flung open the sitting room door in a dramatic fashion and told him exactly what she thought of him, but on second thoughts she rejected the idea, she wasn't dramatic for a start and she had not the slightest idea what to say. She said out loud: 'Listeners never hear any good of themselves,' and Muriel who had just knocked on the door came in wanting to know why she was talking to herself. They went down together to join the men and Muriel asked at once: 'Well, what have you decided to do with the evening?'

Marius was pouring sherry into his beautiful glasses. He said unhurriedly: 'How about all of us going up to De Campveerse Toren for a meal?' Which was so exactly what Tabitha had been expecting that she nodded her head slightly and looked

across to Mr Bow, for he would be the one to answer. She
wasn't disappointed, for he said at once:

'What a splendid idea, Marius, dear boy, but I feel a little
under the weather—the storm, you know. If I could be helped
to bed, I shall be able to manage very well.'

Tabitha picked up her cue; since they were acting, she might
as well make a success of her role. 'I'll stay with you, Mr
Bow, I don't mind a bit, because I've a headache myself.' She
looked round the circle of faces, her smile the bright professional one she wore on the ward to hide her real feelings, although she was unaware of that, but Marius saw it and said
sharply: 'No—' and then stopped, giving her the chance to ask:

'Why ever not? I came to look after the two invalids, if you
remember. So far I've done nothing at all.' Which wasn't quite
true, but sounded right. As though everyone had agreed with
her she said to Mr Bow:

'You shall go to bed, Mr Bow, with a nice supper tray, and
later on I'll give you one of your sleeping pills.'

She smiled round the room again, nicely in control of her
feelings and rather proud of the way she had risen to the occasion, and Muriel who of course knew nothing about it made
it easier by saying: 'Well, if you've got a headache,
Tabby…though it won't be such fun without you. You don't
mind if we go with Marius?'

'Not a bit,' said Tabitha heartily, and saw Marius eyeing her
with speculation and puzzlement though he smiled as he remarked gently: 'You don't seem too upset, Tabby.'

Perhaps she had been a shade too hearty. She smiled directly
at him, although it was an effort. 'There will be other evenings,
I expect. Of course I'm sorry I shan't be coming, but I wouldn't
be much of an asset with a headache, would I?'

They went half an hour later, Muriel a little doubtful at leaving her, but Bill Raynard said nothing and nor did Marius,
although he wished them a cheerful good night and advised
Tabitha to take something for her headache. At the door he
turned round to suggest that she went to bed early—advice she
ignored, for once Mr Bow had been settled with his book, his
spectacles and his glass of water within reach, she wandered

down to the sitting room again and sat in Marius's great chair, leafing through a pile of magazines. Hans was in the kitchen and the house was quiet. She had had her own dinner while Mr Bow partook of a few suitable dainties on a tray and there was nothing to do except flip through *Vogue,* her mind on the dinner party at the hotel; it didn't bear thinking about. She got up and prowled up and down the lovely room and finally went upstairs to see how Mr Bow fared. Since he was supposed to be feeling ill, she might as well treat him as though he were.

He was sitting up in bed, with a book open before him, not reading it but staring in front of him. He gave her a piercing look as she approached the bed and pronounced: 'I am deep in thought, young lady.'

'Pleasant ones, I hope,' observed Tabitha. 'Is there anything you want?'

He answered her absently: 'No—no, what should I need?' and glanced at his old-fashioned watch on the bedside table. 'I had imagined that you would have gone to bed with that head-ache of yours—was it a very bad one?' His blue eyes looked very innocent.

Tabitha could look innocent too. 'No worse than your sudden indisposition, Mr Bow. I daresay we're both feeling better, aren't we?' She smiled at him. 'Now I'm going to bed. Good night and sleep well.'

But she didn't undress immediately, nor did she turn on the light as she went to sit in the chair by the window. She had only been there a few minutes when Hans, accompanied by Smith, went out. She watched them walk stolidly down to the end of the harbour and then back again, with frequent pauses for Hans to greet acquaintances on the way, and still more pauses for Smith to do the same. Ten minutes after they had entered the house again Tabitha saw the Raynards returning from the hotel. Bill Raynard was managing very well with his heavy stick and his wife's supporting arm—at the rate he was going he would be back at work in a couple of weeks' time. There was no sign of Marius; she undressed slowly, lingered over her bath and got into bed, only to get out again and peer out of the window. There were still a number of people about,

for though it was past eleven o'clock the cafés were still open
and the little town's visitors were strolling around enjoying the
warm late evening. The bells had sounded midnight before she
saw Marius walking back by himself. He didn't go into the
house but went to stand by the water, his hands in his pockets.
Presently he went over to the Bentley, got in, and drove away,
leaving Tabitha, quite bewildered, to go back to bed where she
lay thinking up an incredible number of reasons for his strange
behaviour, none of which made any sense.

She was down early the next morning, but Marius was earlier, standing at the open door talking to the postman. He gave
her two letters from the pile in his hand and said: 'Hullo—here
are a couple for you—how's the headache?' He gave her a
questioning smile and looked as though he really wanted to
know.

'Gone,' she said briefly, and couldn't resist adding: 'Mr Bow
has quite recovered too. I went to see him on my way down.'

Marius's eyes met hers; there was a gleam in their depths,
but whether it was laughter or suspicion she couldn't tell. 'I
thought he would be,' was all he said.

They strolled across the cobbles and sat down on the grass
bordering the harbour to read their letters—a lengthy business
for Marius, for he had a great number, but Tabitha's two were
quickly read—one from Meg, full of the unimportant but interesting happenings of home—the milkman's wife had had
another baby, there was a new washer needed on the bathroom
tap and did Tabitha know that the rent was going up in two
weeks' time, and lastly, dear Podger was behaving beautifully
and would Tabitha let that nice Mr Bow know that his pet was
proving a very loving companion which she would find it difficult to part with. Tabitha smiled as she folded this missive
and Marius glanced at her and asked: 'A letter from Meg? I
hope everything is all right at home?'

Tabitha opened her second letter. 'Yes, thank you,' she said
in a voice calculated to discourage further questions, and
started to read the second, longer letter from Sue. Sue had a
great deal to say; the theatre was dull because there were only
the cases from the women's ward and the casualties were being

sent elsewhere. The ward was almost finished—she had sneaked down after duty one day to have a look, and had Tabitha really been allowed to choose the curtains by herself and if so how had she got round Matron to let her do it; and did she know that there were two new housemen? And at the end of a further page of gossip, Sue wrote: 'I'm getting married at Christmas. How about having a go at my job?' At the very end of the letter there was a P.S. 'You didn't mention Mr van Beek—I wonder why?'

Tabitha folded that letter too. It was a little over four months to Christmas, time enough for her to make up her mind if she wanted Sue's job or not, and time enough, too, to know more about Lilith and Marius. She frowned, and Marius, without appearing to look up from his own letters, asked: 'Bad news?'

'No—' Tabitha hesitated, wondering if she should tell him, and decided against it. She sat quietly beside him until he had finished reading and then asked: 'Are there any plans for today?' because that seemed the natural question to ask and would perhaps prevent him from talking about the previous evening. She didn't want to hear how lovely Lilith had looked…besides, he had been looking quietly satisfied with himself ever since they had met that morning.

Marius got to his feet and pulled her to hers. 'How about going down to the Zilveren Schor for a quick swim? I've a luncheon date and I don't expect to be back until after tea—perhaps later.'

She said 'Oh?' in an uncertain voice, longing to ask who he would be with, and went scarlet when he added mildly: 'You're dying to know who with, aren't you, but I daresay you can guess—Lilith and your stepmother. They're going back tomorrow, you know.'

Presumably that was reason enough to spend most of the day with them. She said composedly despite her red face: 'Oh, yes. How quickly the week has gone—too quickly for you, I expect.'

He gave her a long hard look. 'Why, now that you mention it,' he answered coolly, 'yes, far too quickly.'

They went back into the house then and joined the others

for breakfast. They, it seemed, knew about Marius's date and were full of an afternoon's shopping they had planned in Bergen-op-Zoom, and when Tabitha wanted to know why they couldn't go to Middelburg, which was a great deal nearer and surely just as interesting, they put forward so many reasons why Bergen-op-Zoom was the only place to go that she very quickly realized that Marius was going to Middelburg and they were all being very tactful about it.

The Zilveren Schor wasn't very far and they had the wind with them. They tied up to a convenient pole and went ashore and Tabitha discovered that only she and Marius were going to swim, for Muriel declared that she had no energy and the water there was far too deep for her anyway.

There was a very small island off-shore; Tabitha and Marius swam towards it without haste and then lay on its tiny sandy beach. It was pleasantly warm and the sun was bright, so that she lay with her eyes closed, hoping that this might discourage conversation. It did nothing of the sort, for Marius said almost immediately:

'I shall miss these pleasant outings—you're a good companion in the water, Tabby.'

She kept her eyes shut and said 'Um' in an unforthcoming way.

'You're not bad at crewing either,' he conceded.

'Uh-huh,' said Tabitha. 'I'm not much good on a boat the size of the *Piet Hein*—I'm used to dinghies.'

'All the more credit to you,' he went on smoothly. 'You should go back to work feeling like a giant—giantess, refreshed.'

'I shall, thanks to you. It's been a lovely holiday—I've enjoyed every minute of it.'

Which was by no means true and perhaps Marius guessed it, for he said on a laugh: 'Oh, Tabitha, that's a sweeping statement.' He rolled over on his side to look at her. 'Shall I ask Lilith and your stepmother in for drinks this evening so that you can wish them goodbye? You haven't seen much of them.'

Tabitha got up and started to wade back into the water. When he caught up with her she said with a little spurt of anger: 'Are you trying to change me? I can think of no other reason…just because you're going to marry into the family doesn't give you the right…' She stopped because her voice had become a little shrill. 'It would be nicer for you if things were different, but you don't have to be friends with me, you know—it upsets Lilith. We never have got on well and there's nothing you can do about it.'

She dived under the water and then went into a brisk crawl. What with temper and swimming beyond her strength she was breathless when they reached the shore again; it was annoying that Marius was breathing as easily as though he had just got out of a chair. He caught her by the hand at the water's edge. 'Since I am to marry into the family,' he said silkily, 'allow me to tell you that I shall do exactly as I wish to do. You talk wildly, dear girl, and that's not your usual form.'

She pulled away from him and ran away to change, and when she got back it was time to return to Veere. She hardly spoke to him on the way back and when she did he blandly ignored her curtness so that she derived little or no satisfaction from it.

She was in the little walled garden, hanging out the bathing kit in the sunshine when he joined her. 'I'm off,' he said cheerfully. 'Enjoy your afternoon's shopping. There's something I want to give you before you go.'

Tabitha adjusted her bikini top to a nicety on the line. 'What's that?' she wanted to know coldly, and turned round to be caught and kissed soundly.

'Why, a brotherly kiss, dear girl,' said Marius. He held her for a moment longer, staring down at her with twinkling eyes, then deliberately bent his head and kissed her again. He had gone before she had time to get her breath. She went slowly indoors and up to her room to tidy herself for lunch. If that was brotherly behaviour then the quicker she uprooted herself and went to live somewhere inaccessible, like the Highlands of Scotland or a remote part of Wales, where even a Bentley wouldn't reach her all that easily, the better for her peace of mind. Not that he was likely to come after her; Lilith would see to that. She sat combing her hair, wondering where he and

Lilith would live, for she couldn't imagine her stepsister in
Veere. Even if Lilith actually fell in love with Marius she
would still want her own way.

Tabitha flung down her brush and went downstairs to Mr
Bow's room where she knocked and asked if he needed anything. It was purely a rhetorical question, for he was sitting in
great comfort with *The Times* on his lap and a pile of books
as well as a drink on the table beside him. He looked up briefly,
said 'No, my dear,' and then because he was a discerning old
man and Tabitha looked unhappy, went on: 'Come in and keep
me company for a few minutes.'

Tabitha sat down opposite him and looked out of the window
just in time to see the Bentley purr past; Lilith sat beside Marius, Mrs Crawley was in the back. Mr Bow saw them too. By
way of opening the conversation he said: 'Well, well, there
they go.'

Tabitha began to tour the room in a restless way, looking at
pictures and fingering the trifles of silver and china lying
around. Finally she burst out, not really meaning to say it: 'I
suppose when Marius marries he'll live here.'

If Mr Bow found her remark unexpected he made no mention of the fact.

'I imagine so. It is his home, he would choose to be here
for most of the year, I should think.'

Tabitha dumped a small Sèvres dish back on to a side table
with a decided thump. 'Most of the year? Where else should
he go?'

Mr Bow allowed himself a smile behind his magnificent
whiskers. 'Well, he has a flat in Rotterdam because of his work
there, but probably if he had a wife and children here he would
commute…but I would suppose he might have some sort of
residence in England. He's over there frequently, you know,
and with hotels the price they are…' he shook his head and
tut-tutted about the hotels. 'No, Marius would make a home
there too. He has, as you may have observed, my dear Tabitha,
no need to practise economy.'

Tabitha said nothing to this; she was examining a mezzotint
of the house, a charming thing. Mr Bow went on gently: 'Mar-

ius has waited a long time to marry, probably he has been too busy to fall for—er—female blandishments. Now of course he is established in his own field. I daresay he will settle down.'

Tabitha turned her back on the mezzotint and came and stood in front of Mr Bow. Her voice was fierce. 'You really think that?'

'That is my considered opinion, my dear young lady, although I speak only for myself. Perhaps you have your own ideas?'

'Yes,' said Tabitha a trifle wildly, 'I have. I—I think I'll take Smith for a walk before lunch—there's still ten minutes or so, isn't there?'

She was at the door when Mr Bow murmured: 'Marius won't make the mistake of marrying the wrong girl, you know.'

Tabitha thought about that as she and Smith sauntered along the harbour. Because of course, however much Mr Bow and she herself considered Lilith to be the wrong girl for Marius, what difference would it make if he, for his part, thought her the right one?

The afternoon in Bergen-op-Zoom was pleasant, with Hans to look after Mr Bow and Bill Raynard while the two girls went shopping. They got back in the early evening and there was no sign of Marius—indeed, he didn't appear until a few minutes before dinner when he looked in briefly as he passed the sitting room before going to the kitchen to talk to Hans at some length. And when he joined them it was to enter at once into their talk without giving one single inkling as to where he had been or what he had done.

Dinner was gay, almost as though there was something to celebrate, which probably there was, thought Tabitha, being gayer than anyone else, and after dinner they crowded into the Bentley and drove over to Domburg for drinks at the Dolphijn restaurant and talked about everything under the sun except Lilith and Mrs Crawley, who weren't mentioned. Tabitha, peeping at Marius from her seat beside Mr Raynard, came to the conclusion that under the bland façade of his handsome face, he was excited. About Lilith, of course, but why hadn't she been invited to join them? Tabitha remembered that he had told her that he would invite Lilith and her stepmother in for drinks, and here they were in Domburg. She said across the little table between them: 'I thought you were going to ask Lilith…'

He cut in smoothly: 'They have to pack. They preferred to come for coffee tomorrow morning before they leave.' He half smiled at her and turned away, making it impossible to ask any more questions.

They went to bed much later than usual. Tabitha, on her way to Muriel's room with some shopping she had taken to her own room by mistake, was surprised to meet Marius on the lower landing, on the point of going into Mr Bow's room. She stopped short, forgetful of flying hair and a hastily thrown on dressing gown, and whispered: 'You're not going in? You don't mind me saying so, but Mr Bow was very tired when I helped him to bed—don't you think he might be asleep?'

'No,' Marius sounded amused. 'He's expecting me. We've— er—things to discuss.'

Tabitha pinkened. 'I'm sorry, it's not my business, only I thought…'

He nodded and the corner of his mouth twitched. 'Yes, Tabby. Now run along before I forget myself.'

She said good night rather huffily; he need not have been quite so high-handed; she was, after all, a nurse and her duties, however light, surely included seeing that Mr Bow had a good night's rest. She crossed the landing and tapped at Muriel's door and as she went in looked back at Marius. He had made no attempt to go into Knotty's room; he was still standing where she had left him, watching her. She tossed her head and went in to give Muriel her parcel.

'They're up to something,' Muriel confided. 'Bill's still downstairs—says Marius will help him up to Mr Bow's room to have a little chat.' She snorted delicately. 'What about, I wonder?' She looked enquiringly at Tabitha who said she had no idea and after a few more words went away to bed. As she crossed the landing she could hear a steady murmur of voices coming from Mr Bow's room.

Marius appeared at breakfast dressed quite obviously for

something other than a sailing trip. Tabitha, eyeing his well tailored elegance covertly as he took his seat at the table, could well understand that any woman would be glad to have him for an escort. She buttered a finger of toast and then sat with it arrested in mid-air; he was going to drive Lilith and her stepmother to Schipol. Why hadn't she thought of that before, for was it not the most natural thing in the world that he should want to see as much of Lilith as possible? She found herself wishing that her own holiday was over; Marius must be wishing that he was leaving with Lilith...

'Daydreaming again,' remarked Mr Raynard grumpily. 'Here am I begging for butter and all you can do is to stare before you like Lady Macbeth!'

Tabitha begged his pardon, passed the butter and went on with her own breakfast, and presently found herself walking to the post office with Mr Bow, who, as usual, had a great many letters to post.

She said, for something to say: 'I've never met anyone like you—you write letters every day.'

'Yes,' said Mr Bow happily, 'I have written to everyone in the ward as well as to Mr Steele.'

She looked at him with admiration. She had written a great many postcards herself, with a well-tried phrase scribbled on each. 'They'll enjoy them. I had a letter from Sue—the theatre sister, you know—she says the ward is almost ready.'

'Yes—I shall miss my companions there, and you, Tabitha, though I hear that I am to come back into your care for a few days while they do a check-up on my leg.'

Tabitha said worriedly: 'That reminds me—have you somewhere to go? I'm sure I...'

Mr Bow patted her brown arm. 'How kind you are, Tabitha. Marius has my future in his very capable hands, though I shall add that I am free to do exactly as I wish.'

Tabitha put the letters in the box. 'Will you come and live here?'

He became vague. 'Probably, but not, I imagine, permanently. It depends on several factors; nothing can be finally decided until Marius's own future is...'

Tabitha shot the last letter in. 'Oh, yes,' she said quickly because she didn't want to know about Marius's future, not then at any rate. 'Let's go back, shall we, or he'll wonder what's become of us.'

Mr Bow was suddenly meek. 'Why, of course—have we time to go back past those delightful little houses behind the Town Hall?'

She knew the ones he meant, she loved them too; they wandered the short distance, pausing to rest every now and then so that by the time they got back to the house Mrs Crawley and Lilith had already arrived. Everyone was in the sitting room and Marius got up and came to apologise because they had already started their coffee without them. 'We decided to go to Middelburg first,' he explained, 'so we must leave earlier than we had planned.'

Tabitha made a suitable little muttering sound which her hearer could interpret as he wished and went to speak to her stepmother, who listened graciously to her wishes that they would have a pleasant journey and then remarked with the little smile Tabitha so hated:

'I daresay it will be very tedious, but at least Marius will be with us most of the time. Lilith wanted him to come all the way with us, but I advised her not to ask him, for I daresay the rest of you would have objected.' She gave Tabitha an appraisal, half mocking, half scornful. 'Though heaven knows he must be bored with you all by now.' She added with gentle venom: 'Your skin's like old leather, Tabitha—and your hair...you look plainer than ever!'

Tabitha got to her feet. 'I daresay I do—you should be thankful; think what a menace I should be to Lilith if I were pretty.'

She didn't wait to see the effect of her words but moved across the room to where Muriel was sitting. She was so angry that she was trembling a little and her eyes, usually so calm and soft, held a fine sparkle. She put down her coffee cup with a hand which still shook a little and prepared to sit down, to be frustrated by Lilith, who got up from her chair by Marius with the request that Tabitha should take her upstairs to her room so that she might tidy herself, and there was nothing to do but accede to her wish, although it was apparent to Tabitha that Lilith, who looked as much in need of tidying as the front page of *Vogue,* had some other purpose in wishing to get her on her own.

She was right. The bedroom door was scarcely shut behind them when Lilith remarked: 'What a dull lot you are, and how bored Marius must be. I'm glad we came to cheer him up, though we didn't see as much of him as I'd hoped, but of course he kept on fussing about being with his guests. I must say his manners are delightful,' she cast a sideways glance at Tabitha who had gone to look out of the window, 'but you never know what he's thinking, do you—all that charm. I wonder what's behind it? Not that it matters to you.' She gave a triumphant chortle. 'I think I've got him hooked.'

Tabitha didn't turn round. 'How vulgar you are, Lilith,' she said quietly, while her heart raced happily; so Marius hadn't asked Lilith to marry him yet; she wondered why not, and got her answer.

'What a fool you are, Tabby! I've been rather clever, you know. It only needs a little more encouragement from me…but first I want to know more about him. He's—well, vague. He won't talk about himself, only about this dreary little town— I'm damned if I'll live in such a poky hole.'

'Veere is a very lovely place,' Tabitha said hotly, and Lilith laughed again. 'As beautiful as Chidlake? I thought that was the only place worth living in? Don't tell me you've fallen for this potty little town.' She stopped speaking and came and stood by Tabitha. 'Or,' she said slowly, 'perhaps it's Marius you've fallen for?'

Tabitha had expected that. She answered composedly: 'Mr van Beek is a very kind host and I admire him as a surgeon.'

'Oh, pooh,' exclaimed Lilith, 'don't you ever think of anything else but your beastly work? What a dead bore you are!'

She strolled back to the mirror and did things to her already perfectly arranged hair. 'I must say you've done very well for yourself—a cushy holiday with almost nothing to do and this gorgeous room—it's better than mine was at the hotel. Mother said you were going to be a kind of mother's help.' She looked

around her and added spitefully: 'Well, you'll miss it all when
you get back, won't you?'

Tabitha shrugged her shoulders. 'Will you be at home for
the rest of the summer?' she asked, not because she wanted to
know, but it made something to say and Lilith seemed in no
hurry to go downstairs yet.

'Stay at Chidlake? You must be joking! We're off to London.' She paused, her eyes slid away from Tabitha's 'I can't
remember. We're going to Paris too. After that we have to wait
and see.' She jumped to her feet and Tabitha opened the door
thankfully.

'There's one thing for sure,' said Lilith as she went past her.
'Don't expect to be the bridesmaid.'

They went a few minutes later and it was while the farewells
were being made that Marius came and stood by Tabitha, waiting by the door.

'What did your stepmother say to you just now?' he wanted
to know. 'You looked in a fine rage, the place practically burst
into flames.' He frowned. 'And what secrets did Lilith tell you
upstairs?'

She didn't smile. 'It's of no possible interest to you what
my stepmother said, and Lilith has never told me a secret in
her life; she isn't likely to now.'

She thought he looked relieved, though his voice was silky.
'I'm glad of that, but make no mistake, Tabitha, it is of interest
to me. Perhaps you will feel like telling me when I get back.'

Tabitha's temper plucked at her tongue, making it reckless.
'I shall not. In any case, I daresay we shall all be in bed, and
asleep by the time you're home.' She turned on her heel, then
paused to say through her teeth: 'I hope you have a lovely
day,' and was furious when he laughed.

He was back before tea. They were all at the harbour's edge
watching a rather splendid Norwegian yacht edging its way out
into the lake, and it was Tabitha who turned at the soft sigh of
the Bentley stopping behind them. She stared at Marius's face
as he got out of the car to try and read from it how his day
had gone and he returned her look placidly, seeming neither
elated nor cast down. He said: 'Hullo there, how nice to be

back. Schipol is a miracle of modern planning; it is also no place to be in if you happen to want peace and quiet. Have you had tea? If not, I'll be with you in five minutes.'

He was back with half a minute to spare, sitting in his great armchair.

'What shall we do with our evening?' he wanted to know. 'I feel guilty leaving you all day as I did.' He smiled round at them all, looking not in the least guilty but rather very pleased with himself, and, thought Tabitha, studying his face, he was keeping it to himself. He glanced up before she could look away. 'Tabby, I've a message for you—your stepmother asked me to tell you that they intend to be away for several weeks and there will be no point in you going to Chidlake until they return.'

Tabitha's thanks were a little bewildered, for her stepmother had never before bothered to send her messages, good or bad; it was almost as though they didn't want her at Chidlake... She made a strong resolve there and then that just as soon as she could, she would drive over to her home and see for herself. Even if Lilith and her stepmother were going away, there was no reason why she shouldn't go there for her days off. She had in fact done so on several occasions, for it was, when all was said and done, her home. She contradicted herself. It was only her home by courtesy of her stepmother—she had no more claim to it than anyone else now.

She came out of her brown study to find Marius's eyes on her again, and this time the look was guarded and thoughtful, almost as though he had guessed her thoughts. For no reason at all she went pink and when his mouth twitched in a faint, mocking smile, the pink deepened into red just as though she were guilty of something or other. She lifted her chin and turned to Mr Raynard beside her, to plunge into a series of questions about his children, which he, being a kindhearted man and seeing her hot cheeks, answered with a tremendous wealth of detail.

They decided not to go out that evening, instead Marius suggested that he might ask a few friends in for drinks after dinner, an idea which everyone acclaimed, especially Tabitha and Mu-

riel who saw a chance to wear their new dresses and did so
with startling success, even provoking Bill Raynard to say:
'Well, I must say, Tabby, I've always thought you looked very
neat and tidy in uniform, but you'll never be the same again
now, however tight you pull back your hair and starch your
aprons. Marius, what do you think?'

Marius put his glass down and his hands in his pockets. He
spoke mildly.

'But Tabitha isn't going to pull her hair back any more, are
you, my girl? Though I know what you mean, Bill.' His eyes
twinkled although he wasn't laughing. 'Cinderella's ball gown
did the same for her, I believe.'

Everyone laughed and Tabitha with them because it would
have looked silly if she hadn't, and they had a rather noisy
dinner because, for some reason, they all felt lighthearted.

The guests came about nine o'clock. Tabitha had expected
half a dozen of the worthier citizens of the little town, and true
enough, the *burgemeester* and the *dominee* were the first to
arrive with their wives, quickly followed by a sprinkling of
lawyers, doctors and several members of the yacht club, but
these were augmented by several younger married couples from
further afield until the room was full of gay and, as Tabitha
couldn't help see for herself, very well-dressed people. She felt
glad she had on the new dress and began to enjoy herself.

The party broke up about midnight and Tabitha, helping Mr
Bow to bed, had to admit that it had been great fun. She said
so to him now and added:

'I've put your water and glasses and book on the table, but
you won't need a sleeping pill tonight.' His bewhiskered face
looked tired against the pillows; she dropped a kiss on his
cheek and said: 'I'll peep in on my way up in a few minutes,'
and went downstairs. Muriel and Bill were on the point of
going up to their room, but Marius said: 'Unless you're very
sleepy, Tabitha, stay a minute—I haven't seen you the whole
evening.'

She didn't answer but stood rather self-consciously by the
door until Marius said in a voice so unlike his usual mild tones
that she stared:

'For heaven's sake sit!' and before she could do more than feel surprise at his brusque tone, he asked: 'What do you think of my friends?'

That surprised her too, for her mind had been running on Lilith. She said, stammering a little: 'Very nice,' and added idiotically: 'They're all married.'

Marius's eyebrows rose slowly. 'This part of Holland is hardly a hotbed of permissive society,' he observed blandly, and Tabitha frowned and said shortly: 'That isn't at all what I meant—they're all married with children, or all those I spoke to were, and you…you're still a bachelor.'

She was affronted when he burst out laughing and then suddenly unhappy when he said softly: 'Yes, I am, but not for long now.'

She wondered if she should congratulate him or just murmur politely. She had decided on the murmur when he disconcerted her by saying: 'I like your outfit—very dashing and with it. Do you know you've turned into a very attractive woman, Tabitha?'

She got to her feet. The conversation was getting them nowhere.

'Look at me, Marius,' she said flatly, 'and I mean a proper look—not just a kind one, for I know you are kind and you've done all you can to make me believe that I'm not a plain girl,' her voice rose, 'but what is the use? Why did you do it? Look at my face…'

Marius had been tossing a paperweight up and down like a marble; even in her misery she hoped he wouldn't drop it; she had admired it several times, it was a *millefiori* and probably very valuable. She caught her breath as he caught it for the last time and then looked at her. 'I am looking, Tabitha,' he smiled with a hint of mockery. 'I've been looking for a long time.' He sent the paperweight spinning again. 'Go to bed,' he said, his voice suddenly harsh. 'Good night.'

She tried to make sense of the conversation before she went to sleep, but perhaps she was too tired, for she couldn't think rationally and the urge to have a good cry was very great. She blew her sensible little nose with determination and closed her eyes firmly on the tears.

# CHAPTER EIGHT

THE MIRACULOUS weather still held the next morning. Tabitha drank the tea Anneke brought her, laboriously trying out her few words of Dutch on the obliging girl as she did so, and then got up, not wishing to miss a moment of the last two days of the holiday. She was early, but Marius was even earlier; they met in the hall and he greeted her with a cheerful 'Hullo, Tabby, if you've nothing better to do, come into the study—you can browse around the bookshelves while I do some telephoning.'

The little room was cool and quiet and the bookshelves definitely worth exploring. She wandered to and fro dipping into the catholic collection while she half listened to Marius making a succession of calls, all in Dutch. Presently he said; 'Now the letters—you're not bored?'

She looked up from an old copy of *Jane's Fighting Ships* and shook her head, hoping that the letters would take a long time because she was enjoying herself. But they only took fifteen minutes or so, because he dictated them into a Dictaphone she hadn't noticed on his desk. When he had finished, she asked:

'Who types your letters?'

'My secretary—she's on holiday because I am, but she'll be in some time today to deal with these. I couldn't manage without her—she's efficient and quiet, besides, she deals with bills and so forth as well as making appointments.'

Tabitha abandoned her book. 'Do you see your patients here, then?'

'Some. I've rooms in Rotterdam and Middelburg where I see private patients and then I see the *Ziekenfonds* patients in hospital.'

'Every day?'

'Twice a week. I lecture as well.'

179

'But you don't live in Rotterdam?'

'No. Occasionally I spend a night there, but I prefer to go to and fro with the car.'

Tabitha nodded in agreement. 'So would I if I were coming back here each evening. But isn't it a long way?'

He shrugged. 'Sixty odd miles, but the roads are good—it doesn't take me much over an hour.' He smiled and she smiled back because just for that brief while she was happy sitting there quietly with him, and he seemed to be enjoying it too. Even as she thought it he got up from his desk. 'What shall we do today?' he asked.

She didn't answer but said instead: 'There are only two days left,' and walked through the house with him and out of the street door into the sunshine where there was already a cheerful bustle among the boats in the harbour as well as the clatter of the milkman and the postman and the man with a cartload of fruit and vegetables going slowly down the street, to stop each time a housewife appeared at her door. He shouted at Marius as he passed and then pulled up his elderly horse.

'He's offering you a pear, he says he's got some nice ones,' said Marius. 'Go and help yourself.'

'I haven't any money.' She looked at him doubtfully and he said, half-laughing: 'Don't worry about that—Hans is one of his best customers.' But he walked over to the cart with her and waited while the greengrocer chose her the fruit and said something which made the man laugh very much. She had no idea what it was—she bit into her pear and was content.

Muriel joined them shortly afterwards and Tabitha went indoors to see how Mr Bow was getting on with his dressing and investigate the muffled roars coming from Mr Raynard's room, due to the fact that he had mislaid his glasses.

By mutual consent the whole party voted for a day's sailing from which they returned so gloriously tired that drinks at the yacht clubhouse and Hans's excellent dinner, followed by the most desultory conversation, was all that was required to round off a perfect day. It was the same on the following day too, although they returned a little earlier so that they could pack ready for an early start in the morning, and after dinner a few of Marius's friends came in for a drink and to wish them a good trip home, but they didn't stay late and by eleven o'clock Tabitha had Mr Bow tucked up and half asleep in his bed and was on her way downstairs again to wish the others good night, only to find that the Raynards had already gone upstairs and Marius alone in the sitting room. She stood just inside the doorway, trying over a few graceful phrases in her head which would get her upstairs again, when Hans came to call him to the telephone, and she was left alone. It seemed rude to go to bed without saying good night; she waited patiently while the old-fashioned Zaansche clock on the wall ticked away five minutes. Probably he had forgotten she was there. But he hadn't, she had got as far as the arch at the bottom of the stairs when he joined her.

'I see I'm just in time,' he observed mildly. 'I should have asked you to wait.' He opened a cupboard door in the wall and dragged out a thick sweater. 'Put this round your shoulders— it's chilly—and come up to the end of the harbour for a last look at the lake.' They were at the door when he asked as an afterthought: 'You'd like to come?'

'Yes, thank you,' said Tabitha politely, who could think of nothing nicer. She draped the thick wool round her, as it was indeed cool, for it was the last day of August and the evenings were shortening, although the sky was still the deep violet of summer and there were more stars than she could hope to count.

'This time tomorrow we shall be in England,' she said as they leaned over the wall by the hotel to watch the quiet water. Marius flung an arm round her shoulders.

'England in autumn is delightful—I'm looking forward to it.' And Tabitha, hardly sharing his views, made shift to murmur something and was taken aback when he said blandly: 'You don't sound enthusiastic.'

What was the good of telling him she wasn't? And what had she to be enthusiastic about anyway? The ward, the endless broken bones, nurses to train, the constant forays to various departments in search of something needed for the ward and which no one wanted her to have...she loved her work, but at the moment it seemed singularly unattractive.

He said still blandly: 'You haven't answered.'

'No, well—I expect we're thinking of different things, don't you?'

He took his arm from her shoulder and tucked a hand under her elbow and turned for home. 'I'm quite sure we are.' He sounded amused.

The return home went without a hitch, but as everything Marius arranged went smoothly, this wasn't surprising. It was still early evening when they dropped the Raynards off at their house on the outskirts of the city. Tabitha and Mr Bow waited in the Bentley while Marius went to help with their luggage and give Mr Raynard what help he required to get into his house, and Muriel had run back to wish them goodbye and to promise a meeting as soon as it could be arranged. Ten minutes later Marius drew up in front of Tabitha's flat. The end of the journey, she thought, and of a lovely holiday and, with reservations, of the happiest days of my life. She put her hand on the door to open it and it was instantly covered by Marius's own hand. 'No, wait,' he said, 'let me make sure Meg's there first.'

Of course Meg was there, bustling to the door with cries of welcome. He went back to the car and helped Tabitha out and when she asked him if he and Mr Bow would like to come in for a cup of coffee, said yes, of course, in the tone of voice of someone who had expected the invitation, anyway.

'Go on in to Meg,' he advised. 'I'll see to Knotty and your case.'

The flat looked very small after the house in Veere, but it was lovely to fling herself at Meg to hug her and be hugged.

'There's a brown girl,' said Meg with satisfaction. 'My word, how well you look, love!' Her sharp eyes went past Tabitha to study Marius and Mr Bow. 'And the two gentlemen—very content and pleased with themselves they look.'

Tabitha turned round to have a look too. Meg was right; they had the look of men who had planned something which had turned out to be more successful than they had imagined it would. She couldn't think what. She said vaguely: 'We had a lovely time, Meg. Where's Podger?'

Podger came at a sedate trot to greet Mr Bow and sit on his knee while they drank their coffee, and then, at Meg's earnest invitation, ate the sandwiches she offered. And all the time they talked; there was so much to tell and mull over, more than two hours had passed when Marius got to his feet, declaring it was time they all went to bed. Tabitha wondered where he and Mr Bow intended to spend the night, and longed to ask. Instead she thanked him nicely for her holiday, reminded Mr Bow that she would be seeing him in a couple of days, and wished them both good night. If she had hoped that Marius would have anything to say to her, she refused to admit it, her face was calmly friendly as she waved them goodbye—a calm engendered by a hopelessness which she was careful to hide from Meg as they cleared up the coffee cups and got ready for bed. The holiday was over, she couldn't expect Marius to be more than casually friendly in the future; she had made it plain to him that nothing he could do would make her and Lilith like each other, and naturally it would be Lilith he wanted to please—and that meant cold-shouldering her.

She woke in the night and for a few blissful moments, imagined that she was still in Veere and as it was impossible to sleep again, she lay remembering. 'At least I have memories,' she said out loud to Podger, who being sleepy, took no notice at all. But she dismissed the memories in the morning and set herself to entertain Meg with all the details of her stay in Holland and then, because Meg had been having a rather lonely time of it, she drove her down to Torquay, where they had lunch and a pleasant stroll along the sea-front. Meg enjoyed herself enormously, but its bustling holiday atmosphere merely served to make Tabitha sick with longing for Veere again.

The ward, on Monday morning, looked unfamiliar in its fresh coat of paint and the gay new curtains. The patients looked unfamiliar too, excepting for Mr Prosser, who had suffered an infection which had set him back a few weeks. He hailed Tabitha with his usual good humour, however, declared that she looked prettier than ever and wanted to know if she had drowned anyone sailing.

'Good gracious, no,' said Tabitha cheerfully. 'I'm far too good at it.'

'You brought our Dutchman back with yer, Sister?'

She said with dignity: 'Mr van Beek returned with us, yes. Mr Bow too, he's coming in tomorrow for a check-up and to have his plaster off.'

'And the boss—'ow's 'e? Can't think 'ow 'e managed with that great plaster round 'is knee. Sailin', I mean.'

'You'd be surprised!' Tabitha spoke with some feeling, remembering Mr Raynard's activities on board. 'He'll be back very soon now.' She smiled at him very kindly because he had been in hospital a long time and never grumbled. 'Not long now, Mr Prosser, before you're home again.'

He beamed at her. 'Yes, and won't I be glad? Not that you've not been tops, ducks, you and the nurses, but I've 'ad enough 'ospital ter last me. Can't think 'ow yer stand it year after year.'

Tabitha wondered too as she walked away, to bump into George Steele at the ward door. He said with genuine pleasure:

'Tabby, how nice to see you again! We've missed you—no coffee after the round and no cups of tea when we're exhausted.'

'Well, if that's all you missed me for—tea and coffee—the very idea! I might just as well be working for British Railways.'

He laughed. 'Well, can we sample the coffee now while we go over the patients?'

They sat in her office and pored over charts and notes until the coffee arrived. 'Now tell me about your holiday,' he demanded.

Tabitha sipped her Nescafé, so different from Hans's great enamel pot in the kitchen at Veere. 'It was lovely. We went sailing every day—well, nearly every day, and Mr Bow is almost fit again and Mr Raynard can't wait to start work.'

'And van Beek?'

She choked a little. 'He's fine—he's coming back for a few days.'

George eyed her over his mug. 'Yes, I know that—he telephoned me. What else did you do?'

'Well, we sailed and swam and—and talked and did some shopping.'

'What, no dancing and dining by candlelight…' He was interrupted by Mrs Jeffs, who put her head round the door and said in a conspirator's whisper: 'He's in the ward, Sister—he came in through the balcony door.'

'Who?' asked Tabitha, knowing very well.

'Why, Mr van Beek, Sister.' Mrs Jeffs looked a little put out and then broke into a rich chuckle as her head disappeared and Marius came in. He said hullo to them both in a placid voice and then turned to Tabitha.

'How does it feel to be back?' he wanted to know. He eyed the coffee pot. 'I see your staff are already mothering you very nicely.'

'Me!' Tabitha sounded indignant as Mrs Jeffs came in with another mug. 'You're the one who's being mothered!'

'And quite right too.' He disposed his length cautiously on the small wooden chair and added amiably: 'I'm a bachelor with no one to look after me.'

'How about Hans?'

'Hans? A first-class chauffeur, a splendid cook and a wonderful way with children, but I fear he would make a poor wife.'

They all laughed and Tabitha observed: 'But he would have made a splendid husband.'

Marius helped himself to sugar. 'Hans has been married. His wife was killed when Rotterdam was bombed in 1940. She was twenty and they had been married just over one year.'

Tabitha put down her cup. 'Oh, poor Hans—I wish I'd known.'

Marius asked: 'Do you mind if we smoke?' and when she shook her head the two men set about the ritual of pipe filling. When they were nicely wreathed in smoke, Marius asked: 'Why?'

Tabitha hesitated. 'Well, I like Hans, I should have liked to have heard about his wife…'

Marius nodded. 'Probably he'll tell you, he likes you too. He'll be coming over shortly for a quick visit—he won't stay long because of Smith.'

Tabitha wondered why Hans should come to England. 'Will you ask him to come and see me when he does?'

Marius said: 'Yes, of course.' His voice was non-committal and he wasn't smiling, and yet she formed the impression that he was laughing. There was no way of finding out, for he had put down his cup and turned to George, who had been sitting quietly watching them; making no attempt to join in their talk, almost as though he guessed that they had forgotten that he was there.

'Shall we do a quick round, George?' They all stood up and as Tabitha went ahead of them through the door he said: 'I'd like to get away before twelve if I can—I've promised to be at Chidlake for lunch.'

They did the round with ten minutes to spare, and Tabitha, her tanned face serious and withdrawn, did everything she should have done with her usual deftness and good sense, although the fact that she produced the right forms at the right times and handed the correct charts and turned back the right bedclothes was due solely to her excellent training and years of usage, for her mind was on other things. Marius was wasting no time in going to Chidlake; she allowed her imagination to run riot as they went from bed to bed while she made notes of Marius's wishes and held up X-rays for his inspection. It was at the finish of the round, as the men were leaving that Marius asked softly: 'And where were you all this while, Tabitha?'

She gave him a quick look, in case he was joking. He wasn't. 'I was here.' Her voice sounded small.

'So you were,' he agreed blandly, 'but your thoughts were a long way off?'

She looked guilty. 'Oh—did I miss something?'

He shook his head. 'Shall I give your love to your stepmother and Lilith?'

'Yes, please,' and then: 'No, not my love, just—just say I hope they had a good journey back.'

He nodded and put a hand on the patient George's shoulder. He said formally: 'Goodbye, Sister, and thank you.' The men turned away and he went on: 'George, Mr Bow is coming back for a check-up. Can I leave you to deal with him?'

They walked away, deep in talk, and she went back into the ward to help tidy the beds for Matron's round.

There was a heavy list the next day; she didn't see Marius until late in the afternoon after the last case had come back from theatre. His visit was brief—to see his cases and to make sure that they were satisfactory. He looked tired and said nothing at all to Tabitha beyond an absent-minded good evening. And the following day when he came he brought Mr Raynard with him, with his stick and his stiff leg and a tongue which to Tabby's ears sounded sharper than ever. He didn't like the curtains for a start, nor the colour of the paint; she was afraid that he would declare that he didn't like the patients either, but luckily his attention was diverted by the sight of Mr Bow, looking unnaturally brown amongst all the white faces and without his plaster. He drew up a chair and sat down to talk with the old gentleman, which improved his temper so much that he grudgingly admitted that perhaps the curtains weren't so bad after all. 'And what the hell is Prosser doing here?' he demanded of Tabitha, who happened to be nearest to him.

She explained calmly and he heard her out and then declared grumpily:

'She's a different girl, isn't she, Marius? So prim and efficient, just as though she'd never worn a bikini in her life.'

Tabitha, a little red in the face, looked round at the patients to make sure none of them had heard this outrageous remark. Apparently not. She observed patiently: 'Look, sir, I can't do a round in a bikini.'

Mr Raynard laughed, his humour quite restored. 'A different girl, though. Eh, Marius?'

'No,' said Marius deliberately, 'exactly the same girl.' He smiled at Tabitha—he hadn't smiled like that since they were in Veere. She looked away quickly, aware of her heart pound-

ing beneath her starched apron. It was later in the day, when
they had gone, that she remembered that Marius had been to
Chidlake to lunch, yet she herself had received that message
not to go there because they would be away. She frowned over
it and then in a little rush of work, forgot it.

She remembered it the next day when George casually men-
tioned that he would be on call for the next couple of days.
Tabitha frowned. 'But you can't be, George,' she exclaimed.
'Mr van Beek's down on the list in the office.'

'I know, but he wants to be free to go over to Chidlake.'

'But the house is empty—I had a message.'

'Don't know anything about it,' said George comfortably,
and with that useless remark she had to be content, though she
resolved then and there to go to Chidlake at the first opportunity.

There was no opportunity. Marius only operated twice in the
week, but his lists were formidable; he was going back to Holland for a few days in a week's time; he seemed intent on
cramming in as much work as possible. She had already put
off one free day and when Marius stopped for a rare word with
her and remarked that she really ought not to work every day
without a break, her temper flared.

'Chance would be a fine thing,' she declared roundly. 'Just
how do I take a day off when Staff is off with a sore throat?'

'You told me not half an hour ago that she would be back
on duty tomorrow.'

Tabitha fixed him with a smouldering eye. 'And I shall take
a day off,' she snapped.

Marius put down the X-ray film he had been studying.
'Good. What will you do?'

'I shall go to Chidlake.' She hadn't meant to tell him, and
now she frowned with vexation.

He said casually: 'Must you? I want to go up to Umberleigh,' he didn't say why, 'and I thought you might like to
come along for the ride. I'm going to Holland next week, and
taking Knotty with me, by the way. You could go to Chidlake
then, couldn't you?'

Tabitha hesitated. It was quite true, she could just as easily go the following week, and the prospect of a few hours in his company far outweighed the urgency of going to Chidlake. She said finally:

'Well, all right. That would be nice, and as you say, I can just as easily go home next week. I can go on Tuesday, for there won't be any theatre cases, will there?' She sighed, remembering he wouldn't be there on Tuesday. 'I can drive over then.'

Marius said casually: 'Why not?' as he added the X-ray film to the others on the desk. 'I'll come for you about eleven, if that suits you. Now how about some coffee, and do you think you could get George down again? I think we had better put our heads together about Prosser.'

Tabitha wakened the next day to a sky covered by thick grey clouds jostling each other around on the wind. Probably it would rain; she put on a plainly cut peach-coloured linen dress and covered it with a raincoat, as Marius hadn't said what they were going to do. She might as well go prepared for a tramp over Exmoor; she added flat suede shoes and tucked a head-scarf in her pocket, just in case that was what he had in mind. As she did so the thought crossed her mind that it should have been Lilith who was going with him, but perhaps she was already in Paris, leaving him at a loose end. It was a pity that her own outings with Marius were confined to those occasions when there was no one else to bear him company. She voiced this opinion aloud to Meg, who looked shocked and said in an admonitory tone: 'Now, Miss Tabby, that's no way to talk about a nice gentleman like Mr van Beek, for there's no need for him to take you out. He's that handsome and well-to-do I daresay he could have any girl for the asking. You be glad he wants you for a friend, like I said before.' She shook her head quite fiercely. 'There's the door now—that'll be him. There's a nice cup of coffee waiting, so bring him straight in, Miss Tabby.'

Marius seemed in no great hurry to get to Umberleigh, for once they were through Crediton, he turned off through Winkleigh and took to the byroads, winding round the country until

Tabitha, who knew that part of the world well enough, enquired if he were lost.

He glanced at her and smiled. 'No. How would you like to try out the car?'

She sat up straight. 'Me? Drive your car? I've never even sat in a Bentley before I met you!'

'That's no reason for not driving it. Are you scared?'

'Stop,' said Tabitha in a goaded voice; she was already undoing her safety belt. 'I'll drive your car. If I smash it up I hope you won't expect me to buy you another.'

He laughed and drew into the side of the road and they changed places. She found the Bentley surprisingly easy to drive and after the first few nervous moments she found she could handle the big car well enough. Marius let her drive several miles before he remarked: 'Very nice. You use your head, Tabby—I should have no hesitation in going to sleep while you drove.'

High praise indeed; she accelerated slightly out of pure pleasure, although her voice was meek enough as she asked which way they should go.

They were at a crossroads; without hesitation Marius said: 'Go through Burrington and then take the Chittlehampton road—I thought we'd lunch there.'

The High Bullen inn was noted for its good food; they ate *truites flambés au Pernod,* lamb Shrewsbury and *Pêche Melba* with a good claret to wash them down, while they talked of a great many things, but never once of Lilith, although Tabitha tried her hardest to bring the conversation round to this interesting subject. But each time Marius frustrated her because, she suspected, he had no intention of allowing her to ask any questions of a personal nature, although he seemed ready enough to talk about his life in Holland and his friends, even his boyhood, something which he had never enlarged upon before. It was after two o'clock when he said reluctantly:

'I suppose we had better get on—I'm going to see an old patient of mine who lives near Umberleigh. I haven't seen her for some time—you won't mind if we stay a little while?'

'No, of course not, but will your patient mind?'

They were running smoothly along a high-hedged lane. 'I told her that you would be with me,' his tone was casual. 'I thought you might like to see the garden, it's rather nice.'

The understatement of the year, thought Tabitha as he turned the Bentley through lodge gates and drove without haste across a miniature park.

'Capability Brown?' she enquired.

'I believe so. He had a great eye for landscaping, didn't he?'

They ran through a tunnel of rhododendrons and out into a wide sweep of drive before a stone-fronted house of some size. It had an elegant backing of trees and a gate at one side leading to the garden Marius had mentioned. The surroundings were beautiful even under the still stormy sky. They got out of the car and Tabitha said: 'How heavenly! Shall I go into the garden while you see your patient?'

Marius smiled a little. 'I think my patient would like to meet you—this isn't a wholly professional visit, you know. We're good friends too.'

They were admitted by an elderly maid, dressed very correctly in her black and white uniform, and conducted across a vast entrance hall to an even vaster drawing room, most elegantly furnished, and littered with what Tabitha took to be a large quantity of valuable silver and china. There was a small fire burning in the burnished steel grate and beside it sat an extremely fat old lady with a round face and beady black eyes. Her several chins rested on an old-fashioned boned collar and there was a magnificent diamond brooch fastening the rich black velvet folds of her dress. She looked up as they were announced and said in a clear voice like a little girl's: 'There you are, Marius. Come here so that I can have a good look at you.'

He advanced towards her chair and Tabitha, his compelling hand under her elbow, with him. He said pleasantly: 'Hullo, Dolly. Lovelier than ever, I see, and not a day older.'

The old lady looked delighted. 'What did you expect? I shall go on for ever.' She suddenly produced a lorgnette from the vast array of chains and necklaces draped around her ample person and leveled it at Tabitha, who returned the scrutiny with polite interest.

'May I present Miss Tabitha Crawley to you, Dolly? Tabitha—the Dowager Lady Riddleton, who has been my friend for a good many years as well as one of my patients.'

The old lady lowered the lorgnette. 'Do you know about me, Miss Crawley?'

Tabitha shook her head. 'No, Lady Riddleton, I don't,' and added quickly just in case Lady Riddleton should get mistaken ideas into her head: 'I'm a ward sister working at the hospital where Marius operates...' She stopped because the old lady's face had creased into a thousand little folds as she began to chuckle, she drew breath long enough to say: 'He told me,' and went on chuckling. Presently she observed: 'He's a good surgeon, don't you think?'

'Yes, he is,' said Tabitha.

'And a handsome man too—I've no doubt you young women set your caps at him.'

Tabitha bristled and Marius said on a laugh: 'Not Tabitha—she keeps hers firmly on her head. She's got an idea she's a plain girl, you see.'

Tabitha rounded on him, quite forgetting where she was. 'Well,' she breathed fiercely, 'of all the things to say!'

'That's right,' agreed her hostess, 'I like a girl with spirit. I had plenty myself when I was young. Come here, gal, where I can see you.'

Tabitha looked around her rather wildly; the room was empty save for the three of them, and one glance at Marius's face showed her that he wasn't going to be of any use at all; in fact, he was enjoying himself. She gave him a cold look and stepped unwillingly forward to be subjected once more to a prolonged examination through the lorgnette.

'Not plain at all,' pronounced her ladyship. 'Nice little chin, honest eyes, gentle mouth, plenty of hair—good figure too. She'll still be getting admiring glances long after the chocolate box beauties have had their faces lifted.' She paused to get her breath and Tabitha opened her mouth to give vent to her own feelings, but she had no chance. 'Look at me,' commanded

Lady Riddleton. 'Now I was plain and I still am,' she gave a silvery little laugh, 'but no one has called me "poor Dolly" in my life and though I'm turned eighty I've more friends than I can count.' She leaned forward and tapped Tabitha's arm with a podgy, be-ringed hand. 'You thank God you're no raving beauty, gal, then you won't waste the years worrying about getting old and ugly—time is kind to our sort.'

She leaned back in her chair. 'Pull the bell, Marius, we'll have tea—you can look at my legs afterwards. Sit down, Tabitha—and that's a good old-fashioned name. Marius tells me you've been on holiday in Veere. What did you think of his home?' At Tabitha's look of surprise she went: 'Oh, yes, I know it well. We were there with our yacht when I had my accident ten years ago—it was Marius who saved my legs for me.'

Tabitha found this interesting and would have liked to have learned more, but just then tea was brought in and the conversation became general with Lady Riddleton doing most of the talking while she ate her way daintily through a large variety of sandwiches, jam tarts, little iced cakes and a couple of slices of very rich fruit cake. Fortified by these dainties, their hostess bade Tabitha go into the garden, 'For,' she said with rather touching pride, 'I planned some of it myself and it is lovely, although I can't touch the original gardens for beauty. And Marius, ring for Parkes to come down and help me to my room—she can come for you when I'm ready.'

Tabitha went out through the French windows at the end of the room, on to a balcony which led by stone steps to the garden which despite its size had a charming informality as well as beauty. She wandered round, sniffing and admiring and reading labels, happily oblivious of the time. She had crossed the ornamental pond by its little rustic bridge to see what was on the other side and had returned to stroll up the long walk with its herbaceous border when Marius joined her. He had come from one of the shrubbery paths which intersected the walk and she said quickly: 'I've not been bothering about the time. Have I kept you waiting?'

He shook his head and strolled along beside her. 'What do you think of the garden?' he wanted to know.

'Lovely. I should like to take a slice of it back with me. There's a herb garden beyond the pond and a bed of miniature roses…'

'Yes, I know.'

She paused to look up at him. 'You've been here before, of course. A great many times? You know Lady Riddleton very well, don't you? You talked to her as though she was an—an aunt.'

He looked amused. 'She is my aunt, though a very distant one. She and her husband used to visit my parents when I was a boy.'

Tabitha, although interested, refused to be sidetracked. 'She's rather outspoken…that is, I've no wish to be rude, but does your aunt always talk like that?'

'Only to those she likes—otherwise you would have been treated with an icy politeness which would have frozen your marrow in its bones.'

She went on walking. 'How extremely friendly of you to expose me to such a possibility,' she said crossly.

'You malign me,' his voice was silky. 'I knew she would like you.'

Tabitha was on the point of asking why and decided against it. 'You laughed,' she said instead, still cross.

'Kind laughter, Tabitha, you know that, nor was my aunt unkind.'

'Why did you bring me here?'

'I told you, for the ride.' He gave her a sidelong glance. 'No, that's not quite all—I wanted Dolly to see you, because I knew she would tell you what I have been telling you for weeks. You can't very well ignore her opinion of you, although you have always chosen to ignore mine.'

This was a remark which was difficult to answer. Tabitha changed the subject. 'I like Lady Riddleton,' she offered.

He seemed content to follow her lead. 'Everyone does—that is unless they are unfortunate enough to be disliked by her.'

He took her arm and guided her down a small path 'Did you find the dovecote?'

She said no, she hadn't and they went on down the path to come out into a grassy space with the dovecote in its center. It was very old and the doves were flying in and out of its little windows, their wings making a soft whirring sound as they called softly to each other. Tabitha found them enchanting and when one came to perch on her shoulder she laughed like a little girl.

'Look, Marius—do look!' she cried, and was swung round to face him, so tightly held that she could scarcely breathe. She stared up into his face, no longer placid but almost grim. She asked, stammering a little:

'Whatever is the matter, Marius?'

The grim look disappeared. He said lightly: 'Nothing. We've been invited to stay for dinner—you won't mind?'

She still stood within his arms, but now their touch was impersonal so that the thumping of her heart slowed to normal. 'Yes,' she said quietly, 'I'd like that very much.'

So they stayed to dinner, a leisurely meal which lasted all of two hours, what with the amount and variety of the food and Lady Riddleton's conversation, which was very amusing because she had led a very varied life and met a great many interesting people. They took their leave at last and drove back through the cloudy evening, not bothering to talk very much. They had got past the stage where they needed to make conversation, Tabitha thought dreamily, just to be together was enough. She jerked her thoughts away from the idea and applied herself to asking Marius intelligent questions about the house they had just visited.

She saw very little of him for the next day or so. He came and went, sometimes with Mr Raynard, hobbling along with his stick, sometimes on his own, but always on ward business. On Saturday and Sunday he didn't come at all and on the following day he operated for hours, made a brief appearance in the ward to check on his patients, reminded her carelessly that he would be gone for a few days, and went again.

Tabitha went to Chidlake the next day, glad of something to

do now that Marius wasn't there. It was a pleasant enough day with a faint nip in the early autumn air. She stowed a picnic lunch in the back of the car and set out.

She stopped as she always did at the top of the hill above her home. There was a mist coming in from the sea, but she hardly noticed it; her attention was all on Chidlake. She sighed as she looked and went on down the hill. As she turned in at its gate she saw the open windows—presumably her step-mother had left someone in the house—so much the better, she would be able to get some coffee or whatever was going in the kitchen. She opened the front door and went inside and Lilith came out of the sitting room as she did so, to stare at her with such a guilty look that Tabitha said: 'Lilith, whatever is the matter? I know I'm not expected—I thought you were away.'

She went past her stepsister into the sitting room and found Mrs Crawley looking annoyed and even a little guilty too.

'Tabitha!' her voice was sharp. 'Whatever are you doing here?'

Tabitha was bewildered. She knew she wasn't always wel-come, but they were behaving as though they had something to hide, 'I thought you were away—it seemed a good idea to drive over for an hour. Marius gave me your message telling me not to come.' She stopped and asked: 'Didn't you?'

Mrs Crawley had regained her usual poise. 'Oh—did I?'' She got up and went to stand at the window, her back to Ta-bitha.

'Well, since you're here, you may as well know that we've decided to sell Chidlake.' She ignored Tabitha's quick-drawn breath. 'It's mine to sell and really there's no reason why I should tell you.'

Tabitha asked with dry lips: 'When?'

Her stepmother shrugged. 'We want a good offer. How should I know?' she added quickly. 'Christmas perhaps.' She waited for Tabitha to speak and when she didn't, continued in a hard voice: 'This house was left to me, I can do with it exactly as I wish. We—Lilith and I—loathe living here.'

Tabitha found her voice. 'My father would never have left Chidlake to you—you know that, he said so many times; you were to have the money and Chidlake was to stay in the family—I was to have it. Why do you want Chidlake if you hate it so?' The rage she was holding in check turned her quiet voice harsh.

Mrs Crawley laughed. 'My dear Tabby, if only you knew how silly you look standing there insulting me. The house is mine, whatever your father intended to do with it, and I shall sell it for as much as I can.' She smiled. 'In fact I...' she bit her lip and went on, 'you'll not get a penny.'

Tabitha said in a quiet, despairing voice: 'I don't want money. Couldn't you...?'

'No!' Mrs Crawley was triumphant. 'You've got that annuity and far more furniture than you need, you can be content with that.'

Tabitha stood where she was, knowing that there was nothing she could do. Her stepmother was quite right; if she chose to sell the house, she had every right to do so. The older people in the village might shake their heads and disapprove, they might even protest aloud, but no one could do anything. Tabitha tried once more. 'Will you reconsider your decision? The house has been in the family for years—there have always been Crawleys here...'

Mrs Crawley lighted a cigarette before she replied. 'No, Tabitha, I won't. I don't care how many Crawleys have lived here. It's a dump.'

Tabitha bit back a hot rejoinder. 'When did you first decide to sell?'

Her stepmother smiled. 'We had often talked about it; funnily enough it was on Lilith's birthday—during her party—that I had a serious offer for it.'

'You didn't tell me.'

'Tell you? Why should I, it's none of your business. Really, Tabitha, I sometimes think that you're not only plain and dull but stupid as well.'

Tabitha had a sudden vivid memory of Lady Riddleton telling her that she wasn't plain. She said quietly: 'I don't mind any more when you say things like that. I know it's not of the least consequence.'

Mrs Crawley gave her a narrow look. 'My dear Tabitha, you talk like a woman in love. Now I wonder…'

She got no further, for Lilith came into the room. 'It's no good expecting you can stay to lunch, Tabitha,' she said, 'we're going out. I don't suppose you want to anyway—I can see Mummy's told you that…' She paused because of her mother's warning glance. She flung herself in a chair and muttered: 'Oh, well,' and began to inspect her nails. Tabitha, looking at her, thought she had never seen her so pretty; no wonder Marius wanted to marry her. As though she had spoken his name aloud, her stepsister said: 'Marius came to lunch.'

'Yes, I know,' said Tabitha, 'he mentioned it on the ward.'

'I find him rather old,' said Lilith, 'but I shall marry him, you know. All that lovely lolly—after all, he won't be home a great deal, will he with all these lectures he gives?'

Tabitha felt sick. She was sure that Marius was perfectly able to manage Lilith once he had married her, and perhaps he loved her too much to care. She left the house without a word, got into the Fiat and started back up the hill. She stopped at the top and looked back. The sea mist was quite thick now, she couldn't see Chidlake at all.

She got back to the flat as Meg was washing up after her lunch, and she, dear soul, after one look at Tabitha's white face, left the sink and pushed her gently into a chair. 'I don't know what it is that's happened, Miss Tabby, but you look in need of a nice cup of tea.' She put the kettle on and went to draw up another chair. 'Do you want to tell me, love?'

Tabitha's eyes filled with tears. 'They're going to sell Chidlake, Meg.' She drew a steadying breath. 'And I can't stop them. They've been meaning to do it for months and they only told me today because I went h—home.'

'Sell Chidlake?' Meg's cheerful face was shocked. 'They can't—there's been a Crawley there for I don't know how long.'

'I know,' sobbed Tabitha, 'I—I said so, and she called it a d—dump.' She wiped her eyes and blew her nose and sat up straight. 'Meg, what are we to do? I must think of something.'

Meg made the tea and put a cup, very strong and sweet, on the table.

'Drink this up, Miss Tabby. When are they going to sell Chidlake?'

'After Christmas—at least—' she frowned, 'my stepmother said so, but now I'm not sure—but she said Christmas.'

'Time enough to think of something, and depend upon it we shall.'

They thought about it for the rest of the day and were no nearer a solution when they went to bed that night. As they said good night Tabitha exclaimed wearily: 'Oh, Meg, I wish Marius was here; he'd know what to do. Oh, no—I can't tell him, can I? It will look as though I'm trying to make trouble between him and Lilith, and what could he do anyway?'

It was a pleasure to go to work the next morning and find the ward so busy that she had no time for personal problems, and the next day the shock had dulled a little and hope was already beginning to nibble away at her doubts and fears. She went doggedly through the week, longing for Marius's return on Friday. But Friday came and no sign of him and when she asked George what had happened he looked up hurriedly from a patient's notes and said vaguely: 'He's delayed—didn't I tell you? We'll have to manage.'

Tabitha ignored the childish tears pricking her eyelids. She said furiously: 'There's a list as long as your arm, and I'm still a staff nurse short...' And George, who had looked up in astonishment at her sudden outburst, said comfortingly: 'Never mind, old lady, we'll manage somehow. Just our luck the chief's got a cold and can't hobble to our rescue.' He grinned at her. 'Bet you anything you like that we get a whacking great emergency in, just to cap the lot.'

Tabitha swallowed the tears. 'Oh, George, you're always such a comfort,' she cried.

# CHAPTER NINE

THE NEXT DAY began badly. George arrived late for a start and hard on his heels came an emergency—a young railway porter who had slipped and fallen on to the line in the path of a train. He lay, incredibly cheerful, unaware, because of the kindly muffling of the morphia he had been given, that he was going to lose half a leg and face several months of pain and discomfort before he would be able to stand on the other one. He grinned feebly at Tabitha as she checked the blood drip and looked at his dressings and whispered: 'Me for the butcher's shop, I suppose, Sister?'

Tabitha smiled at him, a warm, steady smile that radiated reassurance. 'Well, you do need a bit of repair work done, don't you? Here's the surgeon to have a quick look.'

'I've seen one already.'

'That was the Casualty Officer. This is Mr Steele, the Orthopaedic Registrar.'

She lifted the light cover of the trolley upon which the patient lay, stationing her person in such a way that there was no chance of the patient seeing anything; he was weak with loss of blood and semi-conscious from the morphia, but there was always the possibility that he might want to see the shocking mess under the sterile towel. George stared at it, then without looking at Tabitha said: 'Well, old man, I think the quicker we get up to the operating theatre with you the better, don't you?' He smiled and nodded cheerfully and said 'See you later,' as he walked away.

Tabitha beckoned to a nurse to take her place and went after George.

'Do his people know?' he asked.

She nodded. 'Yes, Cas saw to that—they'll send his wife up as soon as she gets here.'

'Nasty mess,' said George. 'Send him up at the double, will you, Tabby? We'll do the cleaning up. What's he had?'

She told him and he scribbled on a chart. 'Just give the atrophine, then.' He started off down the corridor, saying something as he went, but she was already going in the opposite direction and didn't hear him. She had a great deal to do: the theatre list would have to be reorganized. It was a pity that the first case had already had his pre-med, but there was nothing she could do about that until she knew how long the emergency would take. She telephoned for the porters and then went to take another look at the patient and looked at the clock as she went. It was time to release the tourniquet again for a brief time; she was just readjusting it once more when the porters arrived. She would have liked to take him to theatre herself, but his wife would be coming and she would have to see her. She sent one of the part-time staff nurses and went back into the ward. She did a hasty round first, interrupted several times by telephone calls, dietitians, physiotherapists and an early visit from Matron, who sailed round the ward, towing Tabitha with her, graciously ignoring the disorder of a morning which had started off on the wrong foot.

Mrs Morgan, the porter's wife, arrived shortly afterwards; a large plump young woman who looked at Tabitha with trusting eyes. 'My Dickie will be all right, won't he?' she enquired of Tabitha as she was made comfortable in the office and given tea. 'They said his legs were hurt.'

Tabitha sipped tea she didn't want, but it was easier to talk over the teacups. 'I'm afraid so, Mrs Morgan—one leg is broken in two places; it will be set and put in plaster and he'll be able to use it again, but not for some time, of course. The other leg is crushed below the knee, I'm not sure what is to be done to it, but you can be sure the surgeons will do everything they can to put it right.' She paused. 'Try not to worry too much, Mrs Morgan, your husband looks a big strong man and healthy…they'll get him on his feet again.'

'His own feet, Sister?' Mrs Morgan gave a watery smile. 'Don't answer that, and I don't care anyway, just so long as I get my Dickie back.' The smile faded. 'He's not going to die, is he?'

'No!' replied Tabitha forcefully. 'The operation is being done by an excellent surgeon.' She spoke with a certainty which quite reassured her companion, although she herself didn't feel quite so happy about it. Not that George wasn't an excellent man at his job—he would amputate and do it well, but the unbidden thought that if Marius had been there he would have patched and stitched and pinned and plated the tatters of flesh and bone with all his skill and might, to try and save the leg, because a man's own leg, however scarred and twisted, was still better than the beautifully made artificial one he would be offered in exchange. She left Mrs Morgan in the office and went back into the ward because Sue had sent down a message to say that they were opening the second theatre and would she send up the first case on the list, and when Tabitha asked how Mr Morgan was getting on Sue said hurriedly: 'He'll be hours,' and rang off before Tabitha had time to ask who was taking the second theatre. Surely Mr Raynard hadn't decided to come in—if so, she was heartily sorry for Sue, for Mr Raynard was grumpy enough when he was fit; with a stiff leg and a cold in the head he'd be unmanageable.

But she had no leisure for speculation; there was a great deal to do as the morning wore on full of petty hindrances and annoyances. The third case was already in theatre and Mr Morgan was still not back. Tabitha served the patients' dinners and refused to go to her own; snapping off poor Rogers' head when she suggested it, only to apologise immediately and take her staff nurse's advice to go to the office and have some tea and sandwiches. It was a relief to get away from the orderly turmoil of the ward for a brief spell, besides it gave her a chance to make up the charts. And all the time there was the nagging worry of how she was to prevent Chidlake falling into the hands of a stranger, aching at the back of her mind like a decayed tooth.

Mr Morgan came back an hour later, looking much smaller and very white on the stretcher. It was while they were putting him very carefully back into his bed that Tabitha saw that he still had two legs. The one pinned and plated and ready to go up into extension, the second—the mangled one—was in a half plaster with a heavy dressing from knee to ankle, but unmistakably his five toes bore mute evidence of the fact that there had been no amputation.

She raised a questioning eyebrow at the staff nurse who had brought him back from theatre. 'They saved the leg?'

The staff nurse nodded. 'Yes, Sister—it was a wonderful job. It took nearly five hours.' Her voice held the merest hint of reproach; she should have been off duty an hour ago, a fact Tabitha instantly recalled.

'Poor Staff, I am sorry—do a three-hour stint tomorrow to make up for it. There's coffee or tea in the kitchen, get the orderly to make you a sandwich, but before you go tell me exactly what he had done.'

'Mr van Beek told me not to bother; he's coming down himself to see you at the end of the list, Sister.'

Tabitha said quietly: 'I see, Staff. Do go off duty and thank you for staying.' She took her patient's pulse and charted it, her own hammering almost as fast. So Marius was back and in theatre, and in a little while she would see him. She smiled on the thought and then dismissed him from her mind as she applied herself to the task of keeping Mr Morgan alive. The last case came back soon after and by then it was after four o'clock, and ten minutes later her quick ear heard the murmur of voices in the corridor and a moment later the ward door swung open and Marius and George Steele came in: they were still in their theatre gowns and boots and Marius looked tired. The sight of him and the fact that she hadn't eaten a proper meal for some time made her feel quite lightheaded. She stayed where she was by Mr Morgan's bed and the men came to a halt beside her. George gave her a sidelong glance and said nothing. Marius said pleasantly: 'Hullo, Tabitha—how's our patient?'

She stared up at him. 'You saved his leg.'

'I hope so.' He smiled slightly and waited for her to speak.

'Hullo,' she said belatedly. 'He's fine'—she plunged into precise details and Marius nodded with satisfaction. 'Good—

George, get the electrolytes checked, will you? He's had ten'—
he raised an eyebrow at Tabitha who said: 'Eleven'—'pints of
blood, let's get him on to saline.' He turned back to Tabitha
and gave detailed instructions as to treatment and then said:
'Leave his chart out, will you, Sister? I'll write up the operation
before I go. Now, what about the other men?' He turned away
and said cheerfully to George: 'Quite a day,' then looked at
Tabitha, making her aware of untidy hair and a face which
must by now be devoid of make-up. 'You too, Sister—
shouldn't you be off duty?'

It was true, she should have gone off at half past four, but
Rogers had more than enough to cope with and if she went
home she would only sit and think about Chidlake—she mumbled: 'Oh, well—not really,' which vague remark caused Marius to raise an eyebrow although he said nothing as she led
them down the ward. It was another half-hour before they were
done and then Marius asked to see Mrs Morgan, waiting patiently in the office. He disappeared inside the little room, leaving Tabitha and George Steele standing in the ward.

It was a chance to find out what exactly Marius had done to
save the leg; George explained at some length, ending: 'A nice
piece of surgery; no wonder he's got such a reputation—and
he deserves it. I've written up Morgan's chart, but I'll be down
again this evening.'

'I gave the penicillin at four,' said Tabitha, and remembered
she had already told him that. She blushed and said: 'Sorry,
George—I've said that already.'

'What's on your mind, Tabby?' he asked kindly. 'You've
looked unhappy for weeks and now, today, you look desperate.'

She managed a smile. 'Nothing to worry about, George,' and
as she spoke was struck by an idea so outrageous that she
gasped. 'Oh, George, you've given me an idea—at least, it
came into my head...'

She got no further because Marius came out of the office
with Mrs Morgan. She watched him accompany her to her husband's bedside and settle her in a chair and when he returned
she said very quickly before she could change her mind: 'Could

you spare me a minute, sir? There's something I want to ask you.'

She watched his face as she spoke, but there was no expression on it other than polite interest and he answered readily enough. 'Yes, of course. George, give me a ring this evening, will you? Let me know if you should want me, but everything looks pretty straightforward, given a little luck.'

The two men said goodbye and Marius followed her into her office and waited for her to sit down, but she stayed on her feet; what she had to say had to be said standing. She took a deep breath, and not mincing matters, asked: 'Will you lend me some money?'

Marius was leaning against the door. If he was surprised his face didn't show it. 'How much?' He sounded friendly and she took heart.

'About three hundred thousand pounds.'

His mouth twitched. 'Have I as much money as that?' he queried mildly.

'Well, I don't know.' She raised anxious eyes to his calm grey ones. 'It's all right if you haven't, only I don't know anyone else to ask.'

'Do you need the money so badly, Tabby?'

'Yes—my stepmother told me...' She stopped because her throat ached with sudden tears and it would never do to cry now. She turned her back on him and went on in a resolutely controlled voice: 'She's going to sell Chidlake,' and because her back was still turned to him she didn't see the expression on his face. 'She never liked it, you know—Lilith doesn't either, but I expect you know that. I thought if I could get someone to lend me the money I could buy it...'

Marius hadn't moved. He asked: 'Security?'

'The deeds—wouldn't that do? I telephoned an agent in Lyme Regis and he told me Chidlake would fetch about three hundred thousand pounds. I've an annuity from my mother— I could use that to pay it off and add the same amount from my salary. I'll sell the car and get a job at Lyme hospital and use a bike. Meg and I could manage.' Her voice, despite her efforts, rose a little and shook with excitement. 'We've got our own fruit and vegetables there, you know, and in the summer we could do bed and breakfast—Meg wouldn't mind, and I could help when I come off duty…'

His voice broke into her escalating thoughts. He sounded cool and businesslike. 'It would take you forty years to repay your debt, and you've forgotten the interest.'

'Then I shall pay for more than forty years.'

He let that pass. 'And if you marry?'

Tabitha turned to face him again. She said steadily: 'I'm twenty-five, no one has ever asked me to marry them, and I think it fairly certain that no one ever will.' She swallowed back the cold lump of misery which was threatening to choke her. 'Chidlake's been my home all my life—it's belonged to my family ever since it was built. It's important to me that no—no strangers live there, not while there's still a Crawley…'

She wanted to go on talking, to try and explain how she felt and make him understand, but he interrupted her gently: 'Tabby, I'm sorry—it's no good.'

She said quickly, not looking at him: 'No, of course not—I must have been crazy. I beg your pardon…'

'Chidlake is already sold.'

She stared at him for a long minute. There was a mistake, of course, someone had misinformed him—and how could he know anyway? She said painfully: 'I don't believe it. My step-mother said after Christmas—at least—I'm not sure. It's only a few days ago that I saw her.'

'The house is sold.'

Rising temper and alarm sent her voice soaring. 'Then why wasn't I told—and who to? Do you know?' She felt a small thrust of hope. 'Perhaps I could buy it back.'

Marius said with a calm reasonableness she found infuriating: 'I doubt it—I happen to know that it has been sold to someone who expects to marry—he's not likely to sell, is he?'

She ignored this. 'You know who it is.' She darted a look of fury at him. 'Why didn't you tell me? How contemptible of you! You must have known how much I…'

He cut her short deliberately. 'My dear girl, I'm only just

back from Holland. For all I knew you had come to some arrangement with Mrs Crawley.'

Tabitha said in a bitter little voice: 'You had no reason to tell me. I'm sorry I bothered you with all this—only I—I thought of it suddenly while I was talking to George just now and it seemed such a good idea.' She backed away to her desk and picked up a handful of papers regardless of whether they required her attention or not, but at least he would see that she didn't want to say any more about the whole miserable business. She ventured jerkily: 'Good night. I hope I haven't kept you.' Her voice was cold.

Marius apparently didn't hear the coldness; he said thoughtfully:

'It is just possible that I may be able to help you—at least it's worth a try. I have a slight acquaintance with the buyer of Chidlake. I don't think for one moment that he would consider selling it—or even letting it. I believe that I can find out his solicitors, they might agree to forward a letter. I'll let you have the address.'

Tabitha was staring at him, her eyes very bright. She had missed a great deal of this speech, for her attention had been caught and fired by one word. 'Letting?' she exclaimed. 'I never thought of that—if I could see whoever it is and make him understand. Marius, did you really mean that?'

She became aware of his steady regard. 'Do you think I'm being silly? But I have to try. I'm sorry I asked you for that money…'

A peculiar expression was fleetingly visible on Marius's impassive face. 'What made you suppose that I had such a sum at my disposal?'

Tabitha gave him a quick look. He had behaved indifferently to her—he must surely have known how much she loved her home and he had let Mrs Crawley sell it without saying a word, but at least he was trying to help her now. She explained quickly. 'It was something Knotty said one day—oh, ages ago.' She sighed without knowing it, remembering that happy time. 'He said you were a man of substance and I thought that perhaps a man of substance might have that much money. You

see,' she went on, wanting to explain, 'you're not married like
Mr Raynard with a wife and children to support. I thought...'
Her voice tailed away; she wasn't making much of a success
of it. 'I expect you find us very vulgar talking about money,
but we weren't discussing you,' she added anxiously.

He ignored that. 'Is this what you really want?' he wanted
to know. 'Would you be happy living at Chidlake for the rest
of your life? It wouldn't be easy, you know. You won't have
Meg for ever and as you yourself said, you are twenty-five.'

She cast him a waspish look; it was one thing for her to
remark upon her age, but there was no need for him to do so
too. 'Yes,' she said a shade too loudly. 'Yes, of course it is.'

She suddenly couldn't bear it any longer, for there was nothing she wanted to do other than be with Marius for the rest of
her life—an idea which unhappily enough hadn't occurred to
him. She rustled the papers still in her hands and he said at
once: 'I'm holding you up, I'll say good night. I'll see that you
get that address!'

He turned away and strode up the corridor without another
word or look.

Tabitha stayed awake most of the night wondering if he
would remember, and when she saw his scrawled directions on
her note-pad in the morning, she could have cried with relief
and shame too for ever having doubted him. She tucked the
paper away in a pocket and got on with her work until her
coffee break, when, using hospital stationery with a reckless
disregard for the rules, she wrote a brief, businesslike letter,
enclosed it in a neatly addressed envelope and took it to the
front hall letter box and posted it, having borrowed a stamp
from the head porter, Mr Biggs.

She then went back to the ward and applied herself to her
work once more, resolutely dismissing the matter from her
mind. She did not have the same success with Marius, however;
she thought about him constantly and every time the door
opened she jumped nervously, longing to see him while at the
same time having not the least idea what she would say to him.
It was only on her way home that she remembered that he had
said he wouldn't be in until the late evening.

There was, of course, no letter the next day. It dragged through its interminable length, made longer by George telling her that Mr van Beek found it impossible to come in until after five o'clock and she was off duty at that hour. Although she was sick of her day she hung around until almost half past, and then, beaten by Staff's hurt look at not being left alone to get on with things, Tabitha went. Ten minutes later she crossed the forecourt to the Fiat and passed the Bentley on the way. It was empty and it hadn't been there when she had gone off duty—perhaps Marius didn't want to see her. Now that she thought about it, she realized she had put him in a very awkward position; she could imagine how her stepmother would feel if she discovered that her stepdaughter was trying to get Chidlake back. He must be very sure of Lilith to risk their displeasure. Tabitha clashed the gears, hating Lilith, who was so very pretty and clever enough to get her own way as well as determined.

Tabitha edged the car into the street outside and drove home very badly. She spent the evening mooning around the flat, eating nothing of the tasty supper Meg had prepared and displaying an ill-humour quite at variance with her usual calm disposition. She wasn't on duty until one o'clock the next day so that impatience made her so irritable that even Meg's placid good nature was shaken. When Tabitha had contradicted her for the fourth or fifth time in as many minutes, Meg said in her firm nanny's voice: 'Now, Miss Tabitha, I know you're upset and it's a nasty old patch we're going through, but nothing lasts. It's always darkest just before the dawn.'

Tabitha had to laugh. 'Darling Meg—I promise you I'll cheer up.'

'That's a love,' said Meg comfortably. 'Do you remember how you told me once that Mr van Beek called you Cinderella—well, even she got her glass slipper in the end, didn't she?'

Tabitha, washing smalls at the sink, bent her head over her work. She had been trying not to think about Marius, and now here was Meg talking about him again. She said lightly: 'What a pity life isn't a fairy story. But since it's not, if—if I can't persuade the new owner of Chidlake to rent it to me, would you mind very much if we moved right away from here—it would mean you wouldn't be near your sister.'

Meg glanced at the clock. 'Sit down and eat that bit of lunch I've got for you,' she commanded. 'That's a good idea, love, to move away—right away, as you said. As for my sister, there's still the railway, isn't there, and buses. That's no problem, but don't you worry about that until you need to. Never cross your bridges...'

There was a letter, but because of the sudden spate of work Tabitha was unable to open it at once. It was brief and stated merely that Messrs Stubbs, Cripp and Mann begged to inform her that their client would be at Chidlake on the following even after seven o'clock and was willing to see her. They were glad to be of service and were hers faithfully. She read it through several times, trying to draw hope and encouragement from the dry words. At least she was being given the chance to put her proposition and it seemed like a good omen that she was free the following evening. She would have to plan what she would say, but not until later. Now there was her work. The ward was a heavy one, and for the last week or so it had been getting heavier, culminating in the arrival of Mr Morgan, who, although improving steadily, needed constant care and attention. He had shown great courage and patience and a cheerfulness which defied anyone to pity him, only begging that he should be told should anything go wrong. Marius had gone out of his way to explain exactly what had been done in the theatre, not mentioning that any surgeon might have been justified in amputating, whereas he, by his skill, had saved the leg. It was George Steele, doing a round on his own, who enlightened Mr Morgan as to the extent of the operation. Tabitha, masked and gowned, listened to George's quiet voice and then her patient singing Marius's praise in no uncertain fashion, while she took out a drainage tube and put on another dressing to cover Marius's meticulous stitching.

'There's a man for you,' observed Mr Morgan, 'sewing me leg back on—like new 'e'll be. Going around tidying up arms and legs like 'e does. Daresay 'e's a nice chap too—got a straight eye for all 'e's not English.'

Tabitha, while agreeing with this sincere praise, said nothing, but enquired if her patient was doing his breathing exercises.

'Yes, love, I'm doing 'em, though it's me legs is 'urt; can't see no reason for it meself, but I'll do 'em if you says so, Sister. Proper angel you are, you and the nurses.'

Tabitha fixed the last piece of strapping. 'Why, thank you, Mr Morgan,' she said cheerfully. 'Your wife'll be here in a minute—just in time to have a cup of tea while you have yours.'

She was in the dressing room clearing the trolley when Nurse Betts came in. 'Sister, Mr van Beek's in the ward. Shall I finish the trolley for you?'

Tabitha started to roll down her sleeves. 'Please,' she spoke with her usual unhurried calm while her heart raced. She would be able to tell him about the letter. She hastened into the ward, giving Mrs Jeffs a speaking glance as she did so, which that lady rightly interpreted as a request for her cuffs to be brought immediately. Ward sisters always wore their cuffs when they did a round with the consultant staff, in the same way as men took their hats off in lifts and everyone curtsied to royalty. It was a kind of tradition that was unquestioned. Marius waited now while Tabitha put hers on, and only when she had donned them did he speak.

'Good afternoon, Sister. I've a list for tomorrow, have I not? Perhaps I might see the patients now.'

She led him to the first one and after a moment he said pleasantly:

'Don't bother with me, Sister, I'm sure you have plenty to do. I'll ask a nurse if I want anything.'

Thus dismissed, Tabitha went to her office, where she sat with the requisition books open before her, lost in thought. She wouldn't be able to tell Marius about the letter; in those few minutes together she had sensed his withdrawal behind a cool pleasantness of manner which she knew she wouldn't be able to penetrate. She told herself it was a good thing, for now she could put him out of her mind. She concentrated instead on what she would say the following evening at Chidlake. She was rehearsing a series of speeches calculated to melt a heart

of stone when Marius walked in. 'I'll do that pelvis tonight,'
he said briskly. 'May I use the telephone?'

She pushed the instrument across the desk towards him and
listened while he talked to Sue, with whom he appeared to be
on the friendliest of terms, which made it all the more apparent
to her as he gave her his instructions that he had no intention
of extending those terms to herself. He was still pleasant, but
his manner was guarded and so politely impersonal that nothing
would have persuaded her to so much as mention Chidlake.

She listened to his directions without looking at him, because
she couldn't bear to see his face while he talked in that casual,
distant voice. He got up to go presently and she went at once
into the ward, her face set in a stony calm. She had been unhappy before, but never had she felt quite so desolate as she
did now. It was because she had asked him for money and
help, of course. She had been a fool—if she hadn't been so
desperate. At least she had got her chance of meeting the new
owner of Chidlake, but it had cost her Marius's good opinion
of her. She had thought that he would have understood, and he
hadn't.

She rang for the porters, served the suppers, studied the operation list for the next day so that she could plan the ward
work and went down to supper; the case wouldn't be back until
eight o'clock. She sat with the other ward sisters, eating her
way through egg and chips and college pudding without having
the least idea what was on her plate while she talked with her
usual pleasantness to her companions at table. Afterwards she
was unable to remember a word of the conversation, but as no
one had questioned anything she had said, presumably she had
talked sense.

She and Betts were putting traction on the newly returned
theatre case when Marius came into the ward, finished it for
them, added some more instructions to those he had already
given her and then said: 'A word with you, Sister.'

She accompanied him to the office; perhaps everything was
going to be all right again. She stood just inside the door,
waiting for him to speak. She was mistaken, for he began in
that same coolly casual voice:

'About Morgan—I see you have quite rightly put him on a half-hourly pulse chart. I'd like that changed to a quarter hourly pulse, please. The slightest sign of it going up and you will be good enough to tell Mr Steele at once. Never mind if it is a false alarm—we don't want a secondary haemorrhage. Please make this clear to your nurses.'

Tabitha's voice was so professional it sounded severe. 'Very well, sir. Did you wish to see anyone else?'

She gave him a quick look and found his eyes intent on her, and the wish to fling herself into his arms and tell him how much she loved him was so strong that she clenched her teeth so that her mouth looked quite forbidding. He said slowly, still staring: 'No, not at present, thank you. Good night.'

She watched him make his unhurried way down the corridor and then went back into the ward. There was plenty to do still, and as far as she was concerned a very good thing too.

The following day was busy too; only in the afternoon, when the list was finished, did the work slacken. Marius hadn't been to the ward all day and now it was George Steele who came to check on the operation cases. He wrote up the charts for her and said, 'I expect that will do—you're quite happy about Morgan? I'll pop in later on and have a look at him as Mr van Beek has gone.'

'Gone?' Tabitha lifted a suddenly white face to his. 'You don't mean left?'

George put a chart on the desk and said without looking at her: 'No, Tabby. He'll be here for another week or two while Mr Raynard finds his feet. Didn't he mention it?'

Tabitha shook her head, not trusting her voice. Presently when he had finished writing, she said: 'Thanks for writing up the drugs. Staff's on in a minute. I shall be glad to get off.'

He paused in the doorway. 'You look done in, Tabby. I should have an early night.'

She agreed mendaciously and summoned a smile as she went.

The flat was empty when she got home; she found a note on the kitchen table in Meg's square careful handwriting, telling that she had gone to spend an evening with a friend and had taken Podger with her. Tabitha's supper was in the oven and she was to eat it.

Tabitha read this communication in some surprise; it wasn't like Meg to go out at a moment's notice like that, and certainly not to take Podger. She shrugged her shoulders, ignored the oven, made some coffee while she ran the bath and went to put out her clothes. She had already decided what to wear—the green linen with the white bands round the neck and short sleeves; it was pretty and simple and she wanted desperately to make a good impression. She did her face with all the skill she could muster, and ignoring the clock, took time over her hair. Looking at herself when she was at last ready, she was as satisfied as she ever was with her person; her face looked white and her eyes were puffy with secret weeping, but if she stood with her back to the light, he wouldn't notice. All she had to do was to keep calm and level-headed and put a clear case before him.

She was so late that she had to drive as fast as the little car would go. The evening was already fading and growing cool, but she didn't notice this, for her mind was racing ahead, exploring every possible chance to get the new owner to see how vital it was to allow her to rent Chidlake. That he might not want to do so was something she refused to consider.

It was getting on for eight o'clock when she turned into the familiar gateway and stopped the car outside the front door. It stood open and when no one came in answer to her ring, she walked in, going instinctively to the small room her father had used as a study, and which, after his death, had hardly been used at all. The door was shut and opened under her eager hand into a room which hadn't changed over the years. The French window was open and its faded brocade curtains trembled a little in the light breeze. Her father's desk stood before it with the bookshelves on either wall. There was a small log fire burning briskly with her father's armchair drawn up beside it. And Marius was sitting in the chair.

She stared at him unbelievingly and when he got up and came towards her she exclaimed a little wildly: 'I'm late—has he gone? I didn't expect you would be here too.' She added breathlessly: 'The door was open.'

She hadn't moved and Marius halted in front of her. 'Yes, Tabitha, I left it open.' His voice was gentle, as was his smile, and something in his eyes made her cry out: 'It's you—you've bought Chidlake!'

He took another step towards her so that they were standing very close.

'Yes, I bought it. You see, I want to keep it in the family.' Tabitha felt black despair wash over her. She managed in a shaky voice: 'Lilith?'

'No, you, my darling heart. I've no glass slipper for my Cinderella; perhaps you'll settle for Chidlake instead.'

She stared at him as though he had run mad. 'Glass slipper?' she uttered bemusedly. 'You mean you really own Chidlake?'

Marius smiled very tenderly at her. 'No, you do, my darling.'

'Me?' her voice was a squeak, and then: 'You said my darling.'

'Which you are and have been ever since I first set eyes on you, though I must say you take a lot of convincing.'

She shook her head the better to settle the riotous thoughts which filled it, then forgot them all as he caught her close and kissed her and kissed her again and when she would have spoken, said: 'No, dearest Tabitha, I'm the one to do the talking, but before I start, will you marry me?'

'Yes,' said Tabitha, 'I will,' and was whisked off her feet before she could say more. Her father's chair creaked a little as Marius sat down again, but it had been built stoutly as well as with elegance and its ample proportions were more than sufficient for two. She laid her head against his broad shoulder. 'There are a great many things I don't understand,' she began.

'My darling, it is all very simple. I had made up my mind to marry you before I met your stepmother and Lilith, and when they told me that they wanted to sell Chidlake, I knew that I must buy it for you. You see, Bill Raynard had already told me about you and how much you loved your home. The Johnsons told much the same story too—my problem was to persuade your stepmother to sell me the house as quickly as possible, and without letting her guess that it was you I loved, for I am convinced that she would have refused to sell Chidlake to me if she had had even an inkling. As it was Lilith played into my hands, she was so sure that she had a middle-aged fool in her net…'

Tabitha lifted her head. 'Middle-aged?' she cried indignantly. 'You're not! Don't ever say that again…'

He kissed her. 'I can see that you are going to be a great comfort to me, my dearest. It was a piece of great good fortune that they decided to follow us to Veere, for it was there I finally persuaded Mrs Crawley to visit my solicitor.'

'The day we went to Bergen-op-Zoom,' Tabitha said.

'Yes—and if you remember I took them to dinner at the hotel—that was when they finally promised…'

'The evening Mr Bow was suddenly taken poorly and I pretended a headache!' She sat up once more. 'I heard you, you know—only I didn't understand—I thought you were going to propose to Lilith.'

'And how very mistaken you were, dear love.' He kissed her again to prove how in error she had been.

'You could have told me, Marius.'

'What—and increase the chance of your stepmother and Lilith finding out? I did not dare. But now Chidlake is yours, Tabby.' He went on: 'You know that we can't live here, don't you, my darling? I have to live in Veere, for that is my home and my work lies mainly in Holland, but we shall be able to come here for holidays and a weekend now and again. Could you be content with that? Meg says she will be glad to live here as housekeeper and Knotty can't wait to move into the little cottage next to the garage. It will be a wonderful place to send the children.'

Tabitha drew, if that were possible, a little closer to him. 'I love Veere and I love your home, I can't believe I've got both—I'll never be able to thank you enough, dearest Marius.'

'That is an interesting point we'll take up later.'

'Couldn't you have told me when I tried to borrow that money?'

'Well,' Marius said reasonably, 'you rather took the wind

out of my sails, my dearest. Before I could put two words together there you were asking me for three hundred thousand pounds.'

He shook with laughter and Tabitha made haste to say: 'You may well laugh, but I was deadly serious and I hated it.' She looked up, remembering. 'Oh, Marius dear. I haven't made you poor because of me?'

He laughed again. 'No, Tabby. I am, as Knotty put it, a man of substance—I can well afford it.'

She asked in wonder: 'How does Meg know?—you said she will live here as housekeeper.'

'I asked her. When shall we be married?'

Tabitha sat up. 'I have to give a month's notice.'

'Too long. I'll attend to that in the morning. I'll see about a special licence too. We'll be married here in the village and all your friends shall come.'

Tabitha gave a contented sigh and then exclaimed: 'Goodness, I must go back—I'm on at eight in the morning.'

'You're not going back tonight, dearest. Have you forgotten I'm due in tomorrow too? I'll take you back in the morning. We're going to have supper now. Meg's been busy for the last hour.'

'Meg?' echoed Tabitha faintly.

'Of course. I brought her down with me, with Knotty and of course Podger—Hans is here too. Meg had a lovely time getting your own room ready for you.' He looked at his watch. 'They'll be waiting for us, Tabby, our three old friends.'

They paused in the doorway and she looked back from the shelter of his arm at the peaceful little room. They would come here often, she thought happily. 'Things happen,' she said obscurely, 'lovely things, when you don't think they're going to.'

Marius appeared to have no difficulty in understanding her. 'As you happened to me, my darling.'

Tabitha looked all of a sudden quite beautiful; it was surprising what love could do to even the plainest of features. 'So I did,' she agreed in some astonishment.

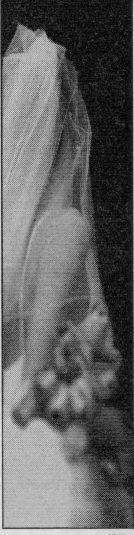

This February—2003—
Silhouette Books cordially invites you
to the arranged marriages
of two of our favorite brides, in

*The*
*Wedding*
ARRANGEMENT

A man fulfilling his civic duty finds himself irresistibly drawn
to his sexy, single, *pregnant* fellow juror. Might they soon be
sharing more than courtroom banter? Such as happily ever
after? Find out in Barbara Boswell's *Irresistible You.*

She *thought* she was his mail-order bride, but it turned out
she had the wrong groom. Or did she? The feisty beauty had
set her eyes on him—and wasn't likely to let go anytime
soon, in Raye Morgan's *Wife by Contract.*

*Look for* The Wedding Arrangement *in February 2003*
*at your favorite retail outlet.*

*Silhouette®*
*Where love comes alive™*

If you enjoyed what you just read,
then we've got an offer you can't resist!

# Take 2 bestselling
# love stories FREE!

# Plus get a FREE surprise gift!